THE CHRONICLE OF ENMERKAR

C. A. ILEY

ISBN: 9798865221135

This is a work of fiction. All incidents, dialogue, and all of the characters with the exception of some well-known places and historical figures, are products of the author's imagination. They are not to be construed as real. Where real-life historical places or persons appear, the situations, incidents, and dialogues concerning those places or persons are entirely fictional. They are not in any way intended to depict actual events or to change the entirely fictional nature of the work. In all other respects, any resemblance to places or persons, living or dead, is entirely coincidental.

DEDICATION

For my children Megan, Joshua, and Elizabeth.
The greatest treasure this life affords.

And for everyone who has ever wondered what lies beyond the far horizon.

CONTENTS

ACKNOWLEDGMENTS

With thanks to my wife Sue for the endless patience and grammar checks. "Speech marks Queen."

Thanks to Hansuan Fabregas for the cover page illustration, and for making his fabulous work freely available on Pixabay.

A E Waite and Pamela Coleman Smith for the Tarot illustrations.

PROLOGUE

They say that history is written by the victor, perhaps they are right and this history will one day be written. But who are 'they?' and how shall we know who the victor will be when the war, which started untold aeons ago, still rages all around us and yet we don't even know it is happening?

Great powers move throughout our world. Some are hidden in plain sight, others drift softly by like the faintest of smoke floating on a gentle breeze, but regardless they all remain unseen by the eyes of everyday men; as we go on with our daily lives, oblivious.

THERE ARE NONE SO BLIND, AS THOSE WHO WILL NOT SEE.

1. THE WAR IN HEAVEN - 483,600 BC.

Enki stood on the bridge of the spaceship looking down on a beautiful green and blue planet about two-thirds the size of his home world. "Such a small, yet precious jewel," he thought to himself. A beautiful paradise that seemed somehow serene, floating incongruously amongst the carnage, in an infinite black ocean. As he watched the sheer horror unfolding all around him, his mind could take no more and it wandered to a small waterfall on a mountain stream where he once played with his brother and sister whilst their mother watched lovingly over them. She was a Queen, regal and beautiful, but there was no formality here, she was laughing as they splashed in the cold water. The children were squealing with delight at every splash, as each released more of the cool droplets which glistened in the sunlight, like diamonds floating in the air.

"Lord Enki, we are ready" said a voice, suddenly dragging him back to a horror that the small boy in the waterfall could never have believed he would ever live to see.

All around them dozens of spaceships had fought their brutal close quarter engagements and now the bodies of his people were floating through space, intermingled with the debris, with the carcasses of the very ships that were meant to be their protection. Along with hundreds of small fighters, the battle cruisers the Enmer, the Shurrup, the Akkad and the Tanis were now nothing more than dead, drifting hulks.

Sargon paused for a moment recognising the pain in his friend's face, then he repeated softly, "Lord Enki, we are ready, we must move quickly while we still can."

"Yes"' he replied, tears welling in his eyes. "Prepare to launch the weapon, move what's left of the fleet to a safe distance and you may fire when ready."

The fusion drive roared to life and what seemed like a mere moment later a huge, intense flash of light illuminated the entire heavens as the energy from the weapon dissipated across the planet's surface. For the briefest of moments there was a deathly silence as all of the electrical systems flickered before the shock wave reached out into space, and several more damaged ships were completely destroyed in its wake.

As the blinding light eventually receded, Enki saw that the entire atmosphere had been ripped from the planet. The once blue and green world; was now a haunting blood red and the bright shining cities of Vorea were no more. The only landmark now visible was a two thousand mile long, radioactive gash across the surface. All hope for life on this once beautiful world was eradicated forever. All that remained below them was a dead world.

The crew cheered; they knew that this was the decisive blow that they had been waiting for. It would mean that not just the battle, but the war would now finally be over. Although he shared the relief that no more of his own comrades would die that day; Enki did not smile. Those on the planet below had not been so fortunate and with his order he had condemned over ten million people to their deaths, including his brother Enlil, and all of his family.

His great armada had won the battle, but at great cost. The lives of hundreds of thousands of people had been lost on both sides in space alone, and another whole world Tiamet, along with at least two of her moons, had already been destroyed. Nothing now but rubble floating in the vast cold reaches of space where she had once been. Tiamet was one of the largest rocky planets in the system it was impossible to know how many innocent lives had been lost but the toll would run to perhaps another fifty million or more.

Enki remained silent for a moment as a wave of intense sorrow rolled over him. There had been no choice left to him, but logic and reason were no comfort. Feeling sick to his stomach, it was taking all of his strength to prevent himself from being overwhelmed, and from drowning in the depths of the shame that he now felt.

Half of the solar system was in ruins; nothing would ever be the same again. He thought absently that the image of the waterfall would be etched in his mind forever.

"Sargon," he said, "please send out the rescue ships, see what life we can salvage from our fleet and when the electromagnetic pulse begins to fade, scan the rest of the system to ensure that none of our enemy has escaped Vorea."

Almost as he gave the order the battle alarms rang again, and as the sensors came back online, they could see there was a small armada of ships headed for the faint, distant light of Einar, currently some sixty million miles away.

"Stop them at all costs Sargon."

"We cannot my Lord" he replied, "they are moving too fast but there are only a few transport ships and small fighters, we will alert home world and hunt them down."

"If they cannot intercept them before they enter the atmosphere then all may yet be lost, said Enki, "it seems that we are in the hands of fate now. Very well, issue the alert, continue with the launch of the rescue ships, and call a council of the commanders, bring them to the flagship. The fighting is over for now but the battle for our survival is not. We must assess the damage across the system and see what we can salvage."

A few hours later Enki, along with the eight remaining Anunnaki commanders, sat aboard the battleship Kilgal. One by one they paid their respects to their Commander in Chief before each relayed their news along with their individual assessment of their current situation, then they waited silently for their orders. Even as Enki listened the weariness was overtaking him, he had not slept for several days, and his mind was beginning to wander again. The horror of the destruction that he had been forced to unleash was already making itself felt. The guilt and shame that he felt were overwhelming.

This day would be a stain on his very soul, and he knew it would haunt him for the rest of his life. Yet even now he could not rest, knowing that their civilisation had been dealt a blow from which it would never fully recover and indeed one that could yet prove fatal. He urged himself on. "This was not the time for repercussion or regret," he thought "there would be time enough for that later and for now he had to focus, it was imperative that they salvage what they could."

"Lord Erish, as the commander of the Enumer deep space squadron, I know that you and your men have been in space longer than any of us and that they are eager to return home but there is one more task I must burden you with. You will head for the outer colonies and assess what damage has been inflicted there. Kill anyone who shows signs of the phage, destroy the colonies from space if you must, and bring the remaining healthy people back to Einar. If you wish to rotate some of your men with the other commanders before you leave, I will understand.

"Thank you, my Lord." he said, "My men will want to complete their mission before returning to Einar but…." he paused hesitant to question his orders.

"Speak freely Lord Erish," said Enki.

He nodded "Yes Sire" he said. "Would our people not be safer remaining in the colonies for now?"

"Perhaps they would" replied Enki, "but that is far from certain. In any event the most likely outcome is that any respite would be short lived. With Tiamet gone and Vorea uninhabitable we cannot continue to supply them from Einar alone. We would simply be condemning them to a slow death from starvation or radiation poisoning. Besides we need their numbers, along with their skills, and their expertise to help us rebuild our world if we still can."

"Do not worry Lord Erish, the stations on the outer colonies will still be there when we are ready to return. We must ensure they are purged. This is our priority, we must ensure that we have left nowhere for the Vori to regroup, this war must be ended, now."

"Yes, my Lord. Our supplies are running too low for a deep space mission," said Lord Erish. "I will speak individually with the other commanders before we depart to see what they can spare." As he looked around the room at his comrades, one by one they all nodded in acknowledgement.

"Very well," said Enki. Report back to me when you are ready to leave.

"Sargon, once we have completed the rescue of the survivors from the fleet, take command of the Kilgal and head out for Tiamet's last known co-ordinates. The planet's destruction has created an asteroid field that will create immense dangers for our world and for all of the colonies. We must begin to track the debris field and bring me news of the moon Marduk."

"But the flagship" protested Sargon, "surely you will need it my Lord."

Enki shook his head. "You are the admiral of the fleet Sargon; you are a worthy commander of our flagship. I will take the cruiser Xisudra. Once on board I will head back to Einar immediately. Their battle fleet has been destroyed; I will not be in any danger. The Xisudra has been shielded from the worst of the fighting and besides, she is faster and more maneuverable than the Kilgal. Once we have assessed the situation and seen what news we have of the surviving Vori, then I will convene the Ennead council to coincide with your return."

They saluted as one, "yes my Lord, glory to Einar."

As the commanders left, Sargon held back and turned to Enki. "I am truly sorry about Lord Enlil, but I do not believe that you had any other choice my Lord."

"Thank you, Sargon, I am not alone, we have all paid a heavy price. I should not grieve for my brother any more than I would for any other of my people and yet…." he could not finish the sentence.

"Take care my friend, the remaining rescue operations will not be easy with so much debris and the Vori may have left some unpleasant surprises."

Sargon nodded. "They will be concluded shortly."

"Then move as swiftly as you can to scan the debris field of Tiamet, I have an uncomfortable feeling that the destruction of that world may yet be our undoing."

2. FEBRUARY 2020 AD.

They sat staring at one another across the rustic wooden kitchen table. Harry ate his breakfast while Sofia sipped her black coffee and finished her cigarette.

“I don’t understand how you are never hungry in the morning;” he said.

"Hmmm," she smiled reminiscing about the early hours and the wonderful sensations they had shared, "I understand why you need to keep your strength up" she teased.

Harry smiled at her; "it's no effort where you are concerned."

Sofia was a beauty, her long jet-black hair complimented by her dark brown smouldering eyes, the smell of her perfume and the softness of her skin always left him intoxicated and craving more.

Although the Tuscan villa and its surroundings were beautiful by any standards and making love with Sofia was beyond delightful; by day Harry was bored stiff.

"Come on Sofia," he said, "we have been stuck in here for three days because of this stupid quarantine. I know we can't head north to go skiing because all the resorts and lifts are closed but the guys from the village are going to hunt for wild boar in the forest this morning, let's go with them."

Even though she did not like the idea of hunting, the truth be told; Sofia was also getting a little stir crazy. They had planned to spend a week skiing together in

Courmayeur, but the virus had put paid to that. Still, she was a doctor, and she took their own health very seriously, so the offer of her parents' villa in Tuscany instead had been a welcome option whilst things settled down. She worked in the Santa Tomassa hospital in Torino and had seen the effects of the virus first-hand. Although she knew she was immune it still frightened her.

"Come on Sofia, there have been no cases here in over a month and besides, the fresh air will do us both good, not to mention the exercise" said Harry, rubbing his midriff. He had to admit he had put on more than a few pounds over the last few months.

Sofia relented and albeit reluctantly, she agreed. They finished their breakfast; Harry grabbed her father's hunting rifle from above the fireplace, found a box of cartridges in the cabinet next to the door, and they made their way down to the village to join the hunt.

"Bella Sofia" shouted Alessandro; "Harry, it is good to see you both."

"It is good to see you also Alessandro, thank you again for inviting us both."

"With a twinkle in his eye Alessandro handed Harry a

small ceramic flask, “we must honour the hunt, yes!”

Harry knocked back the flask then almost choked, “Jesus, what is in that?” he spluttered.

Alessandro and Sofia were both laughing hard.

“It’s the local firewater” she said.

“It will make you go blind if you drink too much, that’s why we keep it in stone jars.”

“Point taken” said Harry, as he raised it again, slowly this time, taking a small sip, and saluting, “to the hunt.”

The hunting party was quite small on this occasion, just a few locals, mainly the men accompanied by their hounds, which were now barking excitedly at the prospect of what was to come. But there were a few women too, sorting through the picnic baskets, making sure there would be food to sustain them during what would likely be a hot and exhausting morning.

The men were huddled together, looking at an outstretched map in the back of a dirty white open pick-up truck and agreeing a general route for the hunt, so as to avoid the possibility of an accident once they were in the woods.

Harry was still reeling from the contents of the flask.

"Pay attention" said Sofia, "I don't want you getting shot accidentally."

It was not long before they were ready and Alessandro shouted, "Harry; come follow us the hounds have picked up a scent at the edge of the forest."

Harry picked up his rifle then he and Sofia followed Alessandro to the edge of the forest. A few minutes later, the barking dogs ran on ahead with the hunters struggling to keep up as they were gradually being thinned out between the trees, getting further and further away from one another.

Although he had been looking forward to the hunt, in the midst of the forest Harry's bravado was now beginning to fade a little as he pondered on their adversary. A wild boar can weigh almost three times as much as a fully grown man, they are extremely powerful, and their tusks and teeth are serious weapons.

He looked back to Sofia. "Stay close to me" he said, "you know how dangerous wild boars can be."

Sofia just smiled, this was not the first hunt she had been a party to, but she liked Harry's tender side and his concern for her was touching.

They were both panting heavily as they crested the ridge when suddenly a shadow appeared out of the corner of Harry's eye. Imaging it to be the frightened boar; instinctively he fired off a shot. To his surprise the shadow whirled away and seemed to head off up towards the Santa Maria church in the nearby glade. The adrenaline was surging now and caught up in the excitement he shouted to Sofia, "I hit it, I am sure I did, quickly follow me."

"Harry wait" she shouted, "Boars are wild animals they are naturally shy of people unless they are threatened. Why would a boar run in to the church?"

He stopped for a moment, "you're right he said that is strange, but that thing just appeared out of nowhere and it moved so fast, it had to be a Boar."

Cautiously they made their way up the church steps and peered inside the open doorway.

"Look' said Sofia pointing to the floor; "that looks like blood."

Suddenly a large brass candlestick holder came hurtling through the air towards them, crashing to the ground and a shadowy figure ran down the stairs towards the church crypt.

Harry raised his rifle and fired a warning shot over the shadow's head. "Don't move or I will shoot you again."

"No Harry, he's hurt" shouted Sofia over the echo of the gunshot still ringing around the crypt.

Cautiously she approached the intruder, who was now slumped against the wall, and he began slowly slipping to the ground.

The figure pulled back the hood of his cloak to reveal an elderly looking man with long grey hair, the most piercing blue eyes, and a strange, slightly silvery glow to his skin.

"Who are you?" she asked.

The figure looked up at her clearly in some considerable discomfort. His breathing was labored.

"My name is Enmerkar, and I am almost the last of my kind."

"What do you mean, your kind? she asked, "almost the last?"

"We call ourselves the Einari. You knew us well

once, but now you know of us only in your dreams and in your myths and legends. In the Middle East you called us the Watchers, the Djinn or the Annunaki, and in Europe you called us the Golden Race, the sons of Zeus, the long-lived ones. We have gone by many names."

Sofia could not help herself as she instinctively reeled back in horror, "are you an alien?"

Enmerkar laughed then winced in pain, "no, of course not, we are from Earth just as you are."

"Then how come we have never heard of the Einari, and how do you know our language?"

Sofia took off her jacket, helped him sit and put it behind his head.

"My race invented your language and much more besides."

"I cannot tell you how long our civilization has existed now; its beginnings are lost in the vast reaches of time. We were not the first, but we were perhaps one of Earth's earlier flowers. Our civilization was at its height around half a million years ago."

Harry stood over him threateningly, pointing his rifle at his head.

"You're injured said Sofia, let me help you I am a doctor."

"No," replied Enmerkar, "you cannot help me, I am dying."

"Stay still, let me look at your wound, it doesn't look too bad."

"Thank you, child, but it is not my wound that is killing me, I don't have much time please listen carefully.

We are indeed a long-lived race by your standard, I was born in 23,580 BC as you reckon time, but the glory of our race has long since faded, and now our time is coming to an end."

"23,580 BC, that's not possible," said Sofia.

"Yes, it is, I am living proof here before you," he paused as he smiled at the irony of his words as he now lay so close to death.

He reached under his cloak and pulled out a small parcel handing it to Sofia. She opened it carefully and inside was a deck of what looked like playing cards.

"The symbols hidden within the cards contain all the secrets of our science, what you would call the secret of eternal life, the fountain of youth and Magic. Take them, use them. You must learn everything you can from the symbols because if we fail, then you are going to need the knowledge they conceal, in order to defeat them."

"Learn what? defeat who?" she asked completely baffled.

"The others" he replied, "the Vori. We have watched over you for almost half a million years, protected you, nurtured you and helped you develop your science to the point where you are ready to explore the stars, but they have challenged us at every step, poisoning your race, destroying every flower of civilization that arose."

Sofia's head was reeling, "….. the, what did you call them, the Vori?

Are they aliens?"

Enmerkar smiled again, "yes and no."

"Yes and no, what kind of an answer is that. What is going on?" she asked.

"You know of them too in your legends, eons ago you called them the Archons but today you know their descendants as the Illuminati. Take my ring; find Erianes if you can, and she will help you finish what must be done."

Sofia stared at the ring, a strange-coiled golden

serpent with Ruby eyes and a blue stone in the centre of its forehead which seemed to glow dimly at first and then with more purpose.

"Where can I find this Erianes" asked Sofia, but as she turned her gaze back to Enmerkar, he appeared to be dead.

"Let's get the hell out of here "said Harry, "I am really not sure what the hell just happened, but this place is seriously giving me the creeps."

"We can't just leave him," said Sofia.

"Looks like we won't have to." As they turned again to look at his body Enmerkar simply faded and vanished like smoke disappearing on a soft breeze.

Harry was now completely freaked out and hyperventilating "Holy shit, holy shit ….no one is going to believe this."

"Calm down, they don't have to believe," said Sofia; holding up the ring and the small parcel, "we have proof."

"Proof of what?" he asked.

As they left the church their friends from the village were beginning to enter the glade. Four of them were carrying a dead Boar on a makeshift litter.

"Hey Harry, what happened here, you look drained, we heard the shots, what have you been shooting in the church? You English are crazy, you know that?" said Alessandro smiling and teasing him.

Harry opened his mouth to speak but Sofia gently squeezed his hand, and gently shook her head, silently imploring him not to share the strange events that had just transpired.

"Erm, it was an accident" he said. "I thought I saw the boar, so I fired off a round but when I realised how close we were to the church I thought I had better come and make sure I hadn't hit anything important. I knocked over the brass candlestick at the door, it probably sounded like another gun going off I expect. "

Alessandro just waved, "you weren't shooting the ghost, were you? People don't come up here much, particularly alone, they are frightened."

"Ghost? What ghost?" said Sofia.

Alessandro just shrugged, "there have always been tales of the ghosts in this place. Come on" he said. "Don't be embarrassed, we all make mistakes, we are heading back to the village for a drink. We must celebrate our good fortune so as not to anger the sisters of fate for their kindness."

"Great" said Harry, "I think we could use one," and they followed the party back down the hill to the village square.

Later that evening back in the villa Sofia and Harry poured themselves another glass of wine and sat silently looking at the golden ring and the deck of cards placed on the table between them.

"I have seen something like these cards before," said Harry.

"They are almost like Tarot Cards, but the pictures are somehow more vivid, more precise, just more…." As he gazed at them, he seemed to go into a trance like state.

"What are you thinking" she asked.

Harry suddenly snapped out of it.

"I don't know what to think," said Harry.

"I don't believe that bollocks about him being twenty-five thousand years old, but I have never seen anyone like him, and I have no idea how he appeared then disappeared like that. He did look like he was well over eighty though and, I if I am honest, he probably moved quicker that I can. He was also very strong, that huge brass candlestick must have weighed almost two hundred pounds. I had trouble just standing it up again before we left. I doubt I could have thrown it like that, in fact if I hadn't seen it with my own eyes, I would have said it was impossible. He was tall too, even though he was hunched up on the floor I reckon he was at least eight or nine inches taller than I am."

Sofia stared at him for moment. Harry was thirty-five years old, six foot four inches tall with piercing blue eyes, straw blond hair and from years of playing rugby he was a ruggedly handsome, muscular seventeen stone man.

Then she thought about the figure hunched on the floor of the church again and she shuddered.

"What are we going to do with these? `` said Sofia, 'we can't just pretend they doesn't exist.'

"Yes, ... yes, we can do exactly that, let's just put them away and never tell anyone about this. "

'Harry, you are a historian, this is one of the greatest discoveries of all time, you can't just sweep this under the carpet and ignore it."

"Oh yes we can" he replied. "I have worked for the British Museum for fifteen years and we sweep stuff under the carpet all the time if it doesn't fit with the academic view of history, and trust me, this definitely does not fit with the academic view of history."

"I am not going to ruin my career over a pack of cards or a ring, although I have to admit it's a strange and beautiful ring and the material the cards are made from is like nothing I have ever seen before."

"Come on Indiana Jones she teased him; let's solve this mystery together."

"Lets' go to bed "he said, "we need to get some rest, my nerves are frazzled" but as they lay next to one another staring out into the darkness sleep would not come for Harry.

The following morning when Sofia arose Harry was already in the living room watching the news.

" Good morning" she said,

"" Hello beautiful" he replied, "did you sleep well?"

"Yes" she said emphatically, almost surprised.

"I am not sure if it was the wine or the excitement, but I was drained, although I am guessing you didn't?"

"No," he said shaking his head, "I have been sitting down here watching CNN and the BBC world service for hours and something has been bothering me. "

"What?" she asked.

"Well yesterday morning I thought this was just another type of FLU and that we're over-reacting with all the travel bans but after the…you know what…. now I am wondering if there is a connection?"

"Look at this" he said rewinding the live play TV.

"Do you notice anything strange about these interviews with the UK Prime Minister and the US President?"

Sofia studied the TV intently, "they both look tired" she said, "and I suppose a little agitated, but with all the restrictions they are putting in place that is not really surprising, they must be under quite some pressure. Why?"

"Exactly" said Harry, "they both seem agitated, it's as if there are implementing something that they don't really agree with, but they are being forced to go along with. Don't you think that is strange?"

"Now that you mention it; yes, it is, do you really think there is a connection?"

"Honestly, I am beginning to wonder" he said.

"Maybe you were right. Maybe we should investigate this.

Sofia smiled. "I have booked us flights to London" he continued. I am ok to travel as I am going home, and you can come as a qualified health worker, so the lock down won't apply to us."

3. THE BRITISH MUSEUM.

By the time they arrived in London and cleared customs, it was already getting late. Although the journey itself had been quite short, they could not help feeling that the formalities of travel due to the covid epidemic were making even the shortest trips unnecessarily arduous. To add to their frustration, neither of them had slept well since the incident in the forest and now it was beginning to catch up on them. They were tired even before they had boarded the plane and now, they just wanted to make the journey into central London as quick and easy as possible. They grabbed their bags, walked through the arrival hall, then headed straight for the taxi rank. A large Asian man climbed out of his cab, picked up their bags and put them in the boot.

"Where to chief?" he asked cheerfully, before pointing out that they should wear face masks whilst inside the vehicle for their own safety.

"The Academy Hotel in Bloomsbury please" replied Harry.

In truth he had not given much to thought to the hotel, he had booked into one that was close to the British Museum.

The following morning after breakfast they took the short walk in the crisp morning air to the Museum through Russell Gardens, along Montague Street where they turned left onto Great Russell Street, and they were soon greeted by the magnificent columned entrance.

"I never tire of this" said Harry, admiring the magnificent

façade through the iron railings.

“I can see why. It is certainly a spectacular building,” said Sofia. “Fitting surroundings for some of the most important artefacts on earth don’t you think?”

“If you had asked me that a few days ago I would have agreed without hesitation, but right now I am not so sure what is important and what is not.” he said.

Sofia nodded. “I know what you mean.”

They walked through the gates and up the steps to the reception desk where Harry smiled, said hello to the security guard and asked if Professor Frederikson had arrived yet.

“Hello Dr Taylor”, he said, “I wasn’t expecting you back at work just yet, this must be your lovely fiancé that you have been telling us so much about?”

“Yes”, he said introducing Sofia, who was now blushing.

“I think the professor has arrived, it is 9.30 am, so I guess he will be in his office by now, would you like me to call up and check for you?”

‘Thanks John” said Harry “that won’t be necessary,” and they made their way up the stone staircase at the rear of the exhibition galleries to a small brown door with the words 'Silence - Reading Room' embossed on them in a very precise, gold italic script.

Harry opened the door just a little and stuck his head around to see that his friend and mentor Professor Frederikson was alone.

"Harry"' he shouted, "my dear boy, come in. What are you doing back already?"

Harry smiled and put his finger to his lips. "Oh, I am sorry' "said the Professor as he fumbled in his jacket pocket, "I haven't turned my hearing aid on this morning, am I shouting again?"

Harry just smiled and nodded his head.

"You do know this is not really a reading room don't you Harry?"

"What?" Asked Harry pointing incredulously at the sign on the door.

The professor laughed. It was a spare door we scrounged from the British library in the 1970s when we were short of funds.

Sofia could not help herself and she too burst out

laughing.

“Ah Sofia, hello there I am so glad you have had time to visit us again, I thought you were staying in Italy until all of this virus nonsense has blown over.”

“Err yes, we were” said Harry, “but you know how it is, we were getting a little cabin fever. Besides I thought it would be a good opportunity to use the time productively and maybe do a little research.”

Professor Frederikson looked rather skeptically over the top of his glasses.

“Research into what my boy?”

“Well, you are always telling me I should broaden my horizons if I want a professorship and tenure so I thought I would have a look at Ancient Middle Eastern history, perhaps the Sumerians” he said.

“Hmmm. I am no expert in that area but as you know our galleries are second to none for the period, but you would really need to see Professor Vishwanath. He is our new expert on Middle and Near eastern antiquities.”

“Who is Professor Vishwanath and why don’t I know him?” asked Harry.

"He only arrived a few weeks ago said the Professor, from the Smithsonian in Washington DC no less. He's very knowledgeable, and quite charming. What time is it......9.45? he usually has a coffee with his interns first thing, but I think he will be here in about half an hour."

"Great "said Harry "we will wait, if that is ok with you?"

"Of course, it is OK my boy. Can I offer you both a cup of coffee?"

"Tell me, how is your father, Harry?"

"He is not well again I am afraid Professor; I am hoping to be able to visit him now that I am back in London, but it all depends on the lockdown, they are quite strict with visitors in the nursing homes at the moment."

The professor nodded. "He's a good man your father, I do miss him you know."

"I will be sure to pass on your regards. He is always talking about the things the two of you got up to when you were excavating the Ring of Brodgar in the Shetlands and the Durrington wall near Stonehenge."

"As yes" he laughed. "The good old days, the time goes by so quickly and there is so much to learn."

"Did you ever finish your book?" asked Sofia.

"Which one my dear?"

"When I was here last you mentioned that you had a manuscript for a book about Stonehenge."

"As yes, that one"' he said. "Yes, we did finish it but" …. his voice trailed off.

"Could I get a copy please?" asked Sofia.

"No, unfortunately that is not possible. You see we never did publish it I am afraid. In the end it was just too controversial for the mainstream. Harry's father and I believed that Stonehenge was only the tip of the iceberg, a very small and minor part of a much bigger system of astronomical observatories that included Woodhenge, Durrington Walls, Avebury, Karnac in north-western France, not to mention the ancient sites in Shetland and Orkney which may be even older.

It seemed like a very sophisticated system to us. All of the evidence we uncovered supported that view and we did try to make the case to the board of the museum, but they kept pushing back. In the end it proved to be just too controversial to keep pushing against the accepted view, which was that our ancestors were somehow savage brutes with little in the way of technology.

Academia sometimes moves much more slowly than I would have liked, but there you have it. Neither of us could afford to lose our positions, so we let sleeping dogs lie as they say. Why do you ask?"

This time it was Harry's turn to grasp Sofia's hand silently imploring her not to reveal anything just yet.

"Oh no reason" she said, "I always loved your tales and thought you both very clever. It can't be easy investigating the past when there is so little to go on. You are a natural storyteller Professor."

"Ah" said the Professor, "you know a beautiful young lady buttering an old man up like a piece of bread is heart warming, and especially welcome on such a cold morning. You should come to visit us more often" and he laughed.

Then he gave Harry a quizzical look, "so much like your father, he would have gotten us into all sorts of trouble if I had let him. A tinge of sadness briefly crept into his eyes; and then, almost casually he added, "perhaps I should have let him, but I wasn't brave enough I am afraid."

A moment later, before they could question him further Professor Vishwanath came in. "Good morning, "said the Professor; "May I introduce you to one of our colleagues and my protégé Dr Harry Taylor. This is his lovely fiancé, Sofia. Harry would like to pick your brains about the Sumerians if you have a little free time."

"Of course, it would be my pleasure" said Professor Vishwanath with a broad smile. Holding out his hand he introduced himself to them both.

"Please, finish your coffee and then we can walk down to the galleries. So, you want to know about the Sumerians?"

"Yes" said Harry, "Professor Frederikson has been encouraging me for quite some time to expand my horizons I thought I could use the lock down to broaden my knowledge a bit."

"I see, very commendable. Well, you have picked quite a difficult topic I am afraid. You see the Sumerians were an interesting lot to be sure, but we know almost nothing about them directly. They are rather shrouded in myths and legends I am afraid. We know more about their gods than the people themselves."

"Perfect" said Sofia, accidentally revealing her growing sense of excitement.

They drained their coffee from the brightly coloured mugs and the Professor suggested they should perhaps start with the Assyrians, so they set off down the stairs to the galleries.

"Why the Assyrians" asked Sophia.

"Well, Sumer was believed to be based in what is today southern Iraq or Mesopotamia as it was known in ancient times. It literally means the land between two the rivers. The rivers in question being the Euphrates, and the Tigris of course. The Sumerians were believed to be a very ancient people, perhaps the oldest civilisation on Earth that we know of, even pre-dating the Dynastic Egyptians. It is at least 8,000 years old, but there are some intriguing references to it being much older than that.

The Akkadians ruled the same area from around 2,500 BC and they then became part of the Assyrian empire. Fortunately for us, both the Akkadians and the Assyrians had a very handy habit of writing things down. Ah, here we are."

The Professor stopped outside of the Assyrian gallery, where he looked up at two massive stone figures, each perhaps ten feet tall. They looked like a giant bull, but with the addition of wings and the faces of bearded men.

"We think they are representations of Cherubim or protective spirits "said the Professor, "magnificent aren't they."

"I thought Cherubim were cute little baby-faced angels," said Sofia.

"Yes, it's a common misconception. In ancient legends the Cherubim were placed outside the Garden of Eden when Adam and Eve were supposedly evicted to prevent them returning and they are also said to have guarded the way to the tree of life with fiery swords. Curious, isn't it?"

Harry was uncharacteristically quiet; he was looking closely at the Cherubim. Although at first glance they looked the same, he soon noticed that they were in fact subtly different, one had hooves and the other had feet that looked more like those of a lion. The professor, noticing his interest continued his explanation; "originally there would have been four of them, two at each entrance to the palace. I see you have noticed the feet; the other two would have had human feet and bird's feet respectively, we are not sure of it was deliberate and held any real meaning or if it's just a decorative thing."

They nodded in acknowledgment of the professor's explanation, but Harry and Sofia were both already beginning to doubt the truth of his orthodox explanation.

Harry had seen these representations before, but he could not quite put his finger on where he had seen them.

4. ENKI, LORD OF THE EINARI.

Even pushing their ship to its limits, by the time the Xisudra made orbit around Einar; Enki already knew that at least some of the Vori ships had made it to the surface and that their remaining forces were wreaking havoc. From his vantage point here, high above the planet, he could clearly see the evidence of the fire fights on the surface below as vast swathes of land seemed be on fire around the central belt. He wondered how they had they managed so much devastation in just a few hours.

His heart sank to see his home on fire. Einar was a beautiful world, like no other in the system. From space it looked like a symmetrical jewel with five distinctive stripes. Two completely white at the poles which stretched for thousands of miles, two alternating blue and green in the temperate habitable zones between the poles and then the central belt which looked like a baked brownish ring around the centre of the planet, that was broken in just a few places by warm tropical seas.

"Call the Ennead council chamber" he commanded.

Nin Kirshag answered the call.

"Sister, it is good to see that you are well," said Enki.

"Likewise; brother. What news do we have of the Vori. "

"We have prevailed thank Anu, but the victory was far from clean. I have sent Lord Erish out to the outer colonies to assess the damage. It seems that our brother Enlil may not have been killed in the attack after all."

"Yes brother, I believe he is here on Einar. His remaining

forces managed to destroy the cities of Cnuth, Eris and Akad. They have also released a pathogen into the atmosphere, we don't know its effects yet, but I would recommend you remain in orbit until we know more.

We think we have the few survivors trapped in the central belt, without shelter and supplies they cannot last long in the heat."

"No "Enki replied, "we will not remain in orbit, we have no choice now, all the outlying colonies have either been destroyed or are likely unsustainable now. They are being purged or evacuated by the Enumer squadron. Our fleet has sustained heavy damage. Much of it cannot be repaired in space, but we may be able to repurpose some of the ships and the crews will need time to honour their fallen brothers. Einar is the only place we have left to call a home, so we will come to aid you and see what can be done to repair the damage to our cities and to the atmosphere. Then we must continue to hunt down Enlil along with all of his followers before they see an end to all things."

"Very well brother": said Nin Kirshag, "I look forward to welcoming you home."

Enki turned to his commander; "send the troops down to

the burning cities Enkidu. Brief the units to look for Einari survivors and wipeout any Vori they encounter. They are not to attempt to capture them. It will cost us time and men, neither of which we can afford to lose. They will seek to get in close so that we are unable to use the firepower from our ships for ground support. If possible, keep whatever distance between them and our men as is possible. I repeat, do not let them engage in close quarter combat.

"My Lord" he said, "they are our brothers, should we not allow them to surrender."

"I give you these orders with a heavy heart Enkidu. Whatever they once were, they are no longer our brothers. Take no prisoners. Please make sure that your men are clear on my orders."

Although Enkidu was clearly uncomfortable, he nodded and acknowledged his commander's instruction, "Yes my Lord."

"Land the Xisudra on the northern continent of Atlan. It's a long way from home, but Enlil won't stay around the central belt. At least while he is trapped there, we have some small advantage, we can maintain some level of quarantine whilst we complete our work."

Three months later Lord Erish returned with what remained of the deep space fleet and the survivors from the outlying colonies. Enki greeted his old friend.

"Welcome Lord Erish, how was your mission?"

"All of the outlying colonies have either been destroyed my Lord Enki or evacuated and we have left their systems on automatic as you commanded."

"How many survivors have returned with you?"

"Approximately one hundred thousand my Lord," said Lord Erish wearily.

Enki looked aghast. "So few survivors, and from so many worlds?" he said.

"Yes, my Lord, the Vori had already started attacking the bases on the moons of the gas giants beyond the orbit of Tiamet. They wiped out seven colonies in total, before we could engage them to destroy what remained of their ships. They had created defensive positions on a further three, around on the moons of the blue world Dumuzid, and as instructed we destroyed them from space.

"Have your actions created anymore debris fields within

the solar system?"

"None that are a threat to home world," said Lord Erish.

"Good" said Enki. "We have enough problems for now. We must report to the council at once and agree how best we can utilise the resources and manpower you have returned with. We are in sore need of both.

You look troubled old friend."

"Are things so bad?" Lord Erish asked.

"The Vori have inflicted considerable damage" said Enki "but we have prevailed."

Enki called the Ennead council together.

The vast stone council chamber was truly magnificent, but somehow today it appeared a little less grand and it seemed to have lost some of the hubris with which it once loomed over the great city of Uruk.

Enki addressed the Ennead, "brothers and sisters, thanks to your steadfast support, skill, and your unflinching bravery we have won a great victory over our enemies, but the price has been almost too much to bear, and we must now consider the future of our race. Our deep space colonies are either gone or mothballed, until we can return. But to do so we must build our supply logistics once again, otherwise we would only be sending our people back out into space to their deaths, and for the moment our resources have been severely depleted.

Home world is now, once again, our last, our only refuge but even here we are not yet safe. The last of the Vori have disappeared and now we know the virus they released proves fatal to almost half of us within a matter of weeks, but we don't know yet know the long-term effects on those who may survive.

Nin Kirshag, please give the council your report, what else do we know of the infection?"

"Thank you, brother. It is a specific pathogen designed to target our chromosomes, but it seems most effective at damaging the Y Chromosomes related to the male sexual reproduction. In the cases where it is not fatal it is also severely affecting the female population in ways that we don't yet understand but we have turned over every resource we have available to work on the problem."

'Thank you, sister," said Enki.

“For all we know, the last of the Vori and Enlil may already be dead but until we find the bodies we must keep searching, it may be that we can gain some additional insight from their own dead flesh.”

Enki continued. “In destroying Tiamet our enemy have created a debris field that represents a threat to the whole system. In spite of our immediate struggles to survive and rebuild we cannot lose sight of the danger this represents. Sargon, what news do we have of Marduk.”

“We were unable to track it beyond the outer rim Lord Enki. Our best hope is that it may continue on its trajectory into interstellar space, but we cannot be sure, and we don’t have the resources to send a ship. I have deployed deep space probes that will hopefully alert us to its return should its orbit stabilise, but there is a lot of space to monitor, and our resources are thinly spread.”

“Yes, I understand. Thank you, Sargon.

Enkidu, what is the status of our ground forces and the general population movements across the globe?”

“It is not good my news my Lord Enki” replied Enkidu “the population is now no more than half a million worldwide. We have a dozen fully operational fighting units, and about half a dozen more seriously depleted, but we are having to cannibalise some of the more badly damaged ships to keep them supplied."

Enki nodded acknowledging the report.

A messenger entered the chamber and hurried to Nin Kirshag causing Enki to pause. "Sister, you wish to address the council again?" he asked.

"Yes brother, we have now discovered that there is another side effect of the pathogen. Those who survive have a marked reduction in reproductive functions. At the current rate of spread, even if we can get the current infection under control, we will be an infertile species within ten generations."

"Ten generations? that is no more than half a million years."

The hall was suddenly completely silent as the council members contemplated the extinction of their species.

Even the mighty Enki looked visibly diminished.

"How can this be?" asked Sargon, we have just destroyed half of the solar system to defeat the enemy and you are saying that all is now lost."

"No, all is not necessarily lost," said Nin Kirshag.

"All is not necessarily lost?" repeated Sargon. "Then what course of action do you recommend to the council?"

"I recommend that Lord Erish, bring the survivors to the cities of Uruk, Ur and Eridu. We have more chance of protecting them here and treating them if we can.

I would propose that we establish a remote laboratory aboard the Xisudra in Atlan where we can continue our work on a cure."

The council murmured in general agreement.

"And there is one more thing…." her voice tailed off. "We need an alternative in case we are unsuccessful. "

"What do you mean an alternative?" asked Sargon,

"Although it has been adapted and engineered, the virus has its origins on Vorea, but somehow it has also managed to adapt to the climactic conditions here. The Vori were our brothers and sisters once, so that is perhaps not surprising. Of more concern should be that they were unable to find a cure despite having access to much of the same technology that we have at our disposal. The one thing we do have which they perhaps did not, is that we have seen how it progresses and so we have a slight element of advantage in time providing we move quickly. So, I repeat, I think it is sensible to consider an alternative, one that will see our race survive albeit our children would be like none who have gone before."

"What exactly are you proposing sister? "Enki asked.

"Well, firstly I would like to create a genetic Ark, but it may already be too late, it is getting harder and harder to find people who have had no exposure to this phage and as I said even those who have recovered are showing lasting DNA damage. I would like the council's permission to engineer the lower species, the hominids to carry our genes before it is too late."

The council exploded in uproar.

"Silence" said Enki calling the council to order.

"You know that hybrid genetic engineering has been outlawed for millennia and for good reason." "Yes brother" said Nin Kirshag, "but with respect council, our race has never been threatened with extinction before and we understand the processes much better than we did when our forebears experimented with it many millennia ago. Our aims this time are very different, we are talking about grafting some of our characteristics into their make-up, using them as a living Ark.

They are a short-lived species, but their breeding capacity is far greater than ours, we could learn much across the course of just a few of their generations. There is strength in numbers when it comes to genetic diversity and our numbers may soon be unsustainable. We will not be making them more docile to enslave them as we did in the past to help us build the mining facilities and establish the colonies. I would not ask this thing in any other circumstances."

Enki was a beloved leader who ruled by right, but he was also astute, he recognised more clearly than anyone their dire situation and there was no one he trusted more than his beloved sister. He knew she was right and but now was not the time to ride roughshod over the council. He looked around at the faces of the council members. They were all weary. Although they too were aware of the situation Nin Kirshag's request had exploded like a bomb and so he weighed his words carefully.

"I think it is clear," said Enki "that we are all uncomfortable with what you are proposing, but it will serve no purpose to debate this in the heat of the moment without some clarity and calm for reflection. What you say is true, we are facing a threat unprecedented in our history, but even so this is not a step we can take lightly.

We will reconvene one Enad from today, bring a detailed proposal before us and I will ask the council to consider your request further.

In the interim, you may set up your laboratory aboard the Xisudra on Atlan to continue the work on seeking a cure. You may also make your preparations for the alternative so that we are ready should an agreement be reached, but in the meantime sister, heed my warning, on pain of death nothing must commence with the hominids before the council has considered the detailed proposal and gives its consent."

Enki scanned the council members again; they were all now nodding in general agreement. "Very well brother, thank you."

5. THE LOST WORLD OF SUMER.

Professor Vishwanath led Harry and Sofia into the main hall of the Assyrian gallery. Sofia took a deep breath as she surveyed the scene before her. The gallery was a magnificent sight, almost two hundred feet long, lined on both sides by intricate stone tablets depicting, wars, hunting, marriages, coronations, and all kinds of other much stranger scenes.

The Professor watched her as she took in the scene, and he smiled. "It often has that effect on people" he said. "Those of us who work in the museum are incredibly privileged to see this every day, but these are some of the greatest treasures on Earth. These are one of the reasons I came to the British Museum. They tell not just the story of a long dead civilisation, they tell our story, and it is a magnificent one. All the more so, because of the huge difficulties we have faced to come this far."

"What difficulties?" asked Sofia, encouraging the Professor to elaborate further.

"Well," he hesitated "a lot of things about the ancient past are uncertain but one thing that is not in doubt, is that civilisations, or perhaps it would be more accurate to call them empires, have risen and fallen many times over the last ten millennia that we know of. War, pestilence, famine have always been common place and more often than not, they were the reasons why they fell, but they varied enormously in size with some lasting significantly longer than others. The most successful of these lasted for many hundreds of years, and others for just the lifetime of one particularly strong ruler. It's not just about the ability to conquer your enemies that is important."

"What do you mean?" asked Sofia.

"Well not to put too fine a point on it, it's also about the ability to breed too if you want to establish a lasting dynasty."

Harry nodded in agreement.

"These carvings are amazing," said Sofia, getting her line of investigation back on track. "Where do they come from, and who are all these people?"

"Most of them come from the ancient city of Nineveh in Northern Iraq, and many are believed to be from the palace of King Ashurbanipal and his forebears."

"What do you think these scenes represent?" she asked.

"For the most part they tell the story of the empire, specifically the rulers but also more generally of what you might call the elite. They show things like important battles, slaves being led away, sieges, chariot racing or hunting. There are even scenes depicting armies swimming across rivers, and this one "he said, pointing to a figure sitting in a chair with three large objects above him, "we think is an astronomical seal of some sort. It depicts Shamash the Sun God, Nanna the Moon Goddess and something called Marduk. "Marduk the destroyer, to be more precise."

"They seem remarkably modern" she said.

"Yes, in some respects they do, when you think of what they had all that time ago and then compare that with how it took Europe many millennia to reach the same level of sophistication."

Harry meanwhile was staring at a panel with a very large figure holding what looked like a Lion in his arms, "he's huge, he must be nine or ten feet tall."

"Ah yes, this panel was very kindly loaned to us by the Louvre in Paris. It is believed to be the fabled king Nimrod, a direct descendent of their line of deities. I suppose he does look rather tall, but it depends on how old the lion he is holding is of course.

It was quite common to show the Kings as being much taller than the rest of the people in these carvings. It added to their sense of power and grandeur you see."

Harry had a quick look along the line of panels, and even seated the rulers were indeed taller than their subjects who were standing before them. He shivered when he thought of the dying figure huddled in the Crypt of the church of Santa Maria.

"What is this?" asked Sofia as she moved on to the next panel, which showed two figures facing what looked like a tree? Above the tree was a winged disk with a small figure inside it that seemed to be looking down on what they were doing. They were both pointing something resembling a pinecone at the tree, and behind each of them stood another winged figure.

"What are these in the background?" she asked.

"Well, if I am totally honest, we are not sure. We think they may be representations of protective spirits or Genies."

"They all look like they are carrying handbags and wearing watches. Their clothes are quite luxurious even by relatively recent standards. Is that some sort of flying craft above them all? I have never seen anything like this, and I never imagined seeing this on something so old."

"Yes" said the Professor, "It is curious that although our modern view of history is one of a long continuous climb up towards civilisation from the barbarous stone age, the evidence really does not always support that view. Civilisation certainly does seem to make huge leaps and then fall back but if you are talking about 'ancient astronauts', I am afraid I cannot subscribe to that view, and I would certainly recommend you don't expound that kind of theory around here" he said glancing Harry.

"I understand" he said, "I guess it would be helpful for the sake of context to maybe understand some of the myths and see where they overlap with what we think we know. After all, Troy was considered a legend too was it not? until Heinrich Schliemann followed the story of the siege and found the site in modern day Turkey."

"Quite true." said the professor, "That is not an unreasonable hypothesis, but Schliemann got lucky. He had the Illiad to follow as his guide. We don't know what sources Homer drew from when he wrote it, but it is very detailed and of course he was also lot closer in history to the real events. Regrettably we don't have anything quite as extensive as the Homeric poems when it comes to the Sumerians."

"What do we have?" asked Harry.

"Well, not as much as we would like. You have to remember that much of the Middle East was subject to

European colonialism. That is even after we take into account the ancient wars that we know of, with everyone from the Greeks and Persians all the way through to Genghis Khan and undoubtedly there were others of which we currently know nothing. As a result, a lot of the historical treasures are either lost or scattered across the world, so it is very hard to get a clear picture.

The Central Museum in Baghdad was actually quite a good source of material thanks to Saddam Hussein of all people, but it has been looted several times as a result of the recent Gulf wars. They even had a battery from that period."

"Excuse me," said Harry.

"Oh yes, a battery" repeated the Professor, "it is quite famous." It is basically an earthen pot with electrodes in it. You put any acidic electrolytic liquid in it, like lemon juice for example, to make it function. We have long known that they could generate small amounts of electricity but what they used it for was a mystery. Academia doesn't really want to know if I am honest."

"Why?" asked Sofia.

"Well, I suppose the obvious thing I would use a

battery for would be electroplating. You dissolve say gold or silver nitrate in water before running an electric current through it and it can be used to coat cheaper materials."

Suddenly the light bulb went on in Harry's mind "……and then most of the ancient golden treasures we have, may not turn out to be quite as priceless as we thought?"

"Exactly "said the professor "As I am sure you know Harry; a lot of this stuff is still in private hands. Most of these collectors are powerful people and they wouldn't take too kindly to their apple cart being upset if you get my meaning."

"So apart from the museum here and in Paris what other good sources do we have for understanding their myths and legends?" asked Sofia.

"Surprisingly the traditional Christian Bible is one of the best sources. The book of genesis is largely a re-written version of a Sumerian legend."

"You have to be joking?" said Harry.

"No, not at all," said the Professor. "We have all heard the story of the Great Flood, yes? Well, here it is on this stone tablet" as he pointed to what looked like intricate indents and scratch marks of several smashed clay tablets that had been roughly placed back together.

"The writing is called cuneiform. We believe they wrote on wet clay bricks using a reed stylus before leaving them out to set in the sun to dry and harden. This one is very famous, and it is a particular favourite of mine. It is called the Epic of Gilgamesh.

It tells the story of a great Sumerian King who had many adventures but one of which was to track down a character called Xisudra or Utnapishtim depending on the translation. He was supposed to be the last survivor from the days before the great flood.

In the story the Gods led by Enlil had decided to destroy mankind long ago, but Enki decided that he wanted to save them, so he warned Xisudra of the coming deluge. On Enki's instructions he built a very strange cube shaped craft and with it he managed to save his family along with lots of the animals that inhabited the earth at that time. As a reward for his bravery and skill, after the flood the Gods decided to not only let him live but they also made him immortal. But it was not so good for the rest of mankind as from then on, the lives of all men were shortened."

Harry looked stunned and he glanced at Sofia who

simply opened her eyes wider in silent acknowledgement of what he was thinking.

"Who were these gods and were they really immortal?" asked Sofia?

"You're getting into the realms of pseudo-science now and I am afraid I cannot follow you there, but if you were still interested, I would recommend you visit the Atlantis book shop just over the road from the museum or Watkins bookshop, in Cecil Court on the edge of Covent Garden. Have a look at the 'Berossus King list', and also there are quite a few works by an author called Zechariah Sitchin, a Russian national who has some interesting ideas, but mainstream archeologists have never accepted them."

"Just one more thing before we go." Harry pulled the snake ring out of his pocket. Have you ever seen anything like this before?" he asked.

The professor examined it closely. "My word that's a beautiful ring, I have never seen craftsmanship like it, where did you find it? "

"I believe it is very old" said Harry ignoring the question, "maybe from the Sumerian area."

"Well, the motif of a snake was also found in the Garden

of Eden of course and there is one tablet in the museum of a naked female figure with claws like those of the lion she is shown standing on. She is believed to be a winged demon but often she is associated with Lilith."

"Who or what was Lilith?" asked Harry

"My dear boy "said the professor, "you really didn't pay attention at Sunday school, did you? Lilith was Adam's first wife before God created Eve for him."

"What happened to her" he asked?

"There are lots of different stories but essentially, as the legend goes, she ran away from the garden of Eden and three angels were sent to bring her back. When she would not return, she was cursed. From then on, she was said to be the slayer of children and the mother of all demons. She is often depicted with a snake motif."

Harry was gob smacked, he had to stop his mouth falling open and a cold a shiver ran down Sofia's spine.

"Thank you so much Professor that has been a really enlightening tour."

"Anytime Harry, I have some work to do and some calls to make today but I will be in for most of the week if you have any more questions."

Saying goodbye, they made their way out of the museum back towards their hotel and stopped at a small coffee shop for a sandwich.

Harry looked at Sofia who was clearly energized by what she had heard. "In Italy we always studied the Romans the Etruscans or the Greeks when it came to history, but I never imagined in my wildest dreams that anything like this was even remotely possible" she said.

"And what about the demon child murderer" said Harry, "how much do we really want to pull on this thread?"

"Let's go to the bookshop after lunch and keep following the trail," said Sofia. "This could re-write the whole of our history, we can't stop now."

"OK but tomorrow I want to see my father too.

Professor Frederikson was trying to tell me something."

6. LILITH.

Across town in the financial district of the City of London, Lilith was sitting in her office. She was playing with a digestive biscuit while she slowly sipped her tea. Somehow this strange little ritual had insinuated itself to become an essential part of her daily routine, one which allowed her to blend in. The people here were fascinated with tea and biscuits. She dipped her biscuit into her cup but she waited too long and it broke in half. "Oh bugger it" she said to herself, "I just can't seem to get the hang of these things," then she reached for a spoon to remove the sludge at the bottom of her cup. "Hmmm she thought there is a real knack to this."

The tea was ruined so she pushed the cup to one side. Staring out sullenly over the skyline she let her mind wander.

She still found it hard to get used to the height of some of the buildings in London. They seemed to loom over the people below, quietly exuding an air of menace, much like the sky which all too often was grey and cloudy here. She wondered why men wanted to live in such cold surroundings where they were completely divorced from the natural world. Didn't they crave the sun? she wondered. It made no sense to her, it was not as if any of them actually, ever seemed to be happy here, in their very own little concrete zoo.

It wasn't that Lilith disliked people; indeed, they were very useful to her most of the time and she could be very engaging socially when it suited her. If she had learned anything from her, very long life experience, it was that perhaps eighty percent of her success had been about how she worked with people. Perhaps it would be more accurate to say, how she got them to work for her. That aside though, there was no getting away from it, she simply found them exhausting. Incapable of seeing things for what they really were, they filled their lives with any number of unimportant, little, things that they worried themselves sick over needlessly, and in the process, they diminished themselves. In her experience they were completely oblivious to the flow of history, to what was really happening in the world around them but saddest of all, to their own magnificent potential. She could forgive them all that because that was not the worst of it. It was their constant whining that really drove her mad.

She thought back to her home, so warm, bright, and full of life that suddenly the world outside her window looked even more cold and austere if that were possible. Still, in more normal time these soulless edifices had certainly made her life considerably easier. People could, and frequently did, disappear in broad daylight almost un-noticed by the multitudes who thronged 'to and fro' across the city with the surge of the morning or evening rush hours. To her they looked like a human tide, mimicking the natural rhythm of the sea, and the life from which they now seemed so completely divorced.

Here she could live in plain sight, she could walk freely amongst any crowd. It mattered not if she could be seen by a thousand eyes. At the same time she would always remain strangely invisible to all of them, they were so wrapped up their own little lives. The cold and cloudy vision outside seemed to make the day draw to a close much quicker but she noted that it was also getting quite late. The city was still, almost eerily quiet now due to the lockdown. Most of her colleagues had long since decided to work from home. They were probably skiving more often than working but that did not concern her. At least she could avoid all that pointless small talk about the weather, Sandra's arthritic cat and the constant arguments about whether Yorkshire tea really was the best that you could get.

Her phone rang, dragging her away from her day dream. She looked at the caller ID and raising an eyebrow in curiosity answered it. "Hello Professor" she said.

The voice at the end of the phone seemed quite agitated as it relayed its news.

"I see," said Lilith "well that is interesting, and you say it was the depictions of the Annunaki that were of specific interest? Did he mention if he was looking for anything in particular?"

"No? Tell me, was he alone?"

"Where are they now?"

"His father?"

"Thank you, that was most interesting, ... yes, you were right to call me, please do let me know when they return, I would love to meet him, he sounds like a very interesting young man. Have a good evening professor Vishwanath" she said as she put the phone down.

"So" she thought to herself... "They have come at long last and the race is on." She mused to herself about what she should do next. "They obviously haven't found it yet so for now nothing changes, for the time being they are not a threat. Eventually our paths will cross, and I will deal with him then......but what to do about her.... hmm."

"Yasmina" a voice called through the half open doorway.

"Yes Mr Thompson" Lilith replied, as she got up and made her towards his office.

She looked around the half open door to see her boss,

Nathan Thompson staring at his computer screen as he always seemed to be. This time he was scanning through his emails but if it wasn't that it would have been something else. Marketing reports, on line discussion groups, LinkedIn, surfing the net for the latest news on hot advertising trends. It wore her out just thinking about it although she did wonder how he had come dull. It was as if by some strange act of self-immolation he had sacrificed himself in order to join his soul with the screen and the digital world beyond it.

Time for the actress within her to take to the centre stage once more. She knew he fancied her so she always dressed provocatively to make sure that he did not forget it. In fact she was one of the few things that ever distracted his attention from the screen in front of him. The attraction was so powerful that she could literally wind him around her little finger. It was it all he could to stop himself drooling over her whenever he stood by her desk, but for now he was safely ensconced behind his own desk on the other side of the room. Lilith was more than adept at playing her flirtatious games, she had been doing it so long it was second nature to her but even she got tired sometimes. Now that she was close to completing her work here in London, this was definitely one of those times, but she smiled at him non the less.

Nathan Thompson himself was unsure why he felt the way he did around her, he was in his late forties, balding, with a greying beard. He was more than a little overweight and he generally preferred tall, blond women who were a little older than his assistant and who also boasted the 'curves' to match his own.

Yasmina was none of these things. She was petite, a little over five feet tall, her hair was almost jet black and he believed her to be in her late twenties or early thirties.

There was no denying however, that whatever that elusive 'sex appeal' or 'animal magnetism' was, she was without doubt its embodiment. Perhaps it was her deep brown, rather soulful eyes. They seemed to him like two deep, dark wells that he could fall into if he looked at them for too long. It was at the same time hypnotic and soothing yet strangely exhilarating.

The firm had hired her just before lockdown, although he wasn't even sure why they had taken her on as she had little relevant experience that she could point to. Yet there was no denying that she had been incredibly useful to the firm. Almost without exception potential clients that came in wanted to sign up to the firm once they had met her, and she had proven to be quite the master stroke when it came to getting them to 'sign on the dotted line' or to bring their invoices up to date.

Just hearing her voice on the telephone seemed to enchant any listener. He found it hard to rationalise, but when she spoke her words seemed to almost have a liquid quality to them. They were able to somehow evoke a soothing feeling, like warm honey, sweet and comforting. It was quite remarkable really. There was no doubt in his mind that Yasmina had played a big part in making NT & Partners not only the biggest, but also the most lucrative, online advertising firm in London in just three short years and for him, the lure of easy money had a very strong appeal.

He looked up from his computer screen and smiled weakly at her.

"Yasmina, I see you have submitted a request for leave."

"Yes Mr Thompson, that is correct."

"Well, a month is a long time and it's our busiest period coming up. We could really do with all hands on deck but….err…."

He paused as she stared at him intently. Her eyes widened

and the corners of her lips curving up into the slightest and most enigmatic of coy smiles.

"…. I suppose that it would be ok," he continued "are you going anywhere nice?"

"Men are so weak" she thought to herself smiling, "I always get what I want, it is amazing they have lasted so long."

"I need to visit my family in Iran" she cooed gently. "My mother has been very unwell. I am so worried about her. As you know the hospitals are full there due to the Covid pandemic and the ongoing international sanctions make it difficult to get medical supplies so I would like to spend some time helping to care for her at home."

The truth however was somewhat different. Yes, she did have family in Iran but for the moment they were a secondary consideration. A family visit would have to wait. She had now finished her research at all of the major museums in London and had reviewed every ancient text she could access. Ironically the breadcrumb trail was now leading back to her homeland and the cold truth was that Nathan Thompson LLP had now served its purpose.

If employing her had been a master stroke for the business, it was certainly, if unknowingly, reciprocated as the firm had provided her with the perfect front. She had made them successful and in return they had sponsored almost every exhibit of interest to her across the city. In the process that had given her privileged access and allowed her to complete her work free from the scrutiny of prying eyes. A little well-placed patronage here and there had also been extremely useful in providing the connections she needed to keep her well informed when prying eyes came calling, as she knew full well that one day they must.

Professor Vishwanath's rather too inquisitive visitors to the British Museum that morning were unlikely to be the last that he would receive. The star or Enlil was still out there somewhere. She could feel herself getting closer to her prize, but with every lead and subsequent dead end, her patience was now wearing thin and the search was proving to be something of a pain. She really didn't mind men killing themselves in their constant wars, but she just wished that they could be a little less enthusiastic about burning everything to the ground in the wake of each petty victory. "They really need to learn the value of good admin" she thought as she waited for her boss to finish his sentence.

"Well please do take care of yourself and take precautions, we can't afford you falling ill, can we?" he said, concluding his monologue.

"I will, take plenty of precautions" she promised. I will be back before you know it."

"Very well then, I wish you and your family all the best."

"Thank you" she said.

"If there is nothing else that you need, I am just about finished for the evening and I was about to make my way home."

"No, nothing else" he said, "Goodnight Yasmina, enjoy your evening."

Then, as if he had been away too long and was answering some siren's call from deep within in him, he turned his attention back to his screen and he was once again lost to the world around him.

A rare tinge of pity invaded her heart. "One day he will be dead" she thought to herself as she turned and left his office "and I am not sure he would even know that he had ever been alive.

7. NIN KIRSHAG.

It was with a strange mixture of sadness and excitement churning inside of her that Nin Kirshag left the Ennead chamber. Her brother had provided enough room for them to begin their work and that would suffice for now. She would submit a detailed report to the council as he had ordered, but both she and Enki already knew that there were some things she could not divulge, not even to the Great Council. She called her assistants to help her make the preparations.

Their world, once a shining beacon in the solar system, was now in chaos. As if the war itself had not been enough, she and her people were about to take on the biggest and the most important task of their lives, trying to save the best of their entire species. Nin Kirshag prayed for success, but regardless of the outcome she already knew beyond doubt, that her world would never be the same again.

They packed the equipment from her laboratory, took the DNA samples both infected and uninfected before boarding the shuttle to take them to Atlan where they would set it down on the broad plane, which was almost completely ringed by a single, almost circular mountain range. As the shuttle came into land, she could not help but be struck by the view. Atlan was indeed a beautiful place. A worthy paradise to be the new birthplace of their race if that was indeed to be their fate.

The continent had always been sparsely populated because of its isolated location but the climate was temperate, and the land was very productive, so it served as both a food hub for much of the planet and a reserve for many different game species. The hominids we also plentiful here. In due course it would be a useful environment to allow her to see how her subjects would progress on their own, as she knew they would eventually have to, relying completely on their own instincts and abilities to survive.

The Xisudra was quite small for a warship, she was a medium sized cruiser about two hundred metres in length, the main structure of the ship was much smaller and almost cube like. The additional external engines, weapon mountings and storage pods needed for deep space exploration and for combat missions had been added later. Enki had suggested she use the Xisudra partly because it was not needed elsewhere, but mainly because it had not originally been designed as a deep space warship. Before the war it had been a research ship supporting the colonization of the outer planets. Relatively little work would be required to refit its laboratories, testing and isolation chambers and crucially the work could be handled by just a few people, so it could be completed without the need to visit a space dock. This was fortunate because the space docks were struggling already to repair what little remained of the fleet and the dock facilities themselves had not completely escaped the ravages of war. It would provide more than enough space for their work. No more than fifty of her staff had accompanied her and it was uncertain what, if any, further help would come.

Two full moons had passed since the last council meeting, and as the end of the Enad approached, Nin Kirshag was preparing to return to the Ennead chamber when Enki called her. "Hello brother" she said, we are almost ready to leave, and we should be with you by dawn."

"No, do not come to the council meeting" he ordered, "use the hologram link only. The city here is not safe for you now. Infection rates have not fallen as we had hoped. The disease is proving more resilient than we had believed possible and many of those helping the sick are showing signs that they are now also infected. This is severely diminishing our ability to hunt down the last of the enemy and although they are only a handful at best, I am sorry to say that some have, at least for now, evaded us. We may have won the war with Vorea, but I fear we are losing the war against the pathogen that they brought here.

We must keep you and your crew isolated from the mainland, it is your only chance to remain uninfected and hopefully it will give you the time you need to complete your work, IF, he stressed, …the council allows it."

"Do you think they will allow it brother?"

"Over the last Enad things have not gone well. I know some of the others have become more convinced of the importance of your work to preserve what we can, and it is my hope that the whole council will concur sister.

There are many challenges here equally worthy of their attention and the moral dilemma has been incredibly hard for many of them to reconcile, but I have spoken to some who feel that this is the only course of action left open to us now and they will petition in your favor. I am sorry that we will not be able to send further help or resources for a while at least."

"What if our world falls?" asked Nin Kirshag

If that happens then you will have to make whatever decisions you see fit, the council would likely no longer be there to assist or hinder you.

"Thank you, Enki."

"There is something else" he said. "I think I know where our brother Enlil is. You and I are the only ones who can follow him there. I think that is how he has managed to evade our ground troops. After the council meeting you and I will discuss our best course of action but for now your work with the genetic Ark and the hominids is our most pressing concern."

When the Ennead was eventually convened, the first order of business was an update on the infection rates and mounting casualties. As Nin Kirshag listened, she was visibly shocked. Enki had not exaggerated when he had spoken of his fears. Despite the heroic efforts of the people, things were not going well.

When the time came for Nin Kirshag to put forward the detailed proposal for a genetic Ark and a request for the support of the council to complete her work, unlike the previous council meeting, this time there was surprisingly little debate. Even that was rather half-hearted and those who had been most vocal at their previous session seemed to have been worn down by recent events. There was clearly a weary sense of resignation amongst the council members. The request was soon put to a vote and unanimously agreed.

"Thank you, council members," she said, "we have collected the DNA samples we need already, and we will begin our work immediately."

"Before you go sister, Sargon and Lord Erish have an update from the outer system." Sargon stood up and addressed the Council members.

"Council, as you know, after the battle at Vorea, Lord Erish was dispatched to the outer colonies on clean up duties. The fleet regrettably had to destroy some of the outposts. Most of the ore mining stations on the smaller moons however were already largely automated and they were unaffected. They were able to leave their automated tracking systems online.

My remaining ships meanwhile have been tracking the debris field from Tiamat and searching for the lost moon of Marduk. I believe that between the mapping we carried out around Tiamet's last position and the automated tracking stations monitoring gravitational changes in the small bodies toward the edge of the solar system, that we have now found Marduk, or at least we can make a reasonable estimate of its position. It appears to be on a very long elliptical orbit around the sun and if that continues it will approach the inner system roughly once every fifty thousand years."

"Does it pose a threat to us?" asked Enki

"I do not believe so my Lord. For now, at least the planet appears to be safe, but we cannot yet determine how the gravity of the other planets it passes on its journey will affect it until its new orbit settles. It is not clear to us yet how long this will take, perhaps eight or maybe ten orbits, is our best estimate."

"Thank you, Sargon, can you please patch the tracking station data links to the Xisudra so that they can continue the tracking from Atlan."

"Yes, my Lord"

"Our best hope now rests with you now, goodbye sister' said Enki and he smiled.

"Good luck and for the safety of you and your team, I would recommend that you do not try to return here until we are in contact again."

Despite his earlier promise to talk again after the council meeting, it seemed to Nin Kirshag that her brother might be saying his final goodbye in case they did not meet again and a great wave of sadness broke over her, but she held back her tears for now. She knew that every one of her scientists had family members they would also be worried about, and they would all have to deal with the separation in their own way. She was a princess of the royal house of Anu, and she had to show them the leadership they needed, no matter how hard. Before she could mourn, Nin Kirshag had first to relay the news of the Ennead's decision to her people. She had to ensure that they could commence their work at pace and without distraction.

Later that night when she retired to her quarters, she prayed for divine help to ensure that they could complete their task successfully, and then she wept. She wept all the tears that would flow, until finally, completely exhausted, she fell into a deep sleep.

8. HARRY'S DAD.

Harry opened the door of Golden Retreat Nursing Home in the leafy suburb of Putney in Southwest London and held it for Sofia to enter first. She smiled as she waked through. They washed their hands using the bottle of alcohol rub situated just inside the foyer, put on their mandatory blue face masks, and made their way to the reception desk where the receptionist was sitting behind a makeshift plastic screen.

"Good morning, I am here to see Professor Simon Taylor" he said.

The receptionist turned her attention from the computer screen, looked up at him and although he could not be sure he felt that she was smiling at him from behind her own blue mask.

"And your name is?" she asked.

"My name is Dr Taylor "said Harry, "I am Professor Taylor's son.".

"I can let you in Mr. Taylor" said the receptionist "as next of kin of course, but strictly it should only be one visitor at a time."

"This is Sofia Morreconi, she is not a visitor, she is a doctor" and for some reason he couldn't quite fathom, he added "specialising in viral induced dementia."

"I see" said the receptionist, "well as she is not the Professor's usual doctor Miss Morreconi needs a certificate showing that she has tested negative for the virus."

"That's ok" said Sofia "I have that," and she handed over

a copy of her test results.

"I was tested at the Santa Tomassa hospital in Torino two days ago."

"Thank you," said the receptionist. "I just need to check this, please make yourselves comfortable, there's a coffee machine in the corner," she said pointing vaguely off to the right," it won't take long."

She left the reception desk heading into the back office before returning a few moments later. She smiled and said "everything is in order thank you. Professor Taylor is in room 102 on the first floor, the lift is just down the hall on your right."

"And may we see a copy of his medical records and treatment history please?" asked Sofia.

"The medical charts and prescription details are all in his room," said the receptionist. "We do not usually provide anything else unless there is a medical emergency."

"Thank you, that should suffice." said Sofia.

As they made their way up to the room Sofia seemed nervous.

"What's the matter?" asked Harry.

"I don't really know. That receptionist just seemed a little 'off.' No one has ever checked one of my test certificates before."

Harry shrugged. "I expect they are just wary. People in nursing homes have been very hard hit with this pandemic and older people are vulnerable. With you coming from Northern Italy…." he paused….. "Well, the area has been hit rather hard."

She nodded. "Yes, you are probably right, perhaps I am just being a little sensitive." Yet still that sense of unease, of being 'watched' would not leave her.

"Hello Dad" said Harry as he poked his head around the door. His father was sitting in a high-backed chair looking out of the window at the traffic in the street below.

"Geoffrey" he replied, "how nice to see you. I knew you would come; it's not finished, is it?"

"Dad it's me, Harry."

"Harry who?"

"Your son, Harry"

"Oh yes, I am so forgetful these days, is Geoffrey with

you?"

"No Dad, I have brought Sofia to meet you."

"I say, you're a good-looking filly, better than the usual dragons that look after me."

Harry rolled his eyes and mouthed "I am so sorry" to Sofia.

"That's quite all right" she said, and a broad smile spread across her face. "It is a pleasure to finally meet you Professor Taylor, Harry has told me so much about you."

"Sofia is my fiancé remember, I showed you her picture the last time I visited you?"

"Yes, yes I am sorry son, where is Geoffrey?"

"Professor Frederikson is at work Dad."

"Is he alright?"

"Yes, he is fine Dad, I saw him yesterday morning and he asked me to say hello."

While Harry tried to make some sense of his father's rambling Sofia stood at the end of his bed and examined his medical records.

"Would you like a coffee Professor Taylor?" she asked.

"Oh yes please, you are very kind, they don't allow me coffee anymore."

Harry looked at her non-plussed, but she just handed over her coffee and he drained the cup almost immediately.

"Do you have any more?" he asked.

Harry handed over his too and again he drained the cup. The transformation was startling; suddenly the Professor was lucid again as if he had awoken from a dream.

"Harry, Sofia, what's wrong? you look pale."

Harry didn't know where to begin.

"Dad, I need your help, I am researching Sumerian history during the lockdown to expand my knowledge and chances of a Professorship at the Museum and Professor Frederikson, Uncle Geoffrey, said you had done a lot of research on some old artifacts that might help."

His father looked at him quizzically. "Ever since you were a little boy I have always known when you were lying son. You were a good boy then and now you are good man, which is why you are not very good at it. Tell me what is going on?"

Harry and Sofia looked at one another. She nodded and Harry started to tell his father the whole tale about the hunting trip and the appearance of Enmerkar in the forest, then he paused waiting for his father to burst into laughter or to pour scorn on their strange tale.

To their surprise the Professor was not at all taken aback by their story, he just nodded.

"So; it is true" he said with a broad smile, "Geoffrey did not imagine it after all, I am so sorry that I ever doubted him."

"Imagine it? Doubt him about what?" asked Harry.

"Where to begin?" said the Professor gathering his thoughts. "Many years ago, we were doing a bit of 'off-piste' researching as they say, and .... well, Geoffrey claimed to have seen one of your 'new friends' but I had always found it hard to believe and I think that was partly why he lost his enthusiasm to continue our work.

Poor Geoffrey, it seems I did him a great dis-service. Looking back on it he was probably in shock and as I couldn't really corroborate his story, it seemed to knock the stuffing out of him. He was terrified of being ridiculed you see, and people have been drummed out of academia for far less you know."

"I know" said Harry, "That's why I have not told anyone else about this."

"That's probably very wise my boy, I would be very careful who you trust. What will you do now?"

"Well, it seems that we need to find this Erianes, but we have no idea who or what Erianes is or even where to start looking."

"Go home." said the Professor emphatically.

"What?" said Harry.

"Go home, ….to the house in Yorkshire Harry."

"You haven't sold it yet, have you?" asked the Professor.

Harry was indignant at the question. "No, of course not Dad, I couldn't do that to you. It's just that I haven't been back for a while."

The old professor smiled. "In the attic, in my old gun cabinet there are some things you should see. It's my life's work really, my journals and some other things. The key is under the incubator in the greenhouse, next to the where I used to keep your mother's tomato plants."

"The key to your life's work is in the greenhouse?"

"Yes" he said matter-of-factly. "Well, it is not much good to me down here, is it? I usually find its better to hide things in plain sight, don't you? When you have read it, I would recommend you head for Muscat in Oman."

"Muscat? Why there?" asked Harry

"It will all make sense when you have read the journals."

As suddenly as he was lucid his father's attention seemed to fade again.

"Is Geoffrey with you?" He asked.

"No dad it's just me and...."

"Who's the new nurse?"

"It's me, Sofia"

"Hello my dear."

"I think it is time to go," said Harry.

"We will call again Dad, I promise."

"Let's go back to the hotel, pack up and we can catch a

train north from Kings Cross this afternoon."

"Where are we going? asked Sofia."

"Great Ayton, it's a little village in North Yorkshire where I grew up."

A few hours later sitting on the train Sofia was very quiet. "What's wrong?" asked Harry.

"I think your father is being kept sedated. Did you notice how quickly the coffee brought him around? When I checked his medication, it seems to have no relation to dementia."

"Well, he does have other health issues," said Harry.

"Yes, but the medicines he has been prescribed were all very heavily based on Aluminium and Mercury compound derivatives, both of which affect the mental capacity and are thought to bring on dementia. Patients who are prescribed these are supposed to avoid coffee and grapefruit."

"Why?" asked Harry"

Well grapefruit can cause a reaction resulting in heart

problems, but coffee specifically interferes with the neuro suppression effects of the drugs and most likely stops them working effectively together. Harry, I think there is more at stake here than we know."

"Yes, I am beginning to realise that" he said. Maybe we are getting in over our heads? I am worn out, we both are, we should try to get some sleep."

Although it took some time the gentle rocking of the train eventually helped Harry to doze off, but this time it was Sofia who could not sleep. Her mind was racing, flitting from one imagined scenario to another and then back again. Although she had encouraged Harry on this journey, she was also now starting to feel anxious about where it might eventually lead them. What could be so important that you would actively sedate a harmless old man?"

Four hours later, after leaving the train at Darlington station they arrived in Great Ayton. The taxi dropped them outside a large white house about half mile from the village green. They retrieved their bags from the boot; Harry paid the driver, and he watched as the car pulled away. The lights slowly disappeared into the distance and a moment later they were standing in pitch darkness under a clear sky, sparkling with countless stars.

"My God, it is beautiful here!" said Sofia as her eyes adjusted to the darkness. "I had no idea you lived somewhere like this."

"Yes, it is, isn't it.? There is not much light pollution here. I haven't been here for so long I had almost forgotten how beautiful the stars are."

He pointed to the southeast, "Look there is the Milky Way." They stared at the sky together drinking in the in wonder of it for a moment then Harry said "Come on, it's freezing outside. Let's get inside and light the fire, there are usually some logs in the garage. It feels like it has been a very long day, and I am badly in need a decent cup of tea.

9. CAPTAIN COOK.

The next morning when Sofia awoke, she found herself alone in the bedroom. Putting on the dressing gown that was hanging on the back of the bedroom door she stepped outside on to the Juliet balcony and for the first time she could really see where she was. There were only a couple houses in the lane, mostly covered by ivy or the now bare wisteria vines, and the land was mostly agricultural. Eastwards the sun was rising over what looked like a small a mountain in the distance. As she scanned the horizon Southwards, she noticed another hill with an obelisk on top and the ring of green hills continued all the way to the west.

"Good morning" said Harry, as he entered the room carrying a tray with a pot of coffee and some croissants.

"Where have you been?" she asked.

"I did not want to disturb you; I have not seen you sleep so peacefully for a while. I know you didn't sleep on the train yesterday, so I put the coffee on and walked down to the village for some milk. Then I called into the bakery to collect us some breakfast."

"Thank you. It is beautiful here Harry. I thought there were no mountains in England" she said pointing towards the rising sun.

He laughed, "no there aren't really, not like there are in Italy anyway, but yes, the hills are lovely here. That is Roseberry Topping, we call it the Matterhorn of the north because of its shape but it is much closer than you would imagine and is only about a thousand feet high. Sofia laughed.

"The obelisk is called Captain Cook's monument."

"Capitan Cook?"

"Yes, the famous explorer, he went to school here in the village. He was a great navigator and explored the Pacific widely from Alaska in the north to New Zealand in the south. He discovered Australia apparently, at least that is what we were taught at school although with the things we are starting to discover I am now wondering if any of what we thought we knew, was actually ever true.

He was a great inspiration for my father though; some of the things he recorded on his voyages were very strange and my father took a lot of interest in his journals. When it comes to historical records there is not a lot that can compete with a sea Captain's logs. Come back inside, it's cold out here; finish your coffee while I run us a hot bath, the boiler has been on for a couple of hours so we should have plenty of hot water now."

An hour later, clean and refreshed they made their way across the garden to the greenhouse where, almost in disbelief, they found the key to the gun cabinet under the incubator, it was exactly where the Professor had said it would be.

Back in the house, standing on a kitchen chair, Harry pushed open the inspection hatch for the attic. Brushing away the cobwebs he pulled down the folding ladder. He climbed up, reached into the darkness, feeling for the switch and he turned on the light.

Sofia followed him up the ladder into the eaves. It was cold up here, amongst the purlins and rafters. The air was stale and the area around the hatch opening was littered with dead flies that had presumably failed to escape the last time the hatch was closed, and they were sealed forever within their airy tomb.

There was a narrow, boarded walkway cluttered with boxes and on either side, they could see rolls of yellow glass fibre insulation laid out between the rafters. "Blimey I remember helping Dad lay all this stuff when I was just a kid." he said. "Be careful, don't stand on that or you will fall through the ceiling. He pointed. The gun cabinet is at the end over there, it's bolted into the chimney breast."

The walkway was alike an Aladdin's cave, full of

unexpected treasures. "What is all this stuff?' asked Sofia?

"No idea." said Harry. "Mum and Dad never liked to throw things out so it could be anything. I am dreading the day I have to look to be honest."

They picked their way carefully amongst the boxes, plastic tubs, and large black bags until they finally reached the chimney breast where Harry began making some room amongst all the clutter before removing the padlock and opening the metal chest. Inside there were a few books, something wrapped in a cloth, his father's journals and over everything were strewn cartridges, 0.38, 0.357 magnum and 9mm shells. He passed the lighter contents to Sofia, who carefully retraced her steps and took them downstairs where she placed them gently on the kitchen table. A moment later Harry brought down the heavy ammunition along with the journals.

"I wonder why he has all this ammunition?" Harry thought to himself.

"This is strange Sofia, Dad hates guns," he said as he examined the cartridges and shells. "He always has. He only kept a shotgun because the farmer next door sometimes needed a hand with the vermin around the farmyard, and to dissuade the odd trespasser from getting a little too curious but the best of my knowledge he never actually shot anyone."

"These are not shotgun cartridges they are military grade shells?" said Sofia.

Harry nodded, "Yes I know, that's what I mean, odd isn't it."

Sofia opened the parcel first. "Oh my God Harry, look at this." Inside, carefully wrapped in a soft chamois leather, was something all too familiar. Harry could only look on in astonishment. Then he reached into his day sack and pulled out the cards that Enmerkar had given to Sofia in the church of Santa Maria, they were identical.

"They are made of the same strange material."

"Yes" said Sophia "and have you noticed how after you have stared at them for a few minutes the images seem to move on the cards as though they are not fixed at all?"

Harry nodded again.

"Open the journals, see if there any more details about how he got them?"

"It says here that my father and 'uncle' Geoffrey, Professor Frederikson, were on a field expedition in Oman in 1976 whilst attached to the British Army. Oman was fighting some inter-tribal disputes with its neighbors and the British military were providing technical assistance but whilst they were there, they embarked on an expedition for the museum to find a lost city called Ubar, but it seems that they never found it.

However, before they left the region the two of them travelled from the capital Muscat, and they visited a place called Majlis Al DJinn or the cave of the Genies. It seems that they were following an old legend tied in with the book they wanted to write.

Harry skipped impatiently past the details of their journey to the cave.

"While they were there Geoffrey had a fall while he was trying to read some petroglyphs carved on a rock face inside the cave but listen to this …. he fell down one side of a small fissure about eight feet deep and he disappeared.

When Dad finally found him, he was on the other side of the cave unconscious. When he came around, he had no idea how he had gotten there, but he had these cards in his rucksack. Feeling someone standing behind him Dad turned around to see what looked like the outline of what he thought was a green-cloaked figure 'fading away like smoke' but he put it down to a simple trick of the light in the cave.

It seems that when Uncle Geoffrey was feeling better Dad questioned him a little more. He still didn't remember much but he said that he had been in a steel room with a tall silver skinned woman and when she touched him, he passed out. They returned to England where they tried to learn more about the cards, but they never told anyone about how they got them, nor did they ever let them out of their sight. There is a lot more about being frustrated with the museum for not taking them seriously and lots of nonsense about the cards being interpreted by some rather shady fortune tellers but eventually he seems to have hit on something.

Listen to this.

'Geoffrey has decided that he cannot risk his academic career and he has asked me to take the cards away from London, so I am taking a sabbatical and returning north with Ellen for a few months.

In the beginning, I thought that perhaps it was the relaxation of being at home after the expedition and the stressful return to the Museum where our ideas were discarded but as I studied the cards in quiet reflection, they seemed to speak to me and I saw the pictures move even though I know this could not be possible, the cards are solid and cannot change.

At first the pictures seemed to be random but the more I studied them the more I began to see links between them, like a web of images but more powerful than I would have believed possible. With practice they evoked deep memories, sounds, smells, and strong emotions within me.

Then one day I hit on it, it was not the cards that changed but my state of mind, so I began to look to the Far East to establish if there was any precedence for this in mediation.

To my great surprise I found that there was indeed something in the resonance of nature. Pictures, smells, and location that can all affect the mind but the easiest way to achieve the effect I was looking for was through music.

Eventually I managed to isolate the effect that made the trance states easier to achieve and that was when I discovered that the cards were resonating, they were vibrating at a frequency of exactly 110HZ, right at the lower end of the frequency range that the human ear can detect. Most people fail to hear it but its effects in stimulating the right-hand side of the human brain are remarkable.

Though my wife Ellen fears for my sanity I have become convinced that the cards have a purpose, they are not random, but they are actually some sort of a machine, they are dynamic in their ability to teach an adaptable mind, but teach it what? This I can only speculate, and as to who made these remarkable objects, I have no clue?

In all our years of study and work with the Museum neither Geoffrey or I have never encountered any artefacts as remotely sophisticated and yet, their age is difficult to determine. I scarcely dare imagine the possibilities this knowledge may unleash or what would happen were they to fall into the wrong hands. Perhaps I should bury them and forget them forever, Geoffrey certainly thinks so, but how can we betray the past, how can we betray the truth that we have spent our whole lives in search of.'

"This can't be a coincidence, Harry. The same thing happening to two members of your family and then to you, the odds are incalculable. I think we should go to these caves and see what is there. There may be some clues to the whereabouts of this Erianes. Could she be the tall silvery woman Professor Frederikson thought he had met or the phantom your father mentions in his journal?"

"I think you are right; we will have to travel back to

London to fly to Muscat anyway so let's see if we can pay him another visit and get him to talk a little more. If we are going to jump into the lion's den, then I would at least like to know a little more so that we can be better prepared."

"Enmerkar did invite us to find this Erianes," said Sofia, "do you really think it will be so dangerous?"

"If it really is her, perhaps not" he said, "but he wasn't very specific about where to find her was he and what if there are more of them?"

"In that case, what should we do?" asked Sofia.

Harry did not answer her question directly, he just shrugged. "Let's just stay here for a few days before we head back. I have to be honest I have enjoyed coming home and there is quite a lot of other stuff in here that may provide some useful clues. If this Enmerkar really was as old as he said he was, then a few more days won't matter. Besides, I'd still like to know what all the ammunition is for. Was Dad afraid of something or someone, and if he has the ammunition, where are the guns?"

"Guns" said Sofia.

"Yes, guns…. there are three different calibres of

ammunition here so, it stands to reason that there must be more than one weapon, right?

Whatever it is we are heading into, I have a terrible feeling in the pit of my stomach that death might not be too far away.

10. THE CAVE OF THE DJINN.

Harry and Sofia's journey to Gatwick was thankfully uneventful and the train to London King's Cross was very quiet, thanks mainly to the ongoing travel restrictions. Even though they were travelling light, the quick jaunt on the underground, first to the British

Museum to speak with Professor Frederikson again, then onto Victoria and finally running to catch the Gatwick express left them feeling rushed but at least they were warm.

As the train pulled away from the station, they looked out on a cold and miserable London. The rain streaking along the train windows blurred the miserable cityscape outside and made it difficult to focus on the passing landmarks. Eventually the city gave way to the suburbs and they could just make out the red roof tops beyond being pounded from above.

"I think I will be glad to see the sun again," said Sofia.

"You and me both," said Harry. "I do love England, but on a day like today you could be forgiven for wishing you were anywhere but here. This weather looks set in for a spell."

"What?" asked Sofia

"Set in for a spell" he repeated, "sorry it's just an expression, it means the rain doesn't look like it will be stopping anytime soon."

"What did you make of Uncle Geoffrey?" he asked.

This caught Sofia off guard. "Your uncle?"

"Well he's not really my uncle but he and Dad have been friends since school and he is my godfather really, but he has always been a part of the family."

Sofia thought hard before answering. "Honestly, I think he is frightened. When you showed him the cards again, he looked like a rabbit in the headlights, it's an old Italian expression" she said and then she started laughing.

Harry smiled, "yes, his reaction was quite curious. I could almost see his eyes glaze over as if he was struggling inside to remember something.

"Does that scare you?" asked Harry.

"If I am honest, yes it does a little, but I keep thinking about Enmerkar. It seems to me that even in his injured state he could have hurt us if he had really wanted to, but he didn't, and we do sort of have an invitation don't we?" She pointed to the small bag which now contained two packs of cards as well as the snake ring.

"Yes, we do" said Harry "but we don't know where we are being invited to, or even how to make use of the invitation yet. I am more than a little concerned about what reception we will get when we arrive, especially after we tell this Erianes that her friend is dead because I shot him."

"Look around us Harry, the world is falling apart, people are dying in every country and across every continent. Why us?"

"I don't know why fate has chosen us" he said, "but at this point I am prepared to take things on a little faith."

When they arrived at Gatwick Airport, they were greeted by a young lady at the check-in desk. "Good morning" she said. Sofia presumed that she was smiling behind the little blue mask, but it was difficult to tell.

"What is the nature of your visit to Muscat."

"I am a Doctor from the Santa Tomassa Hospital in Turin" said Sofia, "my assistant and I are undertaking research on the current virus, specifically its relation to the MERS outbreaks that started in the region in 2012."

"Oh wow" she said "well I wish you every success, this covid is driving people nuts and it's literally killing us in the airlines. I am one of the lucky ones to still have a job, but we are running on a skeleton team at the moment. Do you have your passenger locator forms, and test results please?"

Sofia handed over the documents for both of them.

The assistant examined them and looked back at Sofia questioning her further, "It says here that you are immune to the virus?"

"Yes, I am. My colleagues and I were part of the initial test group for the vaccines they are trying to develop. A curious quirk of fate I suppose but it is lucky for me because it has killed a lot of my colleagues at the hospital."

"I am very sorry to hear that" she said, passing over the boarding cards, "only hand luggage I see."

Sofia nodded.

"You will be boarding at Gate 31 in about forty minutes, have a nice flight."

The flight was not busy, and apart from a little turbulence the seven hour journey was surprisingly relaxed. When they arrived in Muscat they took a taxi to the hotel, checked in and ordered coffee. The taxi driver had told them that the last few days in Muscat had been unseasonably warm, even by the standards of the desert Sultanate.

Harry mused to himself “It wasn't just mankind then, the whole of the planet seemed to be growing increasingly uncomfortable with itself.”

As they sat on their veranda, Harry looked across the western horizon to a crescent moon slowly setting behind the plateau. Billowing clouds seemed to be rising up to meet it and the oppressive air lay heavy about them, filled with the heady scent of Jasmine.

“A storm is coming “he said.

“Yes” said Sofia, “I can feel it too” and she shuddered.

He held her tightly as she leaned into him in spite of the heat, and now they both shuddered at the thought of what might be to come.

“What are you thinking?” he asked.

“I was wondering if we should just turn back and pretend this has all been a dream. Enmerkar, the professor’s stories of the past, Erianes, the 'thing' in the desert and your father's warnings.”

“We can't just forget what we have seen, this is the greatest revelation in the history of the world, and besides I think we are all in very real danger now.

I don't think this storm is all that is coming, let's try to get some sleep we have an early start tomorrow."

Majis Al Djinn, or the cave of the genies, was approximately one hundred miles south of Muscat. Over two and half hours by road. The journey through the baking dry terrain contrasted heavily with the turquoise blue of the Persian Gulf as they travelled south, following the coast as far as possible.

"OK" said Harry, "so what do we know about the cave of the genies?"

"I did a little research on the internet this morning before breakfast," said Sofia. "Just the usual tourist stuff really. It's apparently the second largest cave in the world by surface area. It's three hundred and one metres by two hundred and twenty five metres wide, with a large dome at the top at a height of about one hundred and twenty metres."

"Wow, that is huge, not a bit of wonder people can have accidents down there, Uncle Geoffrey said it was treacherous."

"Yes, apparently it's one of five shafts on the plateau but it is the only one that has no lower entrance."

"That is strange," said Harry." How do people appear and disappear in a cave like that with no other entrance or exit, and where did Uncle Geoffrey get to when dad couldn't find him?"

Then something else suddenly dawned on him. "Hold on minute, are you telling me, that the only way in and out is a vertical climb of almost four hundred feet?"

"Yes" said Sofia emphatically, that seems to be the case." She was giggling now because she knew Harry wasn't good with heights.

After about an hour and half, not far beyond small town of Bimma, they turned west and headed into the mountains where the cave, or more accurately caves, were located. The road into the mountains proved to be the hardest part of their long drive. It was dry, dusty, and chaotic. Hairpin bends made them regularly double back as they climbed the 1,380 metres to the top of the Selma plateau, and all the while they had to be careful to avoid the odd bus, car, or occasional goat herd on the narrow road.

"How exactly are we going to get down into the

cave" asked Harry.

"Well, said Sofia teasing him, "either base jumping or abseiling seem to be the favourite options."

"Hmmm, can I just point out that we have neither parachutes nor climbing ropes" he said, refusing to rise to the bait.

"That's ok," said Sofia. "The ministry of tourism has designated it a cave of cultural interest, so I managed to book a guide in a local village who says he has the equipment to lower us down and to bring us back up when we are ready."

The drive and constant need for total concentration was exhausting and by the time they reached the top Harry was worn out. The village they were looking for turned out to be nothing more than a few whitewashed houses and animal corrals, but rather incongruously there was also a sign for a bus or coach stop where a couple of camels were currently making themselves at home. A few local stalls were selling trinkets to the handful of other visitors and there was a small, round, stone tower that served as both a shelter for the locals from the intense heat of the sun and doubled as a ticket kiosk.

Their guide, Abbas, had agreed to meet them there.

The only other people were a small group from Iceland who were surveying all of the local caves on the plateau in turn, for the department of the interior.

"Curious" said Harry, "maybe I am being paranoid but doesn't it seem strange that in the middle of a pandemic that surveying these tourist caves seems to be a priority for the ministry of the interior?"

Sofia just nodded.

Abbas looked about thirty years of age. He was weather worn, wiry and strong, no doubt from years of helping lazy, overweight tourists explore the caves in the area.

They introduced themselves and were happy to find that Abbas spoke very good English.

"Where did you learn English Abbas?" asked Harry.

"In the Omani Navy" he replied. "I studied at Britannia Royal Naval college in Dartmouth, England he said proudly.

"What are you doing here?" asked Sofia.

"This is my family business" he replied. Since the pandemic we have been unable to put to sea and my father has been ill so I have permission to remain here for a while, but I will return to my own job when I must."

They collected the gear they needed, before Abbas took them to one of the three shafts over the cave where he began to set up his steel framed rig and winch.

"What can you tell us about the cave and the legends surrounding it? asked Sofia.

"Not much" he answered honestly. "Our people do not go down there. The legends say that the cave is the abode of the Djinn, and that they take any they wish, from those foolish enough to venture inside."

"How old are these legends?" asked Harry, trying to ignore their guide's ominous explanation.

"No one knows" he said.

He smiled, "they say that people have disappeared here since the very beginning of time, but do not worry my friends, the chances of you disappearing are very small inshallah. I personally have helped many people descend and ascend again quite safely."

He handed them one of the pair of walkie talkies that he had brought along. Call me when you want to come up. The range on these is approximately one mile but please understand that you will need to be somewhere near to one of the cave entrances for the signal to reach me up here. As long as you can do that there will be no problem."

"And if we can't?" asked Harry.

"Then I will inform your next of kin" said Abbas rather too solemnly for Harry's liking.

Sensing Harry's reservations, Sofia offered to go first. She climbed into her harness and Abbas gently lowered her to the cave floor. Harry followed close behind and moments later unhitched his harness. They stood together on the rocky floor gazing around them in sheer wonder. The cave was surprisingly well lit with natural light from the three large openings overhead that, from their perspective, now looked like giant sky lights letting in huge shafts of sunlight that made the floor and limestone walls appear almost golden.

The cave was comfortably cool too, a full fifteen degrees cooler than the temperature outside which would make their exploration easier. Harry tested his walkie talkie and Abbas replied, so feeling a little more relaxed about their situation they turned their attention to the task at hand.

"I have no idea where to start looking," said Sofia.

"Over there to the left," said Harry without hesitation.

"Look at those rocks and debris. Uncle Geoffrey mentioned falling while looking at some petroglyphs. The floor is flat over to the right, like a dry riverbed so it must have been over there."

Harry's intuition was right, and they soon found the petroglyphs and started examining them carefully, looking for any clue that might help them.

"I think I have seen these symbols before," said Sofia "yes, I am sure I have.

Show me the cards and the ring."

Harry handed them to her, and she pulled out the cards that seemed most closely associated with the symbols on the rock face. She began to concentrate hard.

As she did so the blue stone on the ring began to glow, the wall appeared to vibrate, and the cave seemed to hum.

Harry leaned forward against the wall and as he did so, it seemed to turn to smoke, and he fell right through it, onto what seemed like a floor made entirely of stainless steel. Sofia was more careful; she stepped through behind him before helping him to his feet.

"Oh my god" said Harry," he started panting, "I think I am going to freak out."

"Calm down said Sofia, take a deep breath." He was panting when suddenly a voice behind them said, "Welcome."

Harry jumped. "Mother of God" he exclaimed.

"No, not really," replied the voice matter of factly.

When he recovered his composure, he hoped he had not soiled himself, but he couldn't be sure because he was sweating so much. Standing in front of them was what appeared to be a giantess, well over eight feet tall, with silver skin, wearing robes flecked with gold, green and purple.

"Welcome to Atlan, I am Erianes, and I have been expecting you. Follow me please."

11. ADAM AND THE LAND OF EDIN.

Almost two thousand miles away to the North, on the high plain of North Western Iran, in the city of Tabriz there was a cool early morning breeze blowing. A petite woman, perhaps in her early thirties, with dark brown eyes and black hair clearly visible under her silk head scarf walked through the gardens of Jinnah, past the fountains, and up the steps into the city museum.

To the young men chatting by the fountains, she seemed at home in her surroundings, and she blended in effortlessly, almost invisible like most women in that part of the world. But if any had taken the time to look more closely, they would have noticed that she walked proudly, with an air of authority, one that would meet any challenge, an air to which they would have been unaccustomed in the midst of their very patriarchal society.

She smiled at the security guard, "good morning, Parviz" she said in perfect Farsi smiling as she passed into the inner corridor and on toward to the displays beyond. Although this was a predominantly Kurdish area, most of the official jobs were given to ethnic Iranians, especially those roles considered important, such as maintaining the cultural heritage, and of course controlling the accepted narrative that went along with that. As she walked past him, Parviz could feel himself blush, she always had that effect on him, and he simply waved her through saying "good morning, ma'am."

Inside the main gallery the curator of Persian antiquities Professor Hakim was unpacking the new exhibits that she had come to see. Without looking up, he said "good morning, Professor Hashemi" as her shadow passed over him. "Only you would be here so early to see me unpack these latest finds. How was your time in London, fruitful I trust?"

"Good morning, Professor Hakim" she said. "Yes, London was very informative, the British have many looted artefacts from all around the world. The British Museum is unparalleled in its collection of treasures. Although in fairness to them, many of those treasures may either never have been found or they could have been destroyed had they been left in place. Our own leaders have not always been so kind to these remnants from our past.

I am, however, very happy to be home," she said changing the subject, "and I have been waiting eagerly for these to arrive. I think they may be the missing piece to my thesis."

"Oh yes" he smiled, "the pre-eminence of the Persians over the Babylonians and the Akkadians. No wonder you have no problem getting state funding for your work!"

"You do know that despite our differences that we are descended from the same stock?"

"Of course, I do," she said humoring him, whilst knowing with absolute certainty that this was indeed not the case.

The professor's brain would explode if he knew even half of the history she carried in her head.

"Is it true?" she asked, "have we really found the lost tablets of Cyrus the Great?"

"Yes, I think we may have" he replied.

"Where have they been hidden all this time?" she asked.

"They were found not far from the ancient capital of Persepolis, but strangely they seem to have been hidden in an obscure backwater that later became thought of as a place of the dead."

"A place of the dead" she repeated.

"Yes. The cemetery in the small town of Berdej between Persepolis and Shiraz."

"Well that is certainly a place of the dead" she said.

He nodded and smiled but then continued "It was not the cemetery that I was referring to, it seems to have been placed in Berdej due to frequent sighting of spirits or Djinn. Legend has it that they appeared and disappeared like smoke, if you believe in that sort of thing."

Professor Yasmin Hashemi most definitely did

indeed believe in that sort of thing because she had seen these Djinn her own eyes and she knew them intimately. Professor Hakim passed over the tablets one by one and they arranged them on the floor so that he could plan the exhibition in some sort of chronological order as he saw it. It was indeed remarkable" he said "that Cyrus the Great created an Empire two and a half thousand years ago that spread from the west coast of Turkey to the edge of India in the East, and from the Great Caucus mountains in the North down to the Indian Ocean in the south.

Yasmina could hear her colleague's continual chatter, but she began to tune out and it gradually faded into the background as she examined the reliefs of Cyrus. It was said that he possessed a great and powerful Jewel from ancient times that had fallen from the heavens, a magical jewel which made him invincible in battle but that he kept it secret, and no one knew what it looked like. It seems to have been either a complete fairytale or perhaps it was real but was so outlandish that it was removed from his body before he was buried then hidden away by his followers.

"What superstitious rubbish" she thought to herself. "If they could only understand how far they have fallen." After studying the tablets for a few hours, she eventually hit on it, she knew what she was looking for and there in plain sight in front her was the picture of the artifact she sought. The jewel that was supposed to have fallen from Lucifer's crown when he was cast down from heaven. She had seen it once before, countless years ago, but she had neither realised its power then, nor that it would eventually be the key to both her own survival and to her plan to rid the world once and for all of the threat mankind did not even realise it faced. She would rid them forever of the blight of the Einari and all those who followed them.

"Erm.... professor", she said slowly. "I would like to head over to Yerevan for a few days. I remember seeing some exhibits there that I think can help us with the thematic for the exhibition." Professor Hakim saw no value in this at all but, as he looked into her eyes, to his own surprise he found himself agreeing. "Very well but please promise me that you will be careful, the Armenians are not in much of a sharing frame of mind since their conflict with Azerbaijan. We Muslims are not particularly popular there at the moment. "I will" she said laughing to herself as she was not a Muslim and indeed the Armenians were very much closer to her own people than he would ever know.

The next day the driver she had hired arrived at her house early in a silver Mercedes sedan. She has been waiting for him for almost half an hour, but she hid her irritation as he greeted her. He picked up her bags and put them in the boot of the car, opened the rear door for her, and soon they were heading northwest out of the city.

As she looked around, they passed mile after mile of bleak housing, overpopulated slums, and the stench of the drains in the unseasonal heat was seeping into the cabin. Even the driver involuntarily pulled the loose end of his 'shemagh', the traditional chequered head scarf, over his mouth and nose as if his senses were in a battle with an invisible storm of odors assaulting him constantly. Eventually the houses gave way to a parched landscape, baked hard in the sun. One which offered only poor pasture for the small herds of goats that voraciously consumed whatever they could find.

As they travelled Northwards her thoughts drifted and the scene before her mind's eye changed. She remembered how beautiful this land had once been, long before the population of mankind ran rampant and before the great upheaval. The land of Edin had once been comprised of a great plain between the two great inland seas and a huge crescent that encompassed the whole of the southern shore of the Caspian Sea. In those remote times the land was bounded to the North by the great caucus mountains, and to the south by the lesser caucus mountain range, which was much longer then, as it also took in the Alborz Mountain range which today separates the high plains of Tehran from the northern coastal plain. The climate was almost tropical then. It was always humid, as a rich mist would rise from the land every morning irrigating everything, so that the vegetation was always lush and productive.

Everything then had been in perfect balance; life was rich and easy.

She had been happy then, with Adam her husband. He was the son of the tribal elder and had fallen in love with her the moment he saw her. He had a warrior's countenance, he was tall, fair skinned with light hair, and he was strong. But he was gentle and creative too. He fashioned all manner of things to amuse her.

Then 'they' came down from the high mountain, Ararat the holy place, where they lived, and they took her. When she had awoken, she was terrified as she found herself laying naked on a table, with two very large silver skinned demons looking down at her.

That was where she had seen the jewel. It was mounted in what looked like a diadem in the forehead of the taller of the two figures, the one who seemed to be in charge.

She had been daydreaming for too long when the driver said, "we are approaching the border. I can take you no further madam."

"That's quite alright, the Museum have arranged for a guide to meet me at the border crossing" she said, and she added silently to herself "although I suspect he is more likely to be a state spy than an archeologist."

In Agarak, she met an older man with a beard and greying hair who introduced himself. "Professor Hashemi I presume? My name is Johannes 'Hans' Schmitt. You look somewhat surprised" he said, smiling.

She nodded.

"Yes; I am German, only part Armenian, on my mother's side. I work for the Pergamon museum in Berlin, but I have worked in Yerevan for almost a decade now."

"Yes, I have heard of you. Weren't you the one they said was mad because you believed that Noah's Ark was on Mount Ararat?" she said, pointing westwards.

He just laughed, "Yes, that is me I must confess."

"Good" she said. "Because I don't want to waste my time in going to the museum. I want to go to Mount Ararat."

"The rumors are true then," said Schmitt, "you have found the books of Cyrus and you have seen it. You are looking for the Star of Enlil?" For the second time she looked surprised. "You are either very perceptive or very well-informed Mr. Schmitt, which is it?"

"Well, he explained, I am German, and we grew up with the tales of the stone that fell from Lucifers crown. It is the centre piece of our greatest myth 'Parsifal'. Otto Rahn searched for it before the war in the French Pyrenees and, when he failed the SS murdered him, but they did not give up. They sent Ernst Schafer to continue the search in Tibet. What you call the Star of Enlil, the Christians believe to be everything from the Philosophers stone to the Holy Grail, but it is considered by most to be nothing more than a myth."

"And you Mr. Schmitt, what do you believe?"

"I believe that our ancestors do not get the credit they deserve" he said, "and many tall tales have eventually been proven to have a grain of truth in them."

“Oh, I can assure you it is real” she said. “I saw it once with my own eyes a very long time ago. It is not what you think it is, but let’s just say it holds a great deal of emotional and sentimental value for me and that I am in position to reward you VERY handsomely if you help me find it.” Now it was Schmitt’s turn to be surprised but he eagerly agreed.

We must head into Yerevan, trekking on the mountain is currently forbidden and we would need a permit for an archeological visit, that could take months to arrange” Said Schmitt.

“….and? ....” she asked, pausing for dramatic effect.

“If you have money, my cousin Levon can get us the supplies we need and get us across the border into Turkey to the base of the mountain without any need for the usual permits. We can pick up some trustworthy local guides I know in Yenidogan” and he pointed Westward to the mountain in distance. “If we travel simply, we should not attract too much attention.”

She raised a single eyebrow and looked at him quizzically. “Attention” she said.

“Yes, there are occasional military patrols, but shepherds

are still allowed to roam freely on the mountain."

Yasmina simply smiled and handed over a large wad of notes. "Very well, shepherds it is."

12. ERIANES.

Harry and Sofia followed Erianes as they had been bidden. They made their way into the inner chamber and there on what looked like an altar in an alcove was laid the body of Enmerkar. For the first time Harry could see just how tall he was, probably somewhere between eight and a half and nine feet. Incredibly he looked uninjured, he looked like he was just sleeping peacefully.

"How is this possible?" asked Harry, "I shot him."

"Yes" said Erianes disapprovingly, "I had rather you had not done that. He is dying, but your bullet won't kill him. He scarified himself for you, and for all of us."

"How did he get here?" asked Sofia.

"The same way you did, through the portal."

"Portal, what portal? and exactly who are you, where did you come from?"

"Patience," she said, holding up her hand "all will be explained."

"Stop speaking in riddles" said Sofia emphatically, "Enmerkar did the same when we…. erm" she looked sheepishly at the floor and muttered, "…. accidentally shot him. It's so annoying. Just tell us, who are you?"

"Enmerkar spoke of the others, he called them Vori, what have they to do with this plague and why was he afraid of them?"

"Very well" said Erianes "I had hoped to let you rest a while first but perhaps a brief introduction is in order. We are the Einari, but you know us by many names in your myths and legends."

"Yes, yes" said Sofia interrupting impatiently, "Enmerkar said all that."

Erianes shot her a hard stare then began again. "Our civilisation was at its height almost half a million years ago. The earth was a beautiful paradise and we no longer needed to strip it bare of its natural resources to feed our cities and our people. We had conquered near space and anything we needed was freely available on other worlds in this solar system, which is far richer in its bounty than you currently imagine.

Our main outposts were on Vorea, what you know as Mars and the fifth planet, now destroyed, that we called Tiamet. Tiamet originally orbited in the region between Mars and Jupiter and all that now remains is the asteroid belt that is made up from the planetary fragments. You are on the brink of exploring space again and I envy you the journey you are about to embark upon, but our time is over.

In truth, the people of all of these worlds were once all Einari, but the people of Vorea we eventually came to call the Vori. It means violent ones in our language and even now they are the reason why you think of Mars as the 'god' of war. We had been on these worlds for many thousands of years and worked peacefully together but something, perhaps in the earth, or in the atmosphere of Vorea began to infect our people there and it changed them. It drove them mad, made them prone to excessive violence. It emerged slowly at first, they began to show symptoms of paranoia but soon they began poisoning their own world, they started to focus all of their energies on building machines of war, and without warning or provocation they attacked the colony on Tiamet.

Not content with killing the inhabitants they planted nuclear charges in a ring around the planet's core and they destroyed it in its entirety. The colony on Tiamet called for help and we answered but we were too late. We had never witnessed such devastation and we mustered all of our own resources to defend ourselves.

Harry's jaw fell visibly, "they destroyed a whole planet" he said.

"Yes," said Erianes, "a whole world destroyed and a world that was considerably larger than this one. When our leader, Lord Enki finally destroyed the Vori in their stronghold on Vorea, somehow, some of them survived. Their ships reached Earth; a war of attrition raged until eventually the final few vanished from our sight. Our fleet was over extended rescuing survivors from Taimet's ships and the smaller outposts where we could; whilst at the same time fighting the Vori fleet for our own survival. The losses on both sides were enormous but we managed to protect the Earth.

In the course of these battles, I am ashamed to say that we in turn, made Vorea uninhabitable. When you look at Mars you see a great tear across the surface that looks like the Grand Canyon here on earth; but the Valles Marineris, is four miles deep and almost 2,500 miles long. The final attack stripped away the atmosphere. Your race has already suspected the cause, ever since you sent the first probes to visit the planet where your scientists' discovered traces of the radioactive Isotopes derived from Uranium and Thorium."

"So, the legends of the Annunaki coming from the sky are true?" asked Harry.

"Some are close, but they are mostly confused" replied Erianes. "We, for our part are not gods, and you never thought to look to earth for the source of our race. The planet you think we came from; Nibiru is an incorrect translation of our word for 'home' in your language."

"So, you are not aliens?" asked Sofia.

"No" said Erianes, "we are not aliens. In all of our travels we have never encountered an intelligent species that did not originate of this very unique world".

"What is Marduk, the destroyer?" asked Harry. Was that the weapon you used to destroy them?"

"Erianes looked surprised, "what do you know of Marduk?"

"Not much" he replied truthfully "except that there are lots of references to it in the British Museum and it sounds quite scary."

"Marduk was one of two moons that orbited Tiamet. When the Vori destroyed the planet, Marduk was thrown out of its orbit to embark on a long elliptical journey to the edge of the solar system. After what your legends came to refer to as, 'The war in heaven,' it was assumed that it would drift through the Oort cloud at the edge of our charted space, then out into inter-galactic space, but we were wrong.

Had the Vori not created the plague we would have been able to assess the risk better, but we did not have the resources and after the plague, which almost destroyed us too, it was soon beyond our ability. The best we were able to do was to ascertain an approximation of its orbit and the cadence of its approach to the inner solar system."

"Are we in danger?" asked Sofia.

"Not from Marduk, at least not for another 35,000 years or so." Then almost as an afterthought she added, "he has already left his mark here."

"Just wind back a moment please; what plague?" asked Sofia, "I thought you said that you destroyed the Vori?"

"It's a long and complicated story, we did destroy their stronghold but as I said, a few made it to Earth and their final act was one of self-immolation. They infected all of us with a plague that killed about ninety percent of the population and rendered most of the rest infertile. We are a long-lived species, but our birth rate is very low by your standards and very quickly we reached the point of no return, we faced extinction. That is why you were engineered; although you did provide a ready work force to help us rebuild what we could, you were never meant to be a worker or a slave race unlike your predecessors."

"Excuse me" said Harry "…. our predecessors?"

"Yes, your predecessors" she replied emphatically. "Once, long ago, we engineered other species to help us colonise the outer planets but over time we made genetic experimentation illegal.

Your race was different, we were desperate, and you are, in every sense that matters, our children, and our only hope for carrying on our existence."

Suddenly it was like a light going on in Harry's head. "You are responsible for the rapid rise of art, science, creative thought, agriculture in early humans. We have speculated that there must have been some sort of catalyst but……" his words would not come.

"Yes" she said, "Our journey together began a very long time ago, but you were not ready for everything we could give you and we have still only scratched the surface. I was born in 24,690 BC, but Enmerkar was the last of our kind to be born but we are both infertile. So now that he is dying, the fate of the both the Einari, and mankind is to end with us, unless that is, we can teach you how to use our technology so that you can truly inherit what precious little we have managed to save for you. If we lose, you too stand on the precipice of, at best enslavement or at worst extermination."

"Why couldn't you just leave?" asked Sofia.

"Perhaps immediately after the war we could have, maybe some did, but after we had fought for the remainder of our population, and adapted what we had in order to survive in the new infected world, most likely it was simply too late.

We no longer have the physical technology like spaceships to leave the planet. Our technology is now long since faded and after half a million years we no longer have the knowledge and facilities to reproduce it."

"But you don't need ships" protested Sofia. "We didn't get here by ship did we, wherever here is?"

"At the time of the war, we were already considering transitioning away from ships to the portals, but the technology was in its infancy and their use is more complex than I can explain right now. The portals allow us to travel through space-time instantaneously, that is how Enmerkar returned here with his last conscious thought before he passed out, but he is exceptional. As far as I know no other Einari has even managed this unaided."

"You can't leave the planet, but you can travel at will through space-time?" said Harry.

"There are limits as to how we can use the corridors in

space-time and there is much to explain, please rest a while, I will show you to your quarters and we can talk tomorrow."

Erianes showed them to a simple room with the biggest bed they had ever seen.

"You are safe here" she said. "You will find much that is familiar, there is hot and cold running water in the bathroom, and you can use this to provide any requirements you have for food and drink." She pointed to what looked like a small microwave oven in a recess next to a very large settee.

"Are we prisoners here" asked Sofia.

"No" said Erianes, "but please, for your own safety, allow me to familiarise you with more of my home tomorrow, there are things here that are dangerous for you. Sleep well." With that she left, and the door vanished too, now only a blank silver wall stood where the door had been.

"This place is so cool," said Harry. "I am not sure we are not prisoners here, but I am tired and now that the door has gone, we don't seem to have a lot of choice anyway.

"I wonder where we are?" said Sofia.

When Harry awoke, he assumed it was morning as he could somehow see light penetrating the solid walls of their room despite the lack of any doors or windows. He woke Sofia and when they had showered, and dressed he walked towards where the door had been the previous evening and the wall seemed to melt in front of him letting them out into a wide corridor.

"Well," he said, "it seems we are not prisoners after all."

"No, you are not prisoners." he heard a now familiar voice behind him say. It was Erianes.

Harry jumped. "You really are quite stealthy, aren't you?" he said. Erianes ignored him. "Come this way please, have you eaten something yet?"

"Yes, thank you," said Sofia.

"Good, there is much we need to discuss with you and time is not our friend."

They walked into a small room and there sitting facing them was Enmerkar. "Welcome my young friends" he said.

"It's good to see you well" said Harry rather sheepishly. "Erm, …. about shooting you, I am sorry."

Enmerkar smiled. "It's not the first injury, that a member of your race has inflicted upon me, and as you can see, your bullet caused no lasting damage. Besides it achieved what I had hoped and led the two of you here, although to be honest that is not how I had planned our encounter. If you do not mind, I would not care to repeat it, it was rather painful."

Harry could not help himself as he winced in sympathy. "You planned it?" said Sofia, her eyes almost bulging from their sockets. Yesterday you told us that you had created us."

"Yes" said Erianes, "that is correct, your species was engineered right here, in this place."

"What and where exactly is this place?"

"You are in the laboratory of Nin Kirshag. Before it was converted, it was the battle cruiser Xisudra, and you are in the land of Atlan."

"Are we still on earth?" asked Harry.

"Yes," she replied.

"Well, why haven't I heard of Atlan?" he asked.

"That is probably because we are currently beneath almost

two miles of Antarctic ice. We have been buried here for over twelve thousand years." Erianes gave them a few moments to take it in and then she continued to relate the story of Enki, Enlil and Nin Kirshag.

"In a very real sense she is the true mother of your race, as it is her Mitochondrial DNA that many humans now carry."

"Surely you mean ALL humans?" said Sofia.

"No, unfortunately not, but please be patient. The blending of our DNA was not straightforward. We had manipulated DNA in other species before, but it was more akin to selective breeding within the existing species to bring out specific traits like strength, endurance, or the ability to survive in harsh environments. This task was of a much higher order, and we were effectively giving you what you might call a genetic upgrade, which was far more complex.

You may find it hard to believe but are not yet fully conscious" said Erianes. She paused for a moment to let the statement sink in. "When we created you, it took several attempts to ensure the chromosome grafts would be both successful and pass down the generational line without being weakened but passing on our genes was simple enough and your bodies adapted relatively quickly.

You started to grow taller, your diet changed, then with more balanced nutrition your cranial capacity began to increase but there were problems that Nin Kirshag had not foreseen.

Within our chromosomes we carry a genetic knowledge, which your brains could not handle. It made some extremely violent and we had no choice but to destroy what we had created. Eventually we realised that we had to engineer your brains into separate hemispheres, initially with little direct connection through the central nervous links.

Your ancestors were barely conscious at all in the way that you think of consciousness. They were clever, adaptable, and resourceful but they did not 'think' beyond the immediate requirements of survival. It took almost two hundred thousand years before we could allow the central nervous links to begin to strengthen through the Corpus Callosum, that nexus which connects both hemispheres of your brain. We waited until the very first amongst you started to paint on cave walls. They drew antelope, bison, and many of the things that they saw in the natural world around them. Slowly they began to show their awareness of their own place in the world. With that awareness you began to access the knowledge in your right hemisphere. Your creativity grew and with it your consciousness, along with the ability to deal with concepts and indeed the ability to conceptualise the world around you.

At first you heard this information as 'voices', quite literally the voices of the 'gods.' Your minds have still not developed to the point where you can perceive the world as it truly is, and this is our last task. What remains of our technology can only be accessed through the power of the mind, which is what the cards were created for; the guide was to be our last gift to you, along with the amplifiers."

"Guide? Amplifiers? what amplifiers?"

"The ring" said Enmerkar.

He paused and seeing that his revelations were becoming overwhelming for them he said softly "You are our guests here and the choice is yours, you can decide, but our time is short, either you must leave, or we must begin. If you stay, you must finish what we have started; we believe that the survival of your entire species and perhaps that of all species on Earth now depends upon it."

13. THE FIFTH DIMENSION.

Harry and Sofia looked at one another and slowly they both nodded in agreement. Their world view continued to fall apart around them, but they knew in their hearts that they had no choice.

"Very well" said Enmerkar and he began to explain what their training would entail. I am going to teach you to use the portals as we do and how to kill our foe and her followers. Ideally, we will do this without the need for weapons so that you will be able to leave little or no trace."

"Kill people," said Harry. "I don't want to kill anyone. Why us? What makes you think we can do this after all those centuries of trying."

"It is precisely because you find this abhorrent that you have been chosen. If you do not value the life of others, you would not be worthy of what we are about to share with you; but never-the-less, you must do this or you too will soon die."

"You are both left-handed, yes?"

Sofia looked at Harry, "yes" she replied.

"And both sets of parents were left-handed?"

"Er……yes"

"And their parents before them?"

"I think so," said Harry. "Yes, I remember now, my grandfather telling me that they used to punish him at school for writing with his left hand. Called him a 'cuddy wifter' or something like that, so he started writing with his right hand, he was ambidextrous."

“Most left-handed people are” said Erianes, “or at least they can choose to be. Right-handed people generally find that much more difficult.”

“But why is that important” asked Sofia “surely whether you are left or right-handed is just a random thing.”

“You are a doctor are you not?” asked Enmerkar.

“Yes”

“It is the latent capacity for imaginative thinking which is important here” he continued, “which is controlled by……”

Sofia finished the sentence. “……The right hemisphere of the brain, which is linked with the left-hand side of the body.”

“Exactly. There are few physical signs that would readily mark you out without a detailed DNA analysis which is something your race has only been capable of for a few decades, but this is the one trait that is the most easily recognisable. It almost always signifies that our Y Chromosome is strongly embedded in both of your genetic lines and that you carry, or at least have the potential to carry, our genetic memories. It's the next step in your evolution and this is what will allow you to see the world as it really is, unfortunately it will also put you at great risk."

"But if we carry the genetic memory of your race then they why don't we know about it, why can't we access it?" asked Sofia. "That is a very good question my dear. You must understand that the technology that was used to engineer this ability was ancient even by our reckoning and much has been lost with the passage of time. It is our belief however that you can access them, and you do, although not consciously, and that is a mystery we are still trying to understand.

Your subconscious is very powerful and despite our best efforts it will only reveal things to you when your conscious mind believes that it can handle it. It is most likely an inbred survival instinct that your species already had long ago, before our scientists altered your genetic makeup. This is the reason the 'guides' or tarot cards as you insist on calling them were necessary, because they train your subconscious mind through the use of symbols rather than using logic.

"You still look puzzled? Let me explain how the portals work, this may help. We live in 4 dimensions, yes?"

"4 dimensions? Surely you mean three. Length, breadth,

and height?" said Harry.

"Hmmm" muttered Enmerkar absently mindedly, "this may take a while longer than I had anticipated" he said, glancing at Erianes. He quickly turned his attention back to Harry. "Please try to open your mind. You think of three dimensions all being perpendicular to one another. Let's take first one dimension. A single point. If that point were to move in one direction you would get a line, yes?"

"Yes" said Harry, nodding.

"Now if that line moves perpendicular at 90 degrees you get a plane or 2nd dimension, yes?"

"Yes" repeated Harry.

"And if that plane moves perpendicular, either up or down you get a solid or third dimension."

Harry nodded again. Despite being well out of his depth he was feeling pleased with himself for following the logic so far.

"Well, what are they moving through as they transition from one dimension to another?"

Harry thought hard, visibly trying to wrench an answer from his mind...... "Time?" he said, "of course.... it's time."

"Yes, exactly" said Enmerkar, "time is the fourth dimension, but it is not what you think it is.

We do not move through Time; this is an illusion. In fact it is a stationary field that we exist within. If you were to think of Time as moving then it would be more accurate to think of it moving through us not the other way around.

It is like the subtle skin of the universe. The way you perceive it would be to think of the past, the present and the future. The past is gone, the future has not yet come into being and so you are only conscious of the present as it happens to you. But this only 'seems' to be true. In reality, Time is like a vast sea in which we swim, with waves rolling over it. In this dimension we are always on the crest of the wave, the present, and this is all that we experience, but the rest of the sea still remains. The past and the future are already and forever in existence."

Suddenly feeling like an ant seeking shade from a burning sun in the vastness of an empty desert, the blood drained from Harry's face as he drank in the enormity of what was being explained to him. His world view had disappeared in an instant and the remaining vestiges of his usual self-assuredness, which had already been severely dented since the hunt in the forest, were now stripped away completely.

He suddenly felt very inadequate and very exposed amid this vast new vista that was opening up ahead of him.

"How can this be possible and how do you know all this if it is beyond our experience. You can't simply 'see' higher dimensions......can you?"

"At last," said Enmerkar, "a worthy question. The first of many, I hope. In the long history of this world, it has borne fruit many times and your race is not its first flowering. Nor indeed was our own race.

Whilst much of your mythology is based upon our race, even you have traces of the knowledge of higher dimensions and higher beings. Sometimes they are in plain sight, contained within your most sacred religious texts. You laugh them off as 'fairy tales', the delusional rantings of ancient desert dwellers or dismiss them as simple stories made up by shepherds in order to entertain one another over the camp fires at night. Then there are the artifacts hidden away in the deepest vaults of your museums under the light veneer of respectable archaeology and mainstream education. Your beloved British museum is one such example is it not?"

Although stung by the criticism, Harry had to admit that it was true. Only perhaps ten percent of the artifacts it held were ever on display and anything which was 'difficult' to explain rationally tended to stay well hidden, at least until a theory, or sub theory could be developed to link it to the mainstream narrative.

"At the peak of our technological development over half a million years ago, we had explored the solar system and sent probes way beyond its confines. We had explored our world, dissected every creature, conquered every land mass and Ocean, learned how to rewrite our own DNA as well as that of other species, and we understood the very secrets of nature herself, or so we thought.

Yet, no matter how far we voyaged we came to realise that we would forever be restricted by our dimensional limitations and subject, even as you are, to the effects of time. Slowly at first, we began to realise that the final frontier was not 'out there', and he pointed a long bony finger skywards, it was in here" he said touching his forehead.

"We began to explore the 5th dimension using the latent powers that we had long suspected existed in our minds."

"To what end" asked Harry. "Self-mastery, perhaps?"

"Nothing so noble I am afraid. It was, as it always is, about power."

"Power?" Asked Harry struggling to understand the implications.

"Yes, power Harry. If you take the example that I have just shared with you, a three-dimensional being could see the full spectrum of a two-dimensional world, the whole thing laid out before them, from one end to another and nothing could be hidden from them.

They would be able to touch anywhere at will on the two-dimensional world and, from the perspective of a two-dimensional observer, they would simply have appeared, as if by magic, and from out of nowhere. What is more the two-dimensional being would only see a cross section and would never be able to truly understand the nature of what they were dealing with.

Imagine putting your fingers down on a table. A two-dimensional being would not see your hand, they would only see five roughly spherical cross sections, with no apparent connection to one another.

Well imagine if we could do that with space time if we

could see any point in space or time and simply appear there at will."

"Is it magic or is it really possible?" asked Sofia?

"Yes.....and no"

"Yes and no! What kind of an answer is that?"

"There is a subatomic structure that sits behind what you would call reality. A matrix if you will, a pattern, a force, Chi, Yetzirah, it is called by many names but perhaps quantum mechanics resonates better for you given your current level of scientific understanding. Yes and no, can both be right on this plane.

Two things, worlds apart, can be 'entangled', what affects one affects the other. The distance between them is irrelevant and all outcomes for all possible actions already exist. Crucially ideas are not abstract on this plane, they are in every sense of the world 'real' in this place.

If they are real on this plane, and this is the basis of reality, then any effect in this 'base layer or underlying structure' manifests itself in what we think of as the physical world. This idea is the basis of what you call **both** magic and science. The only difference is the way in which you try to bring those effects about."

Harry and Sofia listened in silence.

“Hocus pocus, Magicians, and witches. It's all nonsense” scoffed Harry.

“Is it?” asked Enmerkar staring intently at him.

“If you don't like that explanation, then let me try appealing to your more rationale instincts. If you could zoom in close enough to any object, at the subatomic level you will see that it is made up of nothing but energy in a state of motion, or more accurately vibration. Matter is only solid because the vibration makes it seem so. It is the nature and cadence of the vibration which gives matter its widely differing characteristics, so we see one thing as gold and one thing as silver for example.”

Harry still looked puzzled.

Enmerkar decided to try again. “What is the difference between steam, water and Ice?” he asked.

“Just the temperature I suppose, “said Harry.

“Exactly, they are all what you call ‘water,’ but the molecules change depending on how agitated they are. The level of agitation is determined by how much energy flows through it, in this case that energy would be in the form of heat."

"I think I understand. So how do you access the fifth dimension and why?"

"Another worthy question my young friend."

"Firstly, by training the mind with these symbols to guide and direct the will", he pointed to the cards. "We came to realise that if we are constantly sitting on the crest of the wave of time, that the first thing we should do would be to try to train our minds to extend our view from the top of the wave. We would start by looking down the sides of the wave and eventually to the horizon in every direction towards both the past and future.

This base layer to reality, opens the door to all of the higher dimensions and there are more than you would imagine. It is peculiarly affected by thoughts, or more accurately the mind, which if carefully trained, can induce changes in it and therefore the structure of the world we live in."

"You already have a famous example in your science called the Schrodinger's Cat experiment. In this experiment a cat is put in a box with some poison. The cat is both alive and dead, but the result only becomes fixed once you observe it. In other words, the act of observation directly affects the sub-atomic realm to crystallise on one option or the other to make it real."

"So, you are saying that you can open these portals with your mind."

"Exactly Harry, but only with help and training".

"Let me get this straight, you can see any point in space or time and simply 'go' there?"

Enmerkar nodded slowly.

"Well then why don't you simply go back and fix the problem?"

Enmerkar closed his eyes and shook his head. "You truly do not understand your world at all do you?"

"I thought I did, at least until I met you anyway," said Harry.

'Let us rest and pick this up later. I grow tired" said Enmerkar.

"Yes" said Harry, "I think a break is a good idea. By the way do you have anything else to eat around here other than vegetables?"

“No” said Erianes firmly, “we do not. As you have already surmised, we do not eat meat.”

“I could do with getting out of here and getting some fresh air” he said.

“I would not recommend it; the surface temperature is currently forty degrees below zero and there is strong wind blowing from the east.”

“I will need my big coat then!” said Harry.

Erianes looked bemused.

“Humour” said Harry, “you do have a sense of humour? Let me guess you gave that to us as well?”

Erianes face softened and for the first time they saw her smile. She was ethereally beautiful, with a tall, perhaps a regal, or even goddess like presence. Her green eyes were absolutely piercing, and her smile seemed to illuminate everything.

Even Enmerkar looked on in wonder and a narrow smile crept over his own lips, it had been too long since either of them had felt joy in their hearts.

14. NOT 'THE ONE'.

After they had eaten and rested for a while Enmerkar asked. "Are you ready to continue your education?"

"Yes" said Harry enthusiastically, and Sofia too nodded. She had remained uncharacteristically quiet during Enmerkar's explanation, but Harry was getting into the swing of things and was beginning to surprise himself. In a matter of days his world had been dismantled completely but he was now coming to terms with it. He knew that nothing would ever be the same again and he was now eager to see the full extent of the view that was beginning to open up ahead of him.

"Yes, I think I am" he said again.

"Then we shall begin again" said Enmerkar.

"You asked me earlier why we couldn't simply go back and fix the problem?"

"Seems like the logical thing to do" said Harry "and it would save us all a whole lot of trouble, wouldn't it?"

Enmerkar smiled. "Yes, it would."

"I can feel an enormous 'but' coming on here," said Harry.

"Indeed, my young friend.

The portals exist in the 5th dimension. They are on one level at least, direct connections to different points in space and time. They allow us to move to any point in space instantly through the 5th dimension, but we are no longer permitted to see or move through time."

“Whoa.... time out,” said Harry.

“I thought I was getting my head around this but you said 'not permitted to’ Not permitted, why?”

“By whom would be more accurate” said Enmerkar.

“What do you mean, by whom” asked Harry.

“By the races that inhabit the 5th dimension, and those beyond.”

Involuntarily, Harry’s mouth fell open as his mind was struggling to take in what he had just heard.

Ignoring the stunned look on Harry’s face, Enmerkar continued. “They have always been aware of us, just as they are of you, but the inhabitants of the world that we occupy, or at least the current races, were of little concern to them. That changed however once we started using the portals. They quickly realised the potential for the madness to spread, not just through this world but also the potential we had developed to cause chaos across many other timelines.

Now they only permit us to travel in space, in one single timeline, and only across this world. They have closed all other aspects of the portals to us for their safety, for the safety of this world and the safety of the younger race. For you.

For you and your descendants to be more precise. We do not know why, but you are important to them, so they permit us to help you. Even with the limitations they place upon us, that is enough for us to complete our work, but we must hurry."

"So are you saying I am some sort of 'chosen one' or Messiah?" asked Harry.

"No" said Enmerkar emphatically, "she is" he said, pointing to Sofia.

Sofia looked stunned.

"It was Sofia I was looking for in the woods in Tuscany.

Your relationship, particularly the strong genes you carry was merely a happy twist of fate, but it is one which will prove useful."

Harry's sense of deflation was now complete, and he sat silently emasculated, and looked at Sofia.

She had been listening intently, the blood was beginning to drain from her face, and now she looked as if she was about to faint. Eventually she spoke.

"You said that the adaptations were so that we could carry your Y chromosome?"

"Yes, that is correct."

"But in humans at least, only males carry the Y chromosomes, females are all XX and males are XY are they not?"

"Correct, but in your case, you somehow have three XXY. The simple fact of its existence in itself is remarkable but there is more. We thought the Y chromosome would have to be completely dormant, but in you, it seems that it is not. That is the reason why you are immune to this Covid outbreak that has killed so many of your colleagues. You have never had a cold or flu, have you?"

"No" she said, "I haven't. How did you know?" she asked.

An expression of deep sadness spread across Erianes face.

"Because we created Covid" she said, "and we closely monitored its spread."

Sofia was horrified, she felt as if she were suffocating and the tears started to run down her face ".... you..., you created it." She ran from the room trying to get away as afar as she could but there seemed to be no exits from the ship and the furthest that she could go was back to their room.

Harry followed her, she was distraught, tears streaming down her face and he just held her while she let it out, reeling off the names of her colleagues, friends and family who had died. The worst of it was that she was here with its creators, and she could not escape. "What are we going to do Harry?"

"I don't know" he said honestly "but whatever we have fallen in to here, I don't think we can avoid it. They could have killed us at any time, in any number of ways, but we do seem to be important to them."

She turned he face into her chest still crying. He could not provide the explanation that she so desperately needed, all he could do right now was to comfort her.

About an hour later Sofia had regained her composure and they made their way back to the laboratory. "Tell me everything" she demanded. "If there are only two of you here, you could not possibly have done all of this without help, even with your advanced technology."

"That is correct" said Enmerkar.

"Some in your governments are aware of us but they are few, carefully placed and only at the highest levels."

"Then why couldn't one of them be your chosen one instead of me?"

They all have the strong genetic marker, but in them it remains dormant. You are unique and even amongst those who have shown the most promising development, none of them has been able to open the portal, except you."

"What about Uncle Geoffrey?" asked Harry.

"Who?" asked Enmerkar who was now also confused.

Harry regaled the story his father had told him about their exploration of the caves and a flicker of remembrance spread fleetingly across Erianes' face. "A simple accident" she said. "I was leaving the cave when he saw me, he was startled and stumbled. He simply fell through the portal I had opened. If I had closed it immediately it would have killed him. I took him back to another part of the cave and your father never got a good look at me, but it seems that your uncle is somewhat adept with his hands. During his very brief stay here he managed to hide the other will trainer, which you now possess" she said, pointing at the cards.

"Then you are not monsters after all?" said Sofia.

"No" said Erianes, "we have told you the truth, we do care greatly for you and for your race. We should have told you sooner but there is so much more that you need to know. When the last survivors of Enlil's Vori disappeared our forebears believed that they would simply die out and they had more pressing matters to deal with.

Once again, we had underestimated them, and we did not know that there was one amongst us in the Ennead council whose allegiance was with Enlil, and she betrayed us. Part of the genetic Ark we set up was stolen. We had thought it destroyed in one of the minor battles before the laboratory was moved here, but Ningal the traitor, had given it to Enlil and in this way, he became aware of our plans. Enlil was completely mad and according to legend his was reward to Ningal was a swift death. A lover betrayed.

Their aim was simple annihilation of your species, retribution for the war, but by then they could not match our resources, so they hid. As far as we know, they are all long dead now but over the aeons they have worked through your own DNA to debase you. There is only one of their direct experiments remaining alive as far as we know, her name is Lilith."

"Lilith: said Harry, "you mean Lilith the demon goddess?"

"Yes" said Erianes "You know of her?"

"Only what we have learned from my colleagues at the British Museum and it seems to be mostly legends supplemented by an awful lot of conjecture and made up theories. Personally I have to say that I doubted she was ever even real."

"Oh I can assure you that she is very real." said Erianes.

"Who is she?" asked Sofia.

"Your progenitor, whom you call Adam, had two mates, the first was called Lilith.

Although the Vori who created her are believed to be long dead, their experiments had been focused on the X Chromosome from our race, which they knew had degenerative properties when combined with the Hominid genes. Although we cannot be certain, we believe that somehow the experiments they performed in the distant past, over the millennia gave rise to a single chance mutation. It was too late before we realised the truth. She became the mother of all-evil in your species."

"Sounds like you really fucked up," said Sofia.

"Your coarseness is not pleasing to my ears, but it is not altogether inaccurate" said Erianes.

"She became the first progenitor of a new species within a species. From her come all those humans with the negative blood groups. Fortunately, they were a minority, albeit a sizeable one, but with careful breeding our Y Chromosome re-established its dominance in most of the population, counteracting the worst effects of the contamination. Thanks to our intervention, with the exception of some minor groups, even those with negative blood groups are now back on the same evolutionary path as you."

Harry shivered, "so that is why she is shown as the mother of demons and the slayer of small children?"

"Yes, …quite…, and what is more she still lives. Her unique mutation seems to have resulted in an incredibly long lifespan even by our standards. We believe she was born over 30,000 years ago and she is both resourceful and clever, but from what we know it is most likely that the sociopathic tendencies which would dominate her make up."

"She doesn't literally go around killing children, does she?" asked Sofia.

"Make no mistake she is deadly" said Erianes, "but no, as far as we are aware the stories of slaying children come from the negative blood group. When parents have opposite blood groups your natural defence mechanisms can attack the foetus, killing it."

"So why didn't you destroy her?"

"To be completely honest with you there is much about Lilith that we do not know. We have spent many years; searching for her and every time we got close, she was always one step ahead, she was deliberately draining our resources which was preventing us from continuing our work. We had to make a difficult choice, so we decided to continue our work with your race and pursue her at a more opportune moment."

"I can sense another very large 'but' hoving into view," said Sofia.

Enmerkar nodded.

"But then, HE Came" said Erianes "and our world was decimated."

15. MOUNT ARARAT.

While Schmitt went into the small café on the edge of town to organise his guides, Lilith stood outside waiting patiently. She looked across the plain and up at the mountains from Yenidogan. The fields around the town were lush with meadow flowers. Poppies dominated the pasture in every direction and here and there the odd birch grove broke up the otherwise flat landscape to the North and to the East. To the West, the two long extinct volcanoes stood side by side.

They were magnificent. They looked like huge and mighty sentinels keeping watch over a great treasure as they rose from the parched landscape below.

"Hello old friends" she whispered to herself.

The snow- capped mountains loomed ominously above the plain. Rising to almost seventeen thousand feet, she knew that the climb would not be easy. As she scanned the terrain, she could see that there would be little cover for their climb and the weather could be treacherous at this time of year.

Her eyes followed the outline of the higher of the two mountains from its base, skywards. The trees soon gave way to rough meadow and the vegetation got progressively thinner until eventually she could see what looked like a simple brown rock, capped with pristine white snow that reminded her of a bride's gown that she had once worn in ages long past. Above it the brooding, cloud fill sky seemed always to be loaded with the thunder and lightning that the mountains were famous for.

She remembered a time long ago. How different

this place had been then.

The snowfields were much smaller, and the snow-capped peaks always seemed reassuring, like huge benevolent guardians watching everything that lived under the gentle blue sky. They only seemed to reach out gently, reaching up into the heavens as if they were supporting the wide arc of the sky above the lush trees of the forest that stretched for miles in every direction and had once provided everything her people had ever needed.

Schmitt came out of the café, saw her looking at the black clouds overhead and interrupted her daydreaming. "Don't worry professor Hashemi, there is often lightening at the top of the mountain, but the storms are usually short lived, and I think that this one will soon pass. The climb would take several days even if we were just to just head straight for the top, but we will need some time to acclimatize on the journey. If we are spending time looking for something, then that is a very big area to cover so I have arranged provisions for ten days and two of the guides will accompany us to about fourteen thousand feet."

"Why were you so long?" she asked.

"They are a superstitious lot and will not go into what they call the ghost lands where they say locals have often been simply 'lost', but like most men they have a price where their greed overcomes their fear."

"Tell me, are you a superstitious man Mr. Schmitt?" she asked.

"I don't believe in ghost stories if that is what you mean" he said. "It is true that shepherds and adventurers alike have been disappearing on the mountain for as long as people have been here and even in recent years well equipped, experienced climbers have been lost. On such occasion those survivors that come back often return with strange stories."

"What do you think happens to the people who are lost on the mountain?" she asked.

"These were once active volcanoes" he said, "and even though they are now extinct, as far as we know anyway, the magma cannot be too far below the surface here meaning that you cannot rule out gas venting from the ground. Combined with strong electromagnetic storms strange things can happen."

"What strange things?"

Compasses and radios don't work, and one can

easily become disoriented. When that happens there are all manner of dangers. Altitude plays strange tricks on the mind when oxygen levels are low and even if you don't fall down a crevasse, getting caught in the icefield can result in exposure and hypothermia. They say that dying that way is like falling into a dream filled sleep so if any were to find themselves rescued it is not surprising that they would be rambling, not knowing what was and what was not real.

Why do I have the feeling that you know all of this, but still you will not be dissuaded?"

She smiled and answered truthfully "this is not the first time I have been on the sacred mountain. I assume our guards will be armed?"

"Yes," he replied, "they always carry their rifles for hunting, and to dissuade the occasionally over-zealous border guards from taking too close an interest in what they are carrying if you get my drift."

Lilith nodded, "and you Mr. Schmitt?"

Schmitt just smiled. "Let's just say that I am no stranger to arduous conditions" he said.

"Come, let us have a warm drink and some food, an early night would be a good idea. The café has a couple of rooms and I have taken the liberty of booking them rather than heading back into town. The accommodation is basic here, but it means that we will be able to make a start at first light, and by doing so it will not attract any attention."

Just before dawn there was a light tapping on her bedroom door. It was Schmitt. "Good morning, Professor" he said as she opened the door. "I hope you are ready; we have a long journey ahead of us."

"Yes, Mr. Schmitt, I assure you that I am only too ready" she replied as they made their way past the last few buildings to the very edge of the town where two guides awaited them. The guides were accompanied by two small brown donkeys on which were packed all of their provisions, other than their own small rucksacks.

"Professor Hashemi, these are my cousin Levon's associates Mehmet and Baris. They will be our guides for the next ten days."

They both smiled and said hello but seemed somewhat uncomfortable to be escorting a woman up the mountain on what would be an arduous climb. "The Jeep won't do us any good from here," said Schmitt. "Once we get through the fields and out of the woods the only way forward is on foot." The sun was beginning to rise across the Eastern plains as they set off into the foothills of Mount Ararat.

Sure enough; once they cleared the last birch grove there were deep ruts everywhere and only narrow tracks, but the donkeys seemed comfortable, and their brays made them seem as though they were laughing. They were grateful for four legs and even with their heavy loads, the joke was on their two-legged companions.

Around mid-day they found a small stone building. A hut that the local shepherds used for shelter, they stopped and set up a small campfire. Sensing Lilith's frustration at the slow pace of their progress, Mehmet smiled and explained that they would need to climb slowly and there were not many places to shelter on the mountain. To walk late into the afternoon would risk them running into the border patrols at this low level. They were heading west and with the sun in their faces they would be seen before they could hide.

"Where exactly are we heading Professor?" asked Schmitt.

"We are heading to the ridge between the two peaks on the Western side of the great mountain" she said.

"That is on the other side of the great ravine and covered in snow at this time of year, it won't be easy. May I ask what exactly we are looking for on the ridge?"

"The entrance" she said.

"The entrance?"

"Yes, Mr. Schmitt, the entrance. The lava that once ran under these mountains has left a maze of tunnels."

"No one has even found any tunnels here." said Schmitt.

"That is because they were not meant to find them."

Schmitt was prepared to go on a little faith, but she could see the doubt written large on his face.

"Once, long ago, long before the Sumerians inhabited this place, a strange race of men lived in these mountains" she said.

"Inside the mountains" said Schmitt …. "If you are talking about the 'watchers', they are just a myth?"

"Yes, Mr. Schmitt, inside the mountains, and the watchers were not just a myth, they were very real, and very dangerous."

This threw Schmitt of guard. "So where and how do we find the entrance?" he asked.

"Let me worry about that, when I see what I am looking for, I will know it" and silently she added silently to herself "and when I do, I will find what I need and use it to kill every last one of them."

"We will set off again just before dawn. The sun rising behind us will give us the advantage in the morning. Try to get some rest" he said.

Lilith made her way into the almost ruined structure and climbed into her sleeping bag, but rest would not come and once again she found herself dreaming of Adam and trying to remember how she had escaped from the mountain.

They set off again in the rose golden glow of the pre-dawn and, as they approached the edge of the great ravine, they could see the goats on the ridge on the other side looking for moss and eating the small alpine flowers that grew in every tiny crevice, each like its own mini ravine. Every flower seemed to ache to reach the morning sun as each in turn was watered by its own tiny river of early morning dew drops, only then to be ripped from its place by a voracious four-legged herbivore seeking its own sustenance.

The whole cycle of life and death played out across every inch of the ravine. They could hear the bells that the goat herders attached to their animals so that they could find them in poor weather and the sound echoed like church bells ringing in a mighty cathedral creating a cacophony in the early morning light.

"We must get to the bottom before the sun is high at our backs" said Baris. "The Turkish patrols will pass around the Eastern ridge around midday."

"That is very specific for a patrol," said Lilith.

"Yes," he replied, "they are looking for Kurdish encampments that they think may be used as terrorist hideaways but many of the soldiers have family connections here so they don't always look too hard" he smiled "but still we must be careful."

At the bottom of the ravine, they took cover in a small copse of birch trees that grew in a crescent shape, shielded by a small wall of solid rock. As they sat eating their cold rations, she asked the guides what they knew of the history of the mountain.

"The locals call this mountain 'Agri Dagi,' the mountain of pain professor," said Mehmet.

"Yes" said Lilith, nodding; she knew well its name and she also knew why it carried its terrible epithet.

"What of the people who lived here?" she asked.

"In the eighteenth century the Ottomans had built a large administrative palace and local capital at Ishak Pasha on the lower slopes. There are a few ruins along the trail of small watch towers and fortifications but there are no buildings from here. Whatever good stone there was, the local shepherds used it to construct their small refuges long ago."

"And what about before the Ottomans?" she asked.

Schmitt added that the Seljuks came here at the time the Mongolian hordes were heading westwards. They were mighty warriors and even the Mongols were wary of them. They had a few small encampments here because they were easily defensible but eventually, they left when they themselves began to conquer, moving south and westward towards Egypt.

"Less than a thousand years, Mr. Schmitt against the backdrop of these ancient mountains it is but a drop in the ocean of time. What of these markings on the rock face?"

"The people of Noah and his ancestors," said Mehmet. He shrugged "no one really knows."

Lilith continued to quiz them. "Tell me Mehmet, have you seen more of these markings on the higher slopes, above the snow line?"

Baris and Mehmet both now looked visibly worried. They looked at one another and eventually Mehmet nodded.

"When we were children" said Baris, "we wandered away from the shepherds and up into the base of the glacier on the western ridge and the weather changed. We thought we would die but we found another small crescent shaped rock refuge like this one but with no ice in it. There were symbols carved on the rocks.

We spent the night there but as soon as the dawn came, we ran as quickly as we could. There were voices all night, demons whispering to us on the wind."

"Yes" said Lilith, recalling to her mind's eye. "Two pillars with a sun atop one and with the moon atop the other. On the left a human body and on the right a human skeleton then below each of them a giant silver figure".

Baris and Mehmet were both now visibly shocked.

"Please, professor we cannot go there again."

"Do not worry my friends you do not need to go there. If you guide us to the snow line, just below the ridge then I will consider your duty discharged. Mr. Schmitt and I will do the rest."

Even Schmitt was starting to look nervous now.

Looking him straight in the eyes she said, "you do not worry either my friend, yes there are devils here to be sure, but together, you and I, we shall bring them in to the light."

He nodded, before almost instinctively moving his hand over the holster of his pistol. "We should get moving again, the patrols should have left by now. Climbing out of the canyon will be tough and we will need the rest of the daylight we have."

As they packed up their things then set off again the weather was beginning to change and the peel of the bells from the animals now had its reply from the thundering clouds above.

16. MARDUK THE DESTROYER.

"Who was 'HE" asked Harry, "and just exactly what did he do?" not sure if he really wanted to know.

"HE was Marduk the Destroyer" said Erianes. 'The one you asked Enmerkar about earlier."

"The lost moon of Tiamet?" asked Harry.

"Yes, the lost moon of Tiamet, and he almost put an end to everything here on this planet. The world you know was very different then. There were no seasons, sea levels were around four hundred feet lower because the icecaps at the poles were much larger."

They could see in her face that she was struggling to remember what to her, was a more familiar and beautiful world. Sofia was dumbstruck but Erianes regained her focus on her visitors and continued.

"Then around 12,500 years ago we detected Marduk returning to the inner solar system. It was then that we realised that it was on a collision course with Earth. We used the last of the ancient resources we had to stop it destroying the planet, we tried to deflect its path but we almost failed and in the course of its journey, it pushed the Earth off its axis, and it now revolves at 23.5 degrees off from Galactic North.

"Yes" said Harry rather excitedly, "that's why we get the seasons, the Zodiac, and the precession of the equinoxes."

"The precession of what?" asked Sofia.

"The precession of the equinoxes." he repeated. "Every 2,160 years or so, at the time of the spring equinox, on

March 21st, the sun rises with a different constellation in the background, and over time it goes backwards through the Zodiac. You have heard of the Age of Aquarius? Well that's what we are just entering, and we are leaving the Age of Pisces."

Erianes smiled, she seemed almost impressed for the briefest of moments, but it quickly passed. "There was a cataclysm and worldwide upheaval, no part of the land or seas were spared. The devastation would be scarcely imaginable had we not witnessed it for ourselves. Every one of your civilizations has legends of a great flood do they not?"

Harry nodded.

"What you call The Ice age, ended abruptly in some parts of the world but in others flash freezing killed herds of Mammoths and other animals, whole civilizations were lost through earthquakes, floods, and fire.

The Einari race was already only shadow of its former glory, but never-the-less we sent out the few remaining members of our species to save as many groups of humans as we could; but even we, were badly affected. The upheaval caused the tectonic plates to shift and our home, Atlan, moved four thousand miles south in just a few hours and is now buried here under what remains of the Antarctic Ice sheet. We watched helplessly as the world above us changed forever."

"That must have been awful," said Sofia.

"Yes" said Erianes "it was a dreadful time and incredibly difficult; but again, by one of those twists of fate it gave us the time we needed to complete our work."

Had Marduk not devastated the world resulting in us being hidden here then we would probably have been hunted to extinction, possibly by Lilith herself but certainly by those who revered the Vori.

Survival in the immediate aftermath of Marduk's return was only the beginning, we had to help you understand what your new world looked like and that would take time, almost five thousand years in total."

Enmerkar looked into the distance remembering old friends. The sadness both in his eyes, and in his voice as he spoke were unmistakable. "We sent one of our number called Uriel, my elder brother, to help you build celestial observatories across the entire world to act as time markers like Stonehenge, Callanish, New Grange and many more so that you could re-establish agriculture and monitor the newly established seasons. Neither he, nor any of those we sent amongst you ever returned to us. Gradually you forgot us. For all but a few, we faded into your mythology.

Marduk was all encompassing in his gift to reshape the world and the followers of the Vori too suffered of course, so we became less of a priority for them in their own struggle to survive. When they believed we were all dead, that is when they took their lesson from Lilith to heart, and they started infecting you directly to wipe you out.

Before what you call the flood, your lifespan was close to one thousand years. Our Y Chromosome does not react well to meat and so you were engineered to be vegetarians like us. It was relatively easy because your ancestors were already plant eaters and quite docile."

"Yes," said Harry, a light coming on in his memory, "I have read that in the book of Genesis, but I never understood it."

Erianes continued, "Photosynthesis was affected by the Earth's displacement, food became scarce, and 'She' came to finish her work. Adam was not the first man but the genetic markers linking him to us were particularly strong in his line. After the flood, food was scarce, and someone, perhaps it was Lilith, convinced your species to eat meat."

"How do you convince a vegetarian species to eat meat?" asked Sofia

"The alternative was brutally simple, extinction through starvation. You adapted to survive, but food became your Achilles heel. The easiest way to infect you using the viruses they created, was to infect other species first. As far as we know Lilith was the first example of a bio-weapon being used directly against you."

"If you don't mind me making an observation, you do seem to be rather vague on the details. Why not just stick to poisoning us through the food supply in order to keep the Einari genes suppressed?" asked Sofia.

"You cannot imagine the scale of the cataclysm we faced" said Erianes, "how much was lost, so yes, we are unable to give you a comprehensive and clear picture of the past. Our records are now incomplete, in fact it would be closer to the truth to say that only fragments survive. But we do know that their aim is not simply to debase you, it is to either enslave you and if they cannot achieve that, to destroy you completely and in the process to wipe out any trace of our species from the Earth, in whatever form it may survive. They will not risk allowing our genes to survive unchecked. I am so sorry. We brought this upon you."

"If this is all true and our existence has been literally hanging on a thread for millennia then why, or how, are we still here?"

"Your reproductive capacity as a species is remarkably strong. After the flood, they realised that the only way to achieve their aim was to wage a series of biological wars against you. That way, they hoped that your immune systems would not have the required time to adapt and to build up resistance.

Every time they tried, we provided the antibodies you needed to survive but she has been growing more resourceful and has nearly succeeded several times."

"Hang on a minute you, you said that you created the virus," said Sofia.

"Yes, this time" replied Erianes matter-of-factly.

"Our aim was to use their own weapon against them. We created it in Wuhan in China, I am only sorry that so many innocents have been affected. Some of those who died were brave volunteers in its development, but we had to spread it to ensure its properties were targeted correctly."

"Volunteers? Targeted correctly?" asked Sofia.

"Yes, as I said, some in your governments at the highest levels have always known of our existence. They know what is at stake and have helped us fight against the enemy. Unfortunately, 'They' too have their followers and this war of which you have been unaware has been raging across this planet since long before the beginnings of your recorded history."

Sofia was aghast. "How could our governments collaborate with this horror?"

"Believe me Sofia when I tell you that you are literally fighting for your survival" said Enmerkar. "We find violence abhorrent but now that the Einari are almost at an end, our only hope to protect you was to wipe them out first. Before we could do that, we had to find them all."

"But so many people have died said Sofia, they cannot all have been our enemies."

"No" said Erianes, "they were not, and there will yet be more." The look of deep and genuine sadness in her eyes somehow darkened them and momentarily, she her regal bearing seemed somehow diminished.

"We know that it is painful for you to hear this, but by isolating the majority of them we will be able to avoid millions more needless deaths."

"Surely there were other ways?" protested Sofia.

"Yes" said Enmerkar softly "and we have used those too. We have guided your technological development to help us. Your Internet was our creation long ago, and we gave the odd nudge here and there helping you to build a digital world where we could at last track them. Your leaders call us the watchers and we have indeed watched patiently. Now we need to restrict their movements and to keep them isolated in so far as we are able, and this is why the most powerful government agreed to create the restrictions."

"How did you get them to agree?" asked Sofia still reeling.

"As I said," he continued "those we have trusted have always known the risks you face. Although most of your people choose to ignore it, and to focus on petty issues, your world is very interdependent. Nothing short of a pandemic would make the isolation of large populations possible.

It only took a few of them agree, the most powerful ones, and other nations soon responded in kind when their citizens were denied the right of travel. Many did not want to close down your transport links; they were afraid of the damage it would cause but what is money when the alternative is extinction?"

"That explains why the Prime Minister and the President looked so uncomfortable making all of those announcements," said Harry.

"Perhaps" said Erianes, "the decision was not an easy one, but in the end they all agreed for the greater good. Our window is short, and we must finish this now. We did create this virus that is true, but they have tried to wipe you out many times.

Tell me Sofia, you are a doctor what do you really know of plague?"

"We have eradicated the plague" she replied.

"Surely you are not that naïve, your recent medical understanding of antibiotics is only a century old, without our help you could have been wiped out many times. The plague of Justinian, the Bubonic plague, or The Black

Death as it is better known, the Spanish Flu, or Malaria to name just a few. It is our belief that, with her help, they created them all. Every flowering of your civilization has been destroyed, each time with the loss of millions of lives; endless numbers lost in the reaches of time but always we have helped you to rebuild, to become stronger and to rise to ever-greater heights. When their followers realised that they we were not dead and that they could not win by force they disappeared, and to our shame we became complacent, we believed the threat had passed."

"Who are 'they'?" asked Harry.

"They are the offspring of those poor beings that Enlil created long ago. They are violent but they are also very clever, and they too at least have the propensity to carry some of the genetic memory that we have gifted to you, although as far as we can tell, they lack the ability to access some of the more subtle aspects encoded within their DNA, so they tend towards being manipulative sociopaths, albeit with normal life spans.

They too have had many names, the one you seem currently most fond of is the Illuminati. The church called the left hand path way to the devil.... the Illuminati controlled them and indeed almost all organised religions. The Spanish inquisition wasn't set up to catch heretics. It was set up to kill every one of you that carried the Einari genetic marker. If you had detailed records, you would realise that every single one of their victims was actually left-handed. Every single one," she said again emphasising the point.

"Even though they did not succeed there were longer term effects on the genetic markers through the generations. There was a marked degeneration in the aspects you inherited from the Y Chromosome we had engineered, and two things happened, your lifespans continued to decrease to a maximum of one hundred and twenty years and as your violent appetites grew it became much easier for our foes to manipulate you.

We have managed to track the last of them down, the virus we created is doing its work."

"Great" said Harry, "job done then. No need for us to be killing anyone."

"No" said Enmerkar "I am afraid not. We can at best reduce them to a level where they are no longer a viable breeding population, but it is inevitable that a few will escape, and they will seek to pollute your gene pool for as long as they are able. We simply don't know what the long-term effects could be."

Erianes added "and the truth is that there is much we still do not know about their leadership and how their evil is perpetuated and controlled from generation to generation."

"So basically, with all of your tampering you have let the genie out of the bottle, and you don't know how to get it back in?" said Sofia.

"Yes, that would appear to be a somewhat accurate, if brutal, summary my dear."

"So that will take care of the majority of them and if you have help, the rest can probably be rounded up over time and we can lock them away somewhere, but what about 'her', Lilith I mean, she seems to be a different kettle of fish.

How do we stop HER?" asked Harry. She seems to be more like what you originally intended, she's clever and has a very long lifespan. What other superpowers does she have that you haven't told us about other than being the 'typhoid Mary' of my nightmares? If she simply starts again and continues spreading her plagues, what can we mere mortals do?"

"Kill her,' said Erianes coldly "and any of her followers, that the virus does not eliminate."

Sofia looked at Harry wide eyed, "she can't be serious, we are talking about killing people!"

"I know" he said, "but I believe her, it all makes sense and if it's a choice between them and us, then what choice do we have?"

"Sofia, I beg you" said Erianes, "we will not be here to help you the next time. Our only hope now is for you to take up this this burden. Come, rest now, you have much to think about."

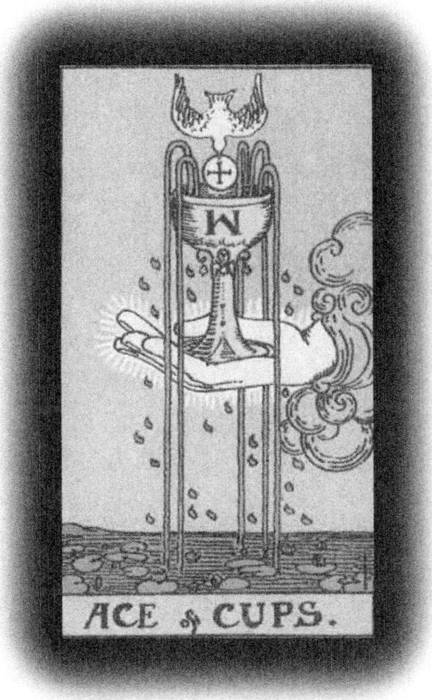

17. THE QUEST.

The following morning Harry woke early, feeling surprisingly refreshed. He glanced at his watch, it was 7am and once again he could somehow see a faint glow outside through the solid walls. "This place is amazing" he thought to himself.

He looked at Sofia who was still asleep.

The previous day had been exhausting both mentally and emotionally for both of them but Sofia had taken some of the revelations very hard indeed. Rather than wake her, he started looking at the cards that she had been given by Enmerkar. He chose a card at random and stared at it. As he did so the images began slowly shifting, melting away and re-combining, changing in front of his eyes and he started to drift off into a trance.

The next thing he knew, Sofia was calling his name "Harry, Harry." .... and she was shaking him, desperately trying to pull him around.

"What?" He asked. "I was just looking at the cards."

"Harry, you have been in another world for almost an hour."

Harry looked at his watch, it was 9.30am.

"That's not possible" he said.

"Ok, let's go and get some breakfast, and coffee, I definitely need coffee, but first I need to jump in the shower, I feel a little bit spaced out."

Enmerkar and Erianes were already in the lab when they arrived.

"Good morning my young friends" said Enmerkar, "did you sleep well?"

"Yes" said Sofia, surprised at herself, but then the revelations of the day before had left her completely drained. They sat down with some coffee and toast and as Sofia looked around the laboratory, she had a dreadful feeling in the back of her mind that the equipment and the whole set up was all eerily familiar. Yes, she had been there for a few days now, but this feeling was something else, something altogether more disturbing.

"Where are our enemies?" asked Harry, getting straight down to business. "How do we find them and how do we get rid of them?"

Erianes smiled at the apparent enthusiasm for their task, but she knew there was lot more they needed to know first. "Mostly they live alongside you in Italy or in Iran, in the mountains to the North of Tehran close to the shores of the Caspian Sea and northwards towards Armenia and the Great Caucus Mountain range."

"Why there" asked Sofia, "that does not seem to be a random distribution."

It isn't random" said Erianes. "They need the high

mountains as their own adaptation makes it harder for them to absorb oxygen at sea level." She smiled. "They also have a few genetic markers that help us to find them. It also helped us manufacture the virus to make sure that it would be deadly to them.'

"What sort of markers?" asked Harry.

"The main one is blood type" said Erianes. "We have used that specifically to find unique components that poison the blood and those it does not kill it will make infertile."

"So that's why the outbreaks in those areas are so prolific," said Sofia.

"Yes," said Erianes, who visibly saddened by the admission.

"And what of the demon queen?" asked Harry.

"We don't know" said Enmerkar truthfully, "but she will find you Harry. In the meantime we will give you the tools that you will need to protect yourself and to destroy her."

Harry gulped, "she will find ME? I thought Sofia was the chosen one?"

Sofia looked thoughtful for a moment; she was studying the variables they were dealing with. "The cards are the key," she said.

"Yes" said Erianes "the cards are indeed the key, and yes Harry she will come looking for you."

"Lilith is looking for something and we believe that she has not yet found it."

"How do you know?"

"If she had, we would probably all already be dead."

"When we first learned about the portals and started to understand how we could use our minds to access them, we developed that technology that you now hold in your hands. The machine is used to help us change our brainwave patterns, to go into trance like state. As you see they are not static symbols, and each can generate a slightly different effect but initially we could not direct our energy sufficiently to open the portal so we developed a focus, a nexus if you will that amplifies our thoughts."

"The ring?" said Harry.

"Yes" said Enmerkar, "the ring that brought you here. It is truly remarkable that you managed to open the portal at all without any training. You were not strong enough without the ring to open it here, and without it you would almost certainly have wandered in the corridors of the fifth dimension endlessly, forever lost to us."

Harry and Sofia both shuddered at the thought.

"Then how come you managed to get back here without the ring after you gave it to me in the church?" asked Sofia.

"Over many centuries of time, with patience and practice the task becomes easier, and we are able to focus our minds on the symbols that are already embedded at each of the places we wish to travel too." He pointed at the floor and there was a peculiar geometric pattern marked out on it.

"Sort of like hitting the home button on your computer." said Harry.

"If that analogy works for you, then yes," he replied, "but as far as I know I am the only one who has ever managed this."

Erianes nodded in confirmation.

"And does Lilith have a ring by any chance?" asked Harry.

"No" said Enmerkar emphatically "she does not."

"Oh, thank God" said Harry, although his relief was short lived.

"But she is looking for one" said Erianes, "if indeed the third artifact was a ring, and eventually, if she has not already done so, she will make the connection with the British museum and through professor Vishwanath to your father, your Uncle Geoffrey and then to you. Men are strangely affected by her, and she manipulates them with apparent ease. So yes Harry, she will almost certainly come looking for you."

"We believe that she ransacked the museums in Baghdad during the wars there, either in person or by proxy, and she has people on every archaeological dig in Mesopotamia. Sorry Iraq," she corrected herself.

Enmerkar continued, "there are only three sets of those cards in existence along with three focal adornments."

"Why three? and why do you say adornments rather than rings?"

"Use of the corridors was relatively new just prior to the war with the Vori. We were not unaware of the power of the technology we were exploring and so for security reasons the exact nature of the portals and how to use them was partitioned information. The full picture was known only to the three most senior members of the house of Anu.

The brothers Enki, and Enlil, and their sister the blessed Nin Kirshag. Each chose a form for the focal adornment, all were different. The ring you now have was that of Enki, the adornment of Nin Kirshag was the golden torc necklace now worn by Erianes and the form of the other is unknown to us. Much has been lost, even to us, over the aeons of time since the three royal siblings walked this earth. These are the only representations we have of Enlil" he said, "it is likely that he had it on him, probably at all times, so there could be a clue here."

"And does she have the cards?"

"No, "said Erianes emphatically "in fact we do not believe that she is yet aware of their existence."

"How do you know?" asked Harry

"Because the cards were created by Enmerkar and they are all here with us. Two sets have always been here on the Xisudra, until Enmerkar gave one to Sofia."

"The third set was lost in the chaos when Marduk decimated the earth and we spent many centuries searching for it. This was found in the cave of the Djinn in Oman in 1976, before the encounter with your father and his light fingered friend. That was what I was looking for in the cave. Until you returned here with them, we had believed them once again lost."

"How did they know?" asked Harry "Dad and Uncle Geoffrey I mean."

"I don't think they did know exactly" said Erianes.

"Many years ago, a young Bedouin boy fell into the caves and was killed. Sometime later when his family went down to collect his body, they saw the cards shifting and changing. They are a superstitious people, and believing the symbols to be living things, they left, taking only the boy's body, warning everyone that the caves were cursed."

"This is what they heard about when they were searching for the lost city of Ubar, and they simply went to investigate?" said Harry.

"Perhaps. Only they know for certain, but their actions have fortunately led to their eventual return to us."

"Wait a minute, if she is looking for me, and she finds out about my father's diary, will he and Uncle Geoffrey be in danger?"

"Perhaps. It is possible that she will try to learn what she can from them; but most likely subtly and without harming them. She is clever, she knows that there is little to be gained by alerting you to either her presence or to her interest in you."

"So, it's a race then, pure and simple." said Sofia "We either find this bitch and kill her, or we are all dead."

"Precisely, if not elegantly put" said Erianes.

It is because she does not have what she needs that she cannot find us here under the ice, but if Lilith learns the secret of the portals there is no limit to the damage she could do and no one……and I do mean no one, would ever be safe from her.

"Then we had better get started hadn't we." said Sofia.

18. TIME AND SPACE IN A DECK OF CARDS.

Enmerkar set them a task. "Spend a few hours this afternoon studying the symbols on the cards and we can reconvene later after dinner."

They set to their task diligently and by the time they were due to eat they were both glad of the break.

"These things are amazing, how can so much information and meaning be crammed into such a small number of symbols? My Dad thought they were a machine of some sort designed to interact with us on an individual basis," said Harry.

"Yes, he was correct in a way, this is what the cards were designed to be. They are what you might call a philosophical machine, to help you train your mind to visualise the portals. Once you can do that, you will be able make full use of all of our remaining technology. You will be able travel the world at will, By the time we have finished your training you must be in a position to protect your race, if you are to free yourself from them once and for all."

"So how do they work?" asked Harry.

It was getting late and he was trying to think of an analogy that he might use as a familiar base for both Harry and Sofia to work from. One that would not require too much explanation. "Think of them as kind of four-dimensional compass" said Enmerkar.

"OK" said Harry.

"There are 76 representations in total. 56 of the cards are

divided into four suits, let us deal with them first."

Harry and Sofia nodded.

"Each suit contains 14 cards. These are the geographical markers that tell where a place is. You could think of them as say, a GPS position but much richer in the information it conveys. The suits each represent a characteristic of the place based on light, heat, moisture, and hardness."

"Earth, Air, Fire and Water, the elements that our ancestors thought the world was made of?" asked Sofia.

"Exactly so," said Erianes. "And the potential number of combinations is so large that it will give you a point for virtually any location on earth."

"It takes time to understand the subtle interactions between the cards but eventually the specific characteristics of a location will become familiar to you as they are to us, and you will be able to bring the location to mind effectively."

"You do know this is the 21st Century?" asked Harry. "We already have GPS satellites and Google Maps" he said hopefully.

Enmerkar was feeling the strain a little, but his

mood lightened when he looked at Erianes who was once again smiling. She was clearly beginning to tune in to Harry's sense of humour. "Yes, quite" he said. "However, apart from the fact you would almost certainly die horribly in transit I suspect you will find it difficult to imagine a place based solely on a set of co-ordinates, which by the way would all be wrong."

"Wrong" said Harry, looking quizzically at him.

"Yes, wrong" said Enmerkar rather impatiently.

Harry stared at him blankly, raised his eyebrows then he just shrugged his shoulders.

"Firstly you need a fixed point for navigation. You currently have three bases for North in your system, grid north, magnetic north and true north. Your satellites are not as accurate as you imagine and as two of the three measures are constantly in motion you would most likely open a portal into a solid rock face and, albeit briefly, die screaming in agony. That is why you have to visualise the place itself, not just work on a set of co-ordinates.

"Oh" said Harry.

"Now shall we continue?"

Now it was Sofia's turn to smile, putting her face into her sleeve as she was trying not to laugh out loud.

"OK, point taken," said Harry.

Enmerkar continued. "Most of your religious monuments are built on what you call 'Ley lines' for a good reason. Ley Lines tap into an energy grid that emanates from the planet itself. This is important because you are not trying to observe or map a location from an external view point. Instead it means you can use the information embedded in the place itself which makes it inherently more accurate. Once you get used to the TRUE world grid system, it's quite straightforward but the characteristics of the place are what help you bring it to mind and to direct the portal. Many of them lead to secluded wooded glades, Church crypts, stone circles etc. Do you think it is a coincidence that these are the places where many of your ghost stories come from?"

"So that explains the suits but why do we need the others?" asked Sofia.

"The other 22 cards are called the Major Arcana and they serve a similar purpose, but instead of the physical location, they help you to locate your journey in time and they make it specific to you."

Enmerkar paused for a moment to let it sink in. "They are representations of the archetypes you pass through on your journey through life, effectively they anchor your journey to this specific timeline in which you live."

"This timeline?" asked Sofia, "how many are there?"

"More than you can imagine" said Enmerkar "but that is a lesson for another day.

Once you can master both of these things, then your mind creates the link in the fifth dimension between the place where you stand and the place you wish to go to, and with the help of the ring or the torc you can simply 'step through'."

"Watch" said Erianes. She raised her left hand slowly as is reaching for something they could not see and with her right hand she touched the golden torc around her neck.

As her breathing slowed, the intense green of her eyes seemed to fade to a grey metallic colour then as suddenly as the colour had faded, her eyes seemed to be filled with millions of stars shining like minute torches in the depths of midnight As they did so, the space in front of her started to dissolve like smoke. As it slowly cleared, they could see the Cave of the Genies before them once again and they stepped through it and then back together.

"That was amazing," said Harry.

"Thank you" said Erianes "but exerting the effort does leave one rather tired. It is getting late. I think that is enough for day."

The next three weeks were surprisingly calm, spent in daily contemplation of, and mediation on, the strange cards and the moving images. They had soon learned to slip into the trances easily and now they found that they could hold them for longer. Moving their attention from their material surroundings and by guiding their thoughts to the world behind the world, they were making ever more links between the symbols in order to anchor their concentration on a particular location.

As they progressed, Erianes gave Sofia her golden torc necklace and every day they practiced their mediation together. Despite agreeing to her training, Sofia was still not sure that they were doing the right thing. It was not just her medical oath 'to do no harm', but her every instinct rebelled against the thought of killing people. Yet each day she saw a little more of Erianes, she came to realise the true extent of the twin burdens of duty and sorrow that both she and Enmerkar had carried for all of their very long lives. The descent of a once truly mighty, race was difficult to contemplate to the point where only the two of them remained and soon all would be gone.

Recognising the questioning and concern in Sofia's eyes, Erianes reached out her hand and she just smiled.

"What will happen to us when you are gone?" asked Sofia softly, almost whispering the question.

"Only you will know the answer to that," she replied.

"Come, the cards are not just the key to the portals, they are a key to many more things on this ship and you need to understand everything."

One evening when they were sitting eating, Enmerkar raised his glass and proposed a toast unexpectedly. "Tomorrow you will face your first real test. You have seen how the portal tires us when we use them, even after all this time and experience with them. You have learned the theoretical aspects that underpin the portals but we must build up your strength in its practical application. It is earlier than I would have wished, but time is against us and the transfer through the portal can kill you if you are not properly prepared. It is our custom to feast on the eve of great adventure so let us toast your success."

"To us, to success" said Harry "and to not dying" he quietly added under his breath. "And may God forgive us for what we are about to do."

That night they went to bed exhausted. Sophie turned in to Harry's chest and she held him tightly. "I am scared Harry."

"Yes, so am I" he replied "but I think we both know we have no choice but to go on. Besides if Erianes and Enmerkar are right then we are already as good as dead unless we finish this."

"Do you really think this Lilith is a monster?" she asked. "Enmerkar and Erianes are quite vague about her and it worries me that they know so little."

"Frankly, I have no idea" he said truthfully "but I would rather be on the front foot and see something coming. I have to be honest, those carvings in the museum and the stories Dr Vishwanath shared about Lilith freaked me out a little. Ever since I found out she was real; I have been getting goose bumps just thinking about her."

Then with his characteristic humour, he tried to lighten the mood a little. "But you'd think she'd stand out in a crowd with a snake wrapped around her and claws for feet so how hard can she be to find?"

Sofia smiled. "Come on let's try to sleep, it seems that we have an early start tomorrow."

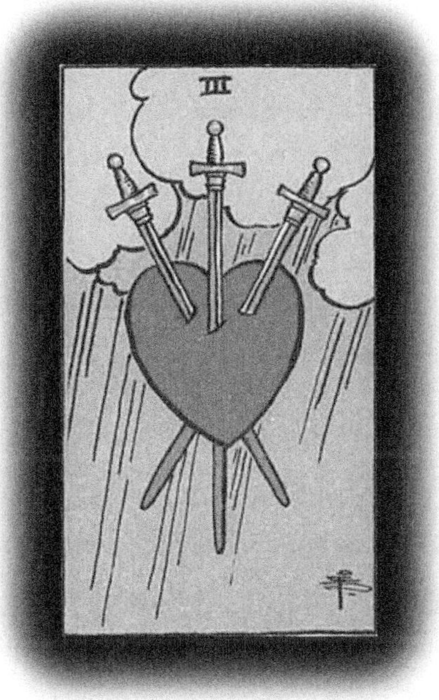

19. THE MOUNTAIN OF PAIN.

As they climbed the mountain Lilith wanted to get to know Herr Schmitt better. Getting to her destination was one thing but what she really needed to know if she could rely upon him in a crisis. A love of history was not going to be enough if she was going to take him all the way to the top with her. Even she did not relish undertaking the final leg alone. She had noticed that he even though he was not a young man, he was not only clever and well versed in the subject of ancient cultures, but he was also unusually strong and fit for a museum curator.

"What exactly is your specialism at the museum and how is it that you spend so much time in the Caucuses?" she asked. "This is a rather dangerous area even for one of mixed heritage such as yourself is it not?"

"That is true" he said "there are dangers, but this is truly my home, at least on my mother's side and I do love the people and their way of life here. It is simple and you can see in everyday life, reflections of the ages long past. I guess for me that is the main fascination, the past that I am somehow always drawn to. Here I do not feel the need to specialise in any one period of history.

It is the history of this region as a whole that fascinates me, it has everything one could wish for, enough to fill a whole lifetime with wonder. It is home to some of the most ancient peoples and stories. Did you know that this was the birth place of St George, the resting place of the Spear of Longinus that killed Christ, even the original location of the garden of Eden was said to be in the Caucuses?"

Lilith nodded. "Indeed they are all wonderful stories, each

worthy of a lifetime of study on their own.

Tell me Mr Schmitt" she said, "is it true that some of the Pergamon museum's artifacts were gathered from active war zones?"

"Yes" he said. "Before you jump to conclusions though," he added, "they only save artefacts where there is a chance of them being looted or destroyed."

"Is that why they recruited you? You have more of the bearing of a military man than of a curator."

Now it was Schmitt's turn to smile. "Professor" he said, "You continue to surprise me."

"I have always found it helpful to be a good judge of people" she said. That was an understatement. In fact it had saved her life on numerous occasions.

"If you must know, I served with the Special Commando Brigade in the German Army from 1996 to 2001" he said. "It was established to fight the threat of terrorism. So yes, that was one the reasons they recruited me" he said. "Most of the threats came as direct result of the first Gulf War. People think the special forces training is all about killing people but in actual fact most of it is about learning to hide in plain sight and to avoid trouble. I spent most of the second gulf war in Iraq identifying, tracking, and cataloguing museum pieces."

"I suppose it is quite difficult for museums to recruit people for that kind of role?" she said.

Schmitt laughed, "the pay is quite good, but the pension and health cover are dreadful."

After two more days of climbing Lilith, Schmitt, Baris and Mehmet were at last close to the ridge and the base of the glacier. The climb had been arduous so far, so much so that on achieving this milestone, the relief was palpable for all of them. Their feet were blistered, their lungs now felt as though they were on fire. With every step and with every breath they took they felt as though their lungs might burst at any moment. Lilith in particular was not accustomed to the altitude, but even Baris and Mehmet who were usually quite talkative and informative, were noticeably quieter the higher they climbed.

A period of acclimatisation would be required before they were able to go further.

After a few days at almost fifteen thousand feet the thin mountain air, although now bearable, was beginning to take its toll on them all. "The mules cannot go any further" said Mehmet "Neither Baris nor I will go with back to that place with you, but we are close now. The wall carvings are up there," he pointed up to a rocky outcrop about five hundred metres above them.

"We should spend the night here and you can make the final stage of your journey tomorrow if the weather is kind. Climbing across the glacier is hard and although it looks to be close, it is still many hours climb from here." The last day of climbing had been really hard work and on the rocky terrain they had not managed to forage much fuel as they travelled so when they eventually made camp, the fire was of necessity small, and they all huddled close to it. They were eager to feel whatever comfort they could.

"You have done very well Professor "said Baris as he watched Lilith apply soothing ointment to the blisters on her feet. "It is mostly only shepherd families that make it this high. Drink lots of water. As well as the thin air, the dust can be a problem up here until you get above the snow line."

"Thank you" she said taking the canteen from his hand.

"It is a curious thing but I think that you will enjoy the

descent" he added.

She smiled, "why do you say that my friend, is it so obvious that I do not belong up here?" she asked.

"Well apart from it becoming easier to breathe, as we descend the air will seem so much thicker with each downward step. We don't normally notice but when you have been up here for a while, one has a peculiar sensation. It feels as though you are 'eating' the air, filling your lungs and your belly at the same time."

Mehmet nodded in agreement. "manna from heaven" he added.

Lilith smiled, "I like the thought of that" she said, "I will try to remember when we return."

As the light began to fade, the clear night sky would bring with it the promise of intense cold but it also had its compensation. The crescent moon was rising in the eastern sky and the backdrop of stars and the Milky Way were breath taking. The air seemed strangely serene too. It was as though mother nature herself was holding her breath, waiting to see what might happen next. Above them they could hear the ice creaking, groaning, as if growling a warning not to travel further. That was not an option for Lilith. In a silent response to the challenge from above; she thought to herself, "I have come too far to turn back now," then as she drifted off to sleep, her thoughts turned once again to Adam and to the garden paradise that once existed below the mountain.

The following morning, they arose with the dawn. The last embers of the fire had long since faded, and it was bitterly cold. They knew that it would get worse once they started climbing on the glacier but at least the sky was promisingly clear.

They ate a simple breakfast, repacked their rucksacks with warmer clothes and some food and water. "Take the rifle Mr. Schmitt" she said.

"The rifle? are we expecting trouble?" he asked.

"We shall see, won't we" she replied.

Mehmet said "Baris and I, we will wait here for you for two days, but no longer.

Goodbye and good luck" he said.

Lilith and Schmitt both nodded, put on their sunglasses to protect their eyes from the glare, then set off together across the ice sheet without a backward glance.

The glare from the white glacier although intense, was softened here and there by the black patches of moraine that it had picked up on its slow crawl across the mountainous landscape. It was a strange, unfamiliar sight for one so used to the warmth of her homeland, almost like soot from a fire, but warmth would stay only a distant memory until they either found the shelter that Baris had told them about, or they returned safely back to the camp.

The snow was soft at first where the glacier was melting, but soon they would need their ice axes to prod the ground beneath them, seeking early warning of the dangerous crevasses that could appear as the ice shifted and to help them balance as the climb grew steeper. After almost four hours of climbing, they reached the small rock crescent where they welcomed the shelter from the cold wind that was once again blowing across the ice.

As they made their way to the rock face, they ran their gloves across the surface to clear away the snow. Slowly at first, they could see the imprint of some ancient markings beginning to emerge. "We are in the right place," said Lilith.

"Here" said Schmitt, pointing at what looked like a small

alcove. There, inside the alcove, was the exact same symbol the Professor had described to him several days earlier when they had been hiding from the patrol in the ravine. As Schmitt cleared the snow it revealed two intricately carved pillars.

He looked at her astonished, "how did you know?"

"I have seen it once before" she replied truthfully, "but it was on the inside of the door not the outside."

"The door?" said Schmitt, visibly shocked.

"Yes Mr. Schmitt, it is the lock for the door, but you need not worry because I have the key. I have always had the key but I did not realise what it was until I read the tablets of Cyrus the Great."

In the middle of each pillar, just above the head of the human figure on the left and the skeleton on the right, were two small red dots. She took off her gloves and pricked each thumb. Once they started to bleed, she placed one on each of the circles, then she waited. Momentarily, next to them the rock seemed to melt, and they were suddenly faced with an open chamber that looked to be made of stainless steel. As they stepped inside, the wall behind them re-formed, but they could still see the reflected light from the snow outside.

The relief from the harsh environment outside was immediate. "Wow" said Schmitt, "this place is amazing, how did you do that?"

"That was a genetically coded lock, I was a visitor here once before, long ago and not of my own free will, I might add." She was visibly tense now and even without her revelation, Schmitt could already sense her anxiety.

They looked around as the lights came on in the corridors running to the left and the right of them and for the first time Schmitt noticed just how big the corridors were. They were almost fifteen feet high. "How old is this place and why are the ceilings so high? "he asked.

She ignored his questioned but said "Now might be a good time to unpack your rifle Mr Schmitt, there are very real dangers here, I can assure you."

The hairs stood up on the back of Schmitt's neck. He did not need to be told twice. He hastily pulled the rifle from his sack and assembled the stock, the barrel, the sights and loaded a magazine. He put two more magazines in his belt then he asked her "what is this place Professor?"

"It is a laboratory amongst other things" then she added

ominously, "and I am afraid that we are the lab rats Mr. Schmitt. I am not expecting there to be anyone at home but just to be clear, if there is anyone here apart from us, then for your own safety it would be wise to shoot them on sight." As if to underline her warning she pulled out a 9mm pistol from inside her jacket.

"Shoot who?" he asked.

"Trust me, you will know if you see them."

"You're not a typical archaeology Professor, are you?"

"No Mr. Schmitt, I am not. I will tell you my story one day but for now let us just be careful and concentrate on the task at hand shall we."

They began to explore the complex and soon came to suspect that they were in fact alone so they were able to relax a little, but Lilith still advised caution. Everything seemed to be on automatic, in stark contrast to the glacier outside the temperature had been slowly rising since they entered the tunnel. It was now a very comfortable 68 degrees. The place seemed eerily familiar to her as if she had seen it, but hazily as if through a dream.

Slowly her memory of what had happened to her

in this place started to return and her long nightmares, although still patchy, began to make sense.

"Professor Hashemi, …Professor…" She heard Schmitt's voice calling her. "You were daydreaming, are you alright" he asked? "This place must be huge. The tunnels look like they could well stretch for miles."

"Yes, thank you I am fine, I just feel a little …. strange. Come, what we are looking for is along here," and she pointed to a corridor on their left.

About halfway down the corridor, she suddenly stopped and faced the wall. She raised her right hand and the wall in front of her began to fade. An entrance appeared to a large square room that was clearly an operating theatre of some kind, with an observation window to a laboratory in the next room.

As they entered the room Schmitt sniffed the air. "It is stale" he said, "but there is a strange odour in here too."

There were a pair of what looked like operating tables in the middle of the room. Along the walls at the back were three translucent tubes, that appear to have been used as cages. Two of them contained skeletons, human skeletons and this time Lilith shuddered. Long ago, the third had been meant for her. There was a bank of what looked like computers on a small island at the head of the tables and in between them, some implements that were clearly meant for invasive surgery of some kind.

Scattered on the floor there was what looked like some broken bottles, syringes and a dark stain that led to the adjacent room.

"Is that blood" he asked

"Yes" she said and her lips curled up in the slightest of smiles, "but it looks like it took her a while to die."

"Her? said Schmitt.

They followed the blood trail making their way into the laboratory and there they found two giant bodies. One was seated behind a desk and the other was prostrate on the floor in front of the first with an arm outstretched as if in supplication or seeking help from the giant seated figure.

"Holy Jesus," exclaimed Schmitt. He raised his rifle scanning the room as the panic rose within him. Neither his historical nor his military training had prepared him for what he was now looking at. "This room has been sealed; these bodies look like they have been here for hundreds of years but they are scarcely decayed."

"They have been here for over thirty thousand years" she said, without looking at him.

"That's not possible" said Schmitt "…. who, …. what, …are they?" he stammered.

"I believe they called themselves the Einari, at least Einar is what they call this world, and they were here long before us" she said, "but we tend to refer to them in academic circles as the Annunaki" and she spat at the floor.

Schmitt was now hyperventilating and sweating profusely, "good god are they aliens".

"Calm down," she said reassuringly.

Regaining his composure, they began to carefully examine the bodies more closely. The smaller of the two, on the floor was probably almost nine feet tall, wearing a green robe covered in blood stains and appeared to be a female with fair hair. The larger of the two wore a deep red robe and there, on his forehead was the diadem with the blue stone in the centre just as she had remembered it.

Schmitt approached the figure cautiously, the "Sangrael" he said softly, and he tried to remove the diadem but it was locked in place on the giant's head. No matter how hard he pulled, it would not budge. As he tried harder to dislodge it, the body collapsed in the chair and Schmitt fell back against the control panel behind him. Putting his hand out to steady himself he managed to avoid the body falling on him but he did not notice that a small light on the panel behind him had been activated.

Lilith meanwhile was completely focused on the diadem and as she reached out for it she felt it react to her touch. It seemed to soften beneath her fingers allowing her to remove it, slowly, with ease from the now prostrate corpse at her feet.

She stood back in a clear space before placing it on her own forehead. It seemed almost to mould itself to her in spite of the fact that the previous wearer was of a significantly larger build. Then she closed her eyes and began to concentrate. Thousands of images floated before her mind's eye like a film playing rapidly, and she fought hard to isolate what she was looking for. She wanted to remember everything that had happened to her, to fill in the gaps of her memory. As she did so the stone began to emit a soft glow.

Schmitt was staring at her transfixed.

And still the small light behind him blinked silently.

20. THE GHOSTS OF TABRIZ.

The last couple of weeks had been physically exhausting. Strangely the combat training and learning about the body's weak spots including how to kill quickly, had not been as much of an issue as they had both feared. Sofia took to it quite easily due to her medical training and Harry had some idea of what hurt from years of playing contact sports.

What had really drained them, had been the sheer mental effort required to master both themselves, and their own physiology. As well as their classroom theory, weapons training, and hand to hand combat, they had also spent several hours of every day meditating, learning to control their breathing. This would allow them to modify their brain waves. Slowly but surely, they had managed to exert a level of control over both themselves, and the movement of the images in the cards. They had managed to focus their attention so that they could both now open and close the portals at will. They were also finding it easier to recognise the geometric patterns that would allow them to travel to a few locations that were regarded as safe in case of unforeseen trouble.

It was still feeling all very surreal, but today was going to be different, it was about to become very real indeed. That morning, Harry and Sofia arose early and dressed in new clothes that Erianes had provided for them.

"Wow, you look fabulous," said Harry.

"You don't look too shabby yourself" Sofia said, then she laughed for the first time in what now seemed like forever.

Erianes explained that the clothes were made of a fabric that responded to mimic its environment and that they would offer them not just some protection from the elements, but they would also appear to bend the light around them. If they stood very still, they would effectively blend in, chameleon like, becoming all but invisible in most environments. "But they are not bulletproof" said Enmerkar emphatically, "so take what we have taught you and what we have given you, then remember to tread softly" he added.

"Where are we going first" asked Harry.

"You should be away no more than a few hours this time. The purpose is not to kill anyone this time you will pleased to know, but to find a clue to the current identity and location of Lilith. You need to go to the museum of Tabriz."
"What for?" asked Harry.

Just after the second Gulf War we became aware that they had come into possession of clues to the location of the great seal of Cyrus. We believe that in the confusion of the war they had sent people to Baghdad and there they found some sympathetic Iraqis who did not want their collection to fall into western hands. With that key as their guide, they were able to locate and retrieve the tablets of Cyrus the Great two weeks ago.

Sofia was confused. She just looked at Harry, spread her arms out and raised her eyebrows.

"I have heard of Cyrus the Great, the first true Persian Emperor of course" said Harry "but I have never heard of the tablets."

"Few have" said Enmerkar, then he relayed the story of Cyrus and his amazing exploits. How much he had achieved, in such a time when this should not have been possible, particularly in the short lifetime of one man.

"So, you think he had help? asked Sofia.

"It is possible, highly likely in fact, but we cannot rule out the possibility that he had somehow come into possession of the third adornment."

"But I thought you needed training to use the portals?" said Harry.

"Yes," said Enmerkar "but the adornments powers they control are not restricted to merely opening doors. Whatever it was that Cyrus managed to wield in his empire building, the secret was lost when he died, but if it was Einari technology it was not buried with him.

Due to the time difference between here and your

destination, it is night-time there now so hopefully this means that you will not be disturbed. Never the less, you must still tread carefully. It is time for you to become the ghosts of the museum" and he smiled. "Take care and we will see you very soon."

Harry nodded then he sat down with Sofia. They both took a deep breath and he dealt out four cards that evoked the place followed by one of the major arcana to establish the point in time he was seeking, then they both let their minds wander until they felt that point of peace between the waking and sleeping world. As they did so, they sensed their own intimate connection to one another as their minds rode the crest of the fifth dimensional wave.

When the picture was clear in his mind, Harry rubbed the ring and the blue crystal in the snake's forehead began to glow, his own blue eyes seemed to fade to a steel grey and then suddenly to radiate a myriad of stars as the world around them shimmered like smoke and began to fade. There, in front of them they could just see the cold stone floors of the dark museum gallery and they stood up together, he put the cards in his robe, then they stepped forward into the room.

The portal closed behind them. "Oh wow"

whispered Harry, amazed at what they had just done, and if he was honest not a little bit relieved that there were both still alive. Sofia let out a deep breath. "Come on let's get started" she said, "I don't want to be here any longer than necessary."

They searched the galleries carefully but could not find what they were looking for. "Let's look in the curator's office," said Harry. "Anything not on display should at least be refenced in his journals".

"Harry," Sofia pointed to the end of the gallery where they could see several beams of light from the security guards' flashlights making their way towards them.

They stood completely still and watched as the beams scanned the walls around them and when one pointed directly at Harry, he expected the game to be up, but the security guards simply kept on with their search.

"It was nothing" one said, just the wind.

As the guards disappeared into the next gallery Harry pointed to the stairs at the end of the room and they made their way upstairs to a dark brown door with a glass pane and a sign in Farsi that Harry insisted was the curator's office.

Inside the office in the desk drawer, they found Professor Hakim's journals.

"I am impressed "said Sofia I didn't know you could read Farsi?"

Harry confessed. "I can't, it was a lucky guess, but I can tell you it is very hard to get an office in a museum so the curator always gets first dibbs."

They scanned the pages. The contents were a mixture of Farsi, English, ancient symbols, and sketches. "I'd say that these look like a draft for a display the are preparing so the exhibits will still be in the warehouse…. most likely in the basement."

Back on the Xisudra Erianes called to Enmerkar to come to the control room. Examining the data she presented to him, he nodded and said "I concur. Someone is trying to access the fifth dimension although it does not seem as though they are trying to open a portal, they are scanning the timeline instead? It has to be her" said Enmerkar, "the only other possibility would be…." then he hesitated. "The only other possibility would be that there are still Vori that are unaccounted for and that they have somehow gained access but, I don't understand how that would be possible after all this time …….and if it is her, what is she looking for?

I know there has been no sign of them for thousands of years but try to recalibrate your scan."

"To look for what?" asked Erianes.

"Scan for Einari or Vori technology, if she has found something it is possible that she may have activated it unwittingly and if fortune favours us, then after all these ages perhaps we may at last catch our elusive prey."

In the basement of the Tabriz Museum, Sofia and Harry found what they were looking for. They scanned each of the tablets in turn and the story of Cyrus and his great prize was laid out before their eyes. "Look Sofia, that has to be what we are looking for;" he said pointing to the crown on the head of Cyrus the Great.

"Why the crown" asked Sofia.

"Our new friends are very advanced and clever but they think like gods, not like men do and they have clearly not read our Holy Grail bedtime stories" he said.

You mean King Arthur and the Knights of the round table she asked?"

"Exactly" he said and Wolfram Von Eschenbach Chretien De Troyes, Geoffrey of Monmouth and all of the others were agreed on one thing.

"In mythology the holy grail was not a cup, it was a stone which fell from Lucifer's crown when he was thrown down to earth after the war in heaven.

Think about if Sofia, if they had always hidden themselves from us; then our ancestors would not know anything about these people and they would make up their own mythology to make sense of what was passed down to them in oral tradition.

Erianes told us our ancestors had been here all along and their experiments on them went on for hundreds of thousands of years. Enlil must have been the one cast down from heaven in the myth. It's the stone, not the crown that is the key."

He had scarcely finished his explanations and was still feeling incredibly pleased with himself when the space behind him seemed to fade and Enmerkar called to him.

"Harry, ……. Harry."

Hearing his voice behind him made him start. "Mother of God will you please give us some warning when you are going to do that?" he said.

"I am sorry my young friend but you need to return to the Xisudra, we have news."

Sofia and Harry held hands and they stepped back through the portal together leaving Professor Hakim's note book on the floor next to the tablet showing Cyrus standing in between two pillars, topped with a sun and moon and two human looking figures one just a skeleton, but each standing atop a giant silver being.

"I would love to be there when he finds his notes" said Harry laughing.

Back on the Xisudra the mood was far from jovial, Erianes and Enmerkar looked distinctly worried.

"What is it?" asked Sofia.

"We believe that we may have found her." said Erianes.

Harry looked dumbstruck. Although he was coming to terms with their mission he was, truth be told, shitting himself at the thought of coming face to face with a demon queen and his throat was suddenly very dry.

"You mean…."

"Yes" said Erianes…. "I mean HER".

"Where?" he asked weakly.

"It seems that she may have gone home" said Erianes.

"Home" said Harry looking puzzled, "I am going to need more of a clue than that."

"To Edin of course" said Enmerkar.

"Seriously? You are telling me she has gone back to the garden of Eden, has she lost her snake or something?" he asked almost sarcastically.

Ignoring Harry's tone, Enmerkar continued. "If we are correct, she is on Mount Ararat in what we believe is an abandoned facility that was once part of the Province of Eshunna.

"And what if you are not correct?"

"Then other dangers may await you. Eshunna was one of the first cities to fall not long after the Vori came to Earth so it would be prudent to take your weapons. With the element of surprise and our adaptive clothing you have some clear advantages, but there is no substitute for keeping your wits about you. Your survival instinct as a species is, fortunately for you, quite remarkable."

"Oh great! This just keeps getting better and better. Tell us about this facility," said Harry.

After they had had been briefed and had some refreshments, they made themselves ready for their journey. Enmerkar proffered two side arms.

Like his father Harry had an aversion to guns and he was initially reluctant but Enmerkar was insistent. "You should probably take these Harry. The first shot will not be fatal but multiple strikes most definitely will be."

Harry's thoughts turned back to the ammunition he had found in his father house then he nodded, whatever they were looking for had most definitely frightened his father enough to arm himself. "Thank you" he said.

Sitting down for the second time that day, Harry dealt four more location cards followed by one major arcana. They both took a deep breath and let their minds wander until once again they sensed their own intimate connection to one another as their minds again rode the crest of the fifth dimensional wave. This time it was Sofia who opened the portal. She held out her left hand and placed her right hand on the golden torc around her neck which soon began to emit a soft golden light. Her deep brown eyes faded to grey and then suddenly seemed to radiate a myriad of stars as the once again the world around them shimmered like smoke and began to fade. There, in front of them they could just see the now familiar stainless-steel floors of another Einari facility and they stepped forward into the long corridor.

"This place is not like the Xisudra" said Sofia, it seems somehow to be older. The technology looks the same but look at the motifs on the floor." She shivered involuntarily, "there are snakes everywhere, do you really think this is where we will find her? All the museum representations of her included snakes."

Harry studied the motif for a moment. "Hmmm, there is something different about these" he said. "Look carefully, they are not random, they are all the same and show the snake biting its own tail, these are representations of the Ouroboros."

"Representations of what?" asked Sofia.

"The Ouroboros" he repeated. "It is generally regarded as a symbol of eternity, the eternal sun, or renewal and rebirth, that kind of thing. It's not usually associated with fear like say a cobra ready to strike, or a constrictor choking a victim to death. It is everywhere so I assume it must have been important to whoever had been the last to use this place and Enmerkar said it wasn't them, so let's be careful."

"Can you hear that, Harry?"

"Hear what?"

"I can hear voices, very faint but I would say they are coming from down there" said Sofia pointing to the corridor on the left.

Harry nodded. "Yes, I hear them now." They both drew their weapons and made their way to an open door about a hundred metres along the corridor.

The voices grew louder as they approached. A man and a woman were talking.

Inside the lab, despite their camouflage, Lilith somehow sensed their approach as they crept stealthily into the room. Schmitt seeing her expression glanced at the lab door which seemed to shimmer and he raised his rifle scanning the space as his mind tried to make sense of what his eyes were seeing. Seeing a movement Schmitt fired his rifle which grazed Harry's shoulder. He cried out involuntarily and returned fire even as the sound of the rifle shot was still echoing around the lab and the corridor outside. He hit Schmitt square in the chest and he fell backwards with some force falling over the lab equipment and scattering glass everywhere.

Harry and Sofia stood pointing their weapons at Lilith who was now bent over Schmitt trying to sit him up.

"Mr. Schmitt, ……. Mr. Schmitt are you alright?" she asked.

Although he was groggy from being stunned, he started to come around. "Yes, Professor I think so" he said. Then he looked at the blood on his hands and started to feel his chest as if expecting to find a bullet hole but fortunately there was no wound.

"It's ok" she said, "it is just a cut from all the glass" Then she turned her attention to the new intruders.

21. REVELATION.

Lilith looked up at Harry and Sofia and suddenly her anger faded. She began to stare as she recognized them both, but she was frozen, as if dis-believing that they were now actually right here, standing before her.

"Who are you?", said Harry, "and what are you doing here?"

Schmitt got shakily to his feet. Not wanting to be shot again he piped up quickly, "I am Hans Schmitt from the Pergamon Museum in Berlin, and this is Professor Yasmina Hashemi from the Museum of Tabriz" he said, holding out his hands rather cautiously.

"Oh, sorry about that" said Harry rather sheepishly, waving his gun in Schmitt's general direction.

"Likewise," he said pointing at Harry's shoulder.

"And may we ask you the same questions?" said Lilith.

"Oh, yes of course, I am Harry Taylor from the British Museum, and this is Doctor Sofia Morreconi, from the Santa Tomassa hospital in Turin."

Harry turned to Sofia who was looking at Lilith. Her brow was furrowed, and she tilted her head as if she was trying to drag some familiar memory from deep within her to the surface. There was something vaguely familiar about this place and about Professor Hashemi.

Then Harry began to stare too, struck by the uncanny likeness between them.

"Well, everyone looks pretty normal so it doesn't look like the demon queen is here thankfully" said Harry "but we should explore this place, see what we can find out and get back as quickly as we can."

"Where is the rest of your team" asked Harry. "You can't have made it up here alone."

"They are waiting for us about five hundred metres down the mountain, below the snowline at the edge of the glacier," replied Schmitt.

"Well, they are safe down there for now," said Harry.

All the while Lilith stood staring at them both. "Adam" …. she paused …. "sister."

"What did you call us?" asked Harry.

"Oh Adam," she repeated "I had not thought this day would come, I have waited for so long."

"Who are you?" he asked again, "and why do I feel that I should know you?"

Suddenly there was a loud bang outside and they could hear voices shouting instructions. Schmitt immediately assumed that it was Turkish soldiers, who he expected would be heavily armed and combing the facility looking for them.

"Quickly, follow me" said Harry, "stay in between us." He wandered out into the corridor first, confident that his camouflaged clothing would protect him from human eyes, but he was dismayed to see two silver giants running towards him dressed in long flowing robes.

"Get back inside" he shouted, pushing them back and closing the door. "I don't know how to lock this" he said but he fired his weapon to the side of where the door had been in the hope that it might disrupt the control system.

"There" shouted Lilith, pointing at a glyph of two pillars on the wall and he fired again. "Get back into the lab over there. Mr. Schmitt, get your rifle, they don't like being shot" he said.

"Don't like it?" said Schmitt clearly puzzled.

"Well put it this way" said Harry, "it won't kill them……. probably, but it tends to contribute to them having a generally bad day and right now I can't think of many options. Sofia, get us back to the Xisudra."

Sofia started to concentrate, holding her Torc, her eyes faded to grey then shone as though they were full of stars and the space in front of her began to shimmer and the portal opened before them.

Lilith had been watching this closely. She could feel the diadem hidden under her jacket, which seemed to resonate as the portal was opened. "So that is the secret" she thought to herself. They stepped through the portal and when Lilith saw Erianes she immediately grabbed Schmitt's rifle from him, but Enmerkar shot her from behind and she collapsed onto the floor. Erianes picked up the rifle and Enmerkar picked Lilith up easily and carried her to the laboratory where she was placed in an isolation room. A very confused Schmitt held up his hands and followed as he was directed.

"Why did you bring them here?" asked Erianes.

"Because they would have been killed" said Sofia, and she relayed the events of their journey. When Harry told her of the silver skinned attackers she asked, "you are sure they were Einari?"

"Well apart from the robes being different to yours, then yes, I would say so."

"This is not possible said Erianes. Only Enmerkar and I remain. All the Vori must be long dead."

Enmerkar emerged from the isolation room with the diadem in his hands, "The star of Enlil" he said. "Now they must both die".

"No wait" said Sofia, "they are just people."

"I am afraid not" said Enmerkar pointing to the Professor laid on the bed behind the glass. "That, my young friend is Lilith and judging by his reactions, I would say that her colleague is no ordinary history student either."

That's nonsense said Harry, look at her, she's just a person not a demon goddess, look….no snakes, talons for feet and besides she can't be more than about thirty years old, and there is something else, she seemed to know us too."

"She knows you?" said Erianes puzzled.

"Yes, she called me Adam and Sofia her sister."

"Enmerkar and Erianes looked at one another. "Could it really be possible?" he asked.

Lilith was starting to come around and this time, Schmitt was trying to help her up. He gave her some water. "Here, drink this" he said. Clearly panicked by her situation she pushed the glass from his hand as she jumped-up, staring wildly, she grabbed anything she could, trying to smash her way out of the isolation room like a cornered, frightened animal.

"Let me go inside," said Harry.

"She is dangerous Harry," said Enmerkar.

"Please, let me go in."

"Harry entered the room and with Schmitt's help he eventually managed to calm Lilith who continued staring wild eyed, searching for a way out.

"Adam" she said, "these things will kill you."

"It's OK" he said, "they are not Vori, they won't hurt you." She eventually calmed down enough to allow him to recount the story of how he and Sofia had come to be on the Xisudra.

"Tell me, are you really who they say you are, are you Lilith?"

"Don't you know me, Adam?" she asked.

To his surprise he found himself saying "yes……yes I think I do but……" and his words trailed off as he seemed to be swimming in the deep pools of her wide brown eyes.

She stood up then staring at Enmerkar, Erianes and Sofia on the other side of the glass wall and she began to recount her story.

"Yes, it is true I am……. I was," she corrected herself…. "Lilith, but neither of us is who, or what they say we are. You are Adam" she said, pointing at Harry.

"Long ago we lived together with your family in the forests of Edin below the mountain.

One day when I was looking for food, I saw the silver ones, like them," she said pointing.

"I thought it was a dream until one of them attacked me.

I must have blacked out or perhaps fainted. The next thing I knew I was waking up in the laboratory on Mount Ararat with two of them leaning over me, one was wearing the diadem you have taken from me. I don't know how long I had been there or what they had done to me, but I could see two more of our kin in the containment tubes. You saw their skeletons, they were your brother and sister Adam, they were once Tubal and Zillah.

They had clearly not expected me to wake up as they had not yet fastened the restraints. While they were distracted by Zillah's cries, I grabbed a knife from the table. I stabbed one of them in the face before the other one grabbed me. He was so strong, but in the struggle, everything was knocked to the floor and the syringes and bottles smashed. I did not know why, but the one holding me seemed to panic. He let go of me and ran to the laboratory and I could see he was struggling to breath. There must have been something in the air that was poisoning them.

I tried to free Zillah and Tubal, but I could not. The one I had stabbed was starting to come around, so Zillah bade me run, and I did. Somehow, I found myself outside tumbling down the mountain and into the forest where I hid. Sometime later, I am not sure how long, three of their kind came after me. No matter where I went, they pursued me, so I ran, and I ran for two days until I came to the edge of the forest to the edge of the land of Nod.

I was exhausted. The people who found me took me to their village where they tended to my wounds. Soon, they grew sick, and in a matter of days they all died. I was grieving for them when the silver ones, who had been pursuing me, found me. I struggled with them again, but they were too strong. They bound me and started the return to Ararat, but they too soon grew sick, and they also died so I was free once more.

It was not long before I began to realise, that whatever

they had done, they had made my body a living poison and that I could not return to you. So, I vowed never to return to Edin, and I stayed in the land of Nod to the East where I waited patiently for Death to meet me, and finally release me from the nightmare that I had endured. But death did not come.

Even through my grief, I realised that they had not finished their work and that they had not been expecting my poison to kill them too, and I hid. Many who helped me paid a heavy price and I have been hiding ever since. I swore to find and kill every one of them. I have searched ever since that time long ago, for the means to destroy them and now I know the diadem is the key to finding the last of them."

"But that was ancient history" said Harry, "how is that possible are you saying you are really thirty thousand years old?"

"No," said Lilith, "of course I am not. I was born in 1989, I am thirty-one." She looked at the glass and pointed. "Beware Adam, they are not telling you everything." Enmerkar and Erianes were listening intently outside.

Erianes spoke to Lilith, "I can assure you that if what you say is true then your enemies are our enemies. Will you stay here, as our guest for a while? We need to learn more, and we will consider your story."

Harry looked at her and nodded in encouragement.

"You will be safe here and I promise you, Sofia, Mr. Schmitt here and I will not leave you alone at any point. One of us will always be with you."

Lilith nodded.

They escorted Lilith and Schmitt to their quarters next to those of Harry and Sofia and motioning at the wall, Erianes opened a connecting door between them. Yours is a unique genetic modification. "We must think on this, and we will talk more tomorrow. We would like to unravel this mystery together. For now, you will be our guests, but you will remain in these quarters for your own safety."

"Harry", said Enmerkar. "Come to the laboratory and let me have a look at your wound." Harry glanced down at the blood on his right shoulder and nodded. The adrenalin had been pumping so much from the chase and subsequent realization of who their new guest was that he had almost forgotten about it, but it was hurting him now things were calmer, and he was starting to stiffen up.

Once in the laboratory, Enmerkar noticed that

Harry winced as he tried to take off his Einari clothing, he could not stop himself from smiling.

"What's so funny?" asked Harry.

"It hurts, doesn't it?" said Enmerkar. The irony of him having shot Enmerkar on their first meeting was not lost on Harry.

"Yes, it does actually" he said, but as the anesthetic began to take effect, he too found himself smiling.

"Well, I told you that they weren't bullet proof," said Enmerkar. "It is nothing serious but it is a valuable lesson for what may be to come" and he finished applying a dressing.

"Thank you" said Harry, "that does feel a lot better."

"Do you think we can trust her, Lilith I mean?"

"I do not know yet, but I must be honest, she is not what I had expected. It is not clear if the Vori who tortured her, chose her by accident but I am certain that they could not have been responsible for her remarkable abilities. It takes something very special to be able to access the higher realms without any training. We will be safe, while she is in the quarters we have assigned, and Erianes is taking some additional precautions to keep us all safe for now. We will find out more tomorrow and if she is a threat or not…." and his voiced tailed off.

"If she is a threat, what will you do?" asked Harry.

"We will kill them, both of them." He said matter of factly.

"Why didn't you kill her when she came through the portal with me instead of just incapacitating her?"

"This whole ship is a laboratory Harry, if there had been a biological hazard associated with her presence, then the sensors would have activated immediately and isolated the entry point. It would seem that there is at least some truth in her story, but just how much, we do not yet know.

Good night, Harry."

Harry went back to his room where the others were waiting. Lilith seemed both surprised and relieved to see him. She examined his wound. "So they have given you medical treatment as they promised. My sister has told me your story, perhaps they are not all the same and there are differences between these Vori and Einari, but I am certain that we are all still in danger."

22. MORTAL AFTER ALL.

The following day they were all called in to the laboratory and Erianes began summarizing the results of her analysis of Lilith.

"It seems that you are mortal after all Lilith. You do not carry any pathogens. These must have died out long ago but," she paused and turned to Sofia, "it seems that she truly is your sister, and she too carries the XXY chromosome combination and perhaps now we have a clue as to what it does, other than make you immune to most pathogens. What do you know of your genetic make-up?" she asked Lilith.

"Not much" she said truthfully, "although I have been trying to piece together what happened to me, I have been more focused on finding a way to destroy you all for what your kind did to us." Erianes ignored her last remark. "Just start from the beginning" she said, "please, tell us what you do remember."

"My name is Yasmina Hashemi" she said, "I was born in 1989 in Tehran. There was nothing unusual as a child growing up, I lived the same life as all of the other children; we played games and helped our mothers in the kitchen occasionally, it was quite unremarkable really. Then one day when I was about thirteen, I started to have what I can only describe as strange visions."

"What kind of visions?"

"As I said they were strange, they were disjointed. I could make no sense of them at first. It was like waking in the morning when you know you have been dreaming. Vivid dreams, but the dreams jump for place to place and when you try to think of them in the morning it is like trying to grasp smoke in your hands. Over time they seemed to become more concrete, more real. Somehow, I knew that they were dreams of a world from long ago and that I should be cautious about revealing too much.

When I eventually told my parents, they thought it was just puberty coupled with my vivid imagination, but luckily, rather than lock me away as they may have chosen to do, they encouraged me to study history and archaeology as it seemed to make me calmer. It was as though a pathway was opening up before me; and I knew that no other road would ever be possible, so I studied everything I could find and for a while everyone was happy. I felt as though I had found my purpose. I was happy to become the studious, dutiful daughter that my parents had always wanted.

Over quite a long period of time, perhaps ten years or more, I found in my studies many things that corroborated my visions and eventually I came to understand that they were not visions at all, they were real memories. I remembered the life of one called Lilith as if it was my own, even though logically I knew that was impossible. Gradually I remembered the life of every other Lilith that has lived since that time. Not just visual memories, but every sound, every smell, all of their fears, and their moments of joy.

Then I came to realise that in every life, Lilith had been hunted. Hunted by your kind," she pointed her finger accusingly, "or by men who have served your kind. At first, I became afraid because I knew that they would come for me too and then as I came to understand more, I felt an anger rise in me. An anger that has lived for thousands of years and so I carried on our work."

"What work?" asked Harry.

"The work she started, to kill them all of course" she replied. "It is not in Lilith's nature to simply lay down and die."

"At long last we have found it Erianes "said Enmerkar.

"Found what?" asked Lilith. "These are the genetic memory traits we gave you. This is your heritage, the last embers of our race and the gift we, the Einari, bequeathed to you. It seems that it does not descend linearly through family lines, but it emerges randomly from time to time……… but how is that possible?" he asked himself rhetorically. "There are yet many unanswered questions here.

"That would explain how you have managed to elude us for so long" said Erianes.

"That's just as well don't you think? As you would keep killing us otherwise," said Lilith.

"Probably" said Erianes truthfully.

"That's how it protects itself and us. Each time it arises in a generation there will be a twelve- or thirteen-year hiatus before the host reaches puberty."

"And by then you have learned to hide?" added Sofia.

"Exactly, why do you think I am living in a shitty bedsit in East London, avoiding social media and spending my time working for a small PR firm in a city where everyone is invisible, at the beck and call of a fat old boss who is constantly trying to get me to sleep with him."

Harry winced.

"If we weren't in danger from their kind" she said pointing at Erianes "I would be living like the Queen of Sheba or a bloody Kardashian, wouldn't I?"

The tension was becoming palpable now, and when Harry laughed involuntarily, it lightened the mood in the room.

"It is curious" said Erianes "that you can remember these things, even more so that you can recognise your former kinsmen, but that they cannot recognise you, nor one another? You do indeed share the same genetic code as Sofia and there are similarities with Harry but not an exact match. Perhaps there is a trigger we have overlooked."

"Then what of him?" Sofia said pointing to Schmitt who had remined silent throughout, stunned by the revelations he was hearing.

He raised his arms in supplication. Erianes pulled up the results of Schmitt's scans and tests then glanced through them quickly. "Nothing remarkable as far I can see. He shows no propensity for accessing the DNA enhancements, no chromosome variations from standard or any enhanced resistance to infection. He seems to be simply…… human."

Although relieved, Schmitt was almost sure that he had just been insulted.

"It is possible that the Vori may have understood some of this and that were perhaps trying to reverse the genetic modification. When they realised that they could not, they decided to kill the whole human race using you as their first agent of death."

"I guess we will never know" said Lilith "but I for one don't ever plan on having a conversation with one of them.

Anyway, their poison worked for a while, almost without exception everyone who came in to contact with me died. When the original Lilith died, the poison died with her but by then her legend had been created. They had found the method very effective, and it would appear, that they have been trying to replicate it ever since and have managed to do so on several notable occasions throughout history."

Harry, Sofia, Enmerkar and Erianes all looked at one another, then in silent unison, agreed that this would not be a good time to mention that it was Erianes and Enmerkar who had manufactured the latest wave of pandemic which was currently sweeping across the globe.

"We had not believed that any had survived that long, and you say there are still some left alive? If you are correct, then this changes everything. It seems we have been looking in the wrong place for so long, and it is they who truly fear you."

"With good reason" she said proudly. "I …. we; have killed almost thirty of them that I can recall."

"Most efficient" said Enmerkar almost with a hint of admiration in his voice. "That would be a heavy toll given our rate of reproduction, and our kind do not die easily."

"No" she said smiling, "but you bleed like everything else on this planet, so you do have your weaknesses. They made sure that the Legend of Lilith lived on so that I would be hated and hunted by all. Even you would have gladly completed their work for them, if Adam……sorry if Harry," she corrected herself, "had not stopped you."

Noticing that Harry looked shocked she turned her gaze to him, and Sofia then added softly "I told you truthfully, I am not a threat to you. You are my Adam and my sister Eve, but you just don't remember it."

"Mr. Schmitt' said Erianes, "perhaps it is time for you to leave us. We may have need of you again but for the moment we will take you back to your companions on Mount Ararat. Go back to Yerevan and we will come for you when we are ready. In the meantime if you speak a word of what you have witnessed here …. " Enmerkar slowly drew his finger across his throat. "You do understand that there is nowhere that you can hide from us."

Schmitt was nodding his agreement almost frantically; despite his training he was already terrified and did not need any further warning.

"Very well, let us take a break."

Half an hour later Harry opened a portal just below the glacier on Mount Ararat and Schmitt walked through it with him. It was early evening; the moon was rising but there were storm cloud coming from the east. "You must go quickly Hans" said Harry, "Good luck, that looks like a nasty storm front heading in," and with that, he turned and walked back through the portal which closed behind him.

Schmitt returned to find Baris, and Mehmet huddled over a small fire in the shelter provided by the crescent shaped rock formation where he had left them two days earlier. They were surprised, but relieved to see him.

"Come sit by the fire" said Baris offering him some of his bread, "we saw the patrol above us on the glacier and we heard gunshots, we had thought you gone and planned to leave but we had to hide until they stopped searching. We are planning to leave at first light. Where is Professor Hashemi?"

Schmitt just shook his head. "Break camp as soon as possible" he said, "we must get off this mountain, we are in danger here."

23. TWELVE MINUTES TO MIDNIGHT.

Over the next few days Lilith's mood continued to improve. She became less anxious whenever she was in the presence of Enmerkar and Erianes who were frantically trying to fill in the gaps that the devastation of Marduk had left in their knowledge of their enemy. She recounted everything she could recall about how she had hunted the Vori, where they were hiding and who she knew, or at least had good reason to believe, they were controlling.

She could tell by the expression on Enmerkar's face that he was beginning to realise there was quite a lot that had eluded them. "You have been deceived by some of the governments you have been trying to help" she said. They are not working for you, they are working for them, or at least some factions within the governments are."

"Yes, so it would seem" he admitted.

"They do not call themselves the Illuminati by the way" she said. "All that tosh was leaked to give the conspiracy theorists something to do."

"Why would they leak information about a conspiracy if there really was a conspiracy?" asked Harry, who was now totally confused.

"Sometimes things happen that make it obvious that something is going on, so by creating a conspiracy theory, they don't have to actually then go on to explain it. People just accept that there is one. They wink at one another and nod knowingly, but the real point is to keep them looking in the wrong places. It's a double bluff. It's quite clever really."

"What do they call themselves then?" Enmerkar

asked. Lilith looked puzzled for a moment. "You said they don't call themselves the Illuminati?"

"No. They call themselves the Twelve Minutes to Midnight," she said,

"Why twelve minutes to midnight?"

"Because that is how close they are to winning, and because their human disciples are twelve in number. There are five remaining Vori as you call them, and seven humans, presumably controlled or adapted by them in some way, like us" she said gesturing at Harry and Sofia. "Then a further five apprentices waiting in the wings.

They are declining in number for sure," she said with a deep look of satisfaction on her face, "so I assume that like you are they are a sterile and dying race. That's what the other five humans are for, when one of them dies their human apprentice takes their place at the top table. At the moment they don't have full control of everything, but their influence is immense. When they are all in place, then it will be "midnight" and the signal for them to thin out humanity."

"Thin out humanity……why?" asked Sofia?

"Look around you Sofia, the world is in a chaos of our

own making," said Lilith. "They are gradually gaining control over all of the assets of the world but without order it will do them no good. When the population is finally thinned out, to maybe three hundred million, they will be able to establish a single world government so that they can control everyone and everything. Eight billion people and two hundred countries are currently making this impossible for them; and this is the true globalist agenda."

"But that is genocide," said Harry. "They would have to kill almost seven and a half billion people!"

"And they will, without hesitation if we let them" said Erianes.

"At least on this we are all agreed" said Lilith "they need to be stopped."

"Do you know who these humans are that are in control, and who are the apprentices waiting in the wings?" asked Sofia.

"They are cautious too" said Lilith "and not necessarily the most immediate names you can think of, but I do know that the five Vori apprentices are based in Tibet, Israel, The Vatican, Saudi Arabia, and Iran.

"Why those places specifically?" asked Harry

"It's not random," said Lilith. "There they have been able to quietly influence every one of the major religions of the world. Hinduism along with its offshoot, Buddhism, Christianity, Judaism, as well as both branches of Islam."

"Over the centuries they have stoked much racial and religious hatred. They have initiated many wars, which in turn have encouraged an endless cycle of escalation and retribution. Within all of the religions some fanatical souls have arisen who were only too willing to kill for them if it served their own twisted interpretation of their faith. The role of these few here is a simple one. To corrupt men's faith, their ideals, and in the process to turn one against the other.

The Vori themselves have also used their technology and their appearance to sow division where they could, and they have actively supported the fanatics to do their work for them. Reading some of the ancient texts it points to the fact that they have actively intervened on occasion. In some battles or major turning points they have done so in order to sway the course of history in their preferred direction."

Harry nodded. "And we have helped them by being all too

ready to dismiss things we did not understand as fairy tales."

Lilith nodded.

"You said there were twelve, what of the other seven?"

"I believe their role is much more mundane, but it is important to them non the less. It is simply about controlling money and economic resources. They are based in the seven largest economies of the world. The USA, China, UK, Japan, Germany, France, and India. They are not the leaders of these countries as you would perhaps assume, but they work from within. They are the hidden voices that whisper their poison into powerful ears.

They set up monopolies and controlling interests in finance, space exploration, electronics manufacturing, food production, medicine, pharmaceuticals, and transport. Anything that they can potentially utilise to choke the world's economies or bring the nations to a global consensus. Mostly they achieve their aims through the companies they control. Companies that people have never heard of but in the background, they control large corporations, stock markets etc. Failing that, they are not above using much more direct methods. If I was a gambling person, I would guess that they already exercise control over perhaps two thirds of the world's resources."

"The two pillars," said Sofia, who was suddenly having something of an epiphany. "The symbol on the door of their facility where we found you."

"Exactly" said Lilith.

Harry looked on; he was clearly still confused.

"The twin pillars of force and form Harry, of God and Mammon, of belief and reality, call them what you will. You can't control mankind unless you can control both his body and his mind. Their work is nearly done, so are we going to stop them together or are you going to give me the diadem and let me go and complete my work?"

"What do you know of the power of the diadem?" asked Enmerkar.

"I know that Cyrus the Great managed to control the known world with it somehow nearly three thousand years ago. I seem to have been drawn to it. Besides it's obvious that I need a powerful weapon to stop them so I am willing to go on a little faith that I can learn how to use it."

"That is very interesting" said Enmerkar, "and

what exactly did you feel when you held it?"

"It was very hazy but when I held it, it became malleable in my hands and then, when I wore it, it seemed as though I could visualize where they were and what they were planning. But seeing as you showed up shortly afterwards, I am guessing it works both ways and perhaps, that is how you and then the other ones found me? Would I be correct to assume that it also has something to do with the way those portals work? A key perhaps?"

"You are very perceptive Lilith, but at least in some of these things you are mistaken. Yes, Erianes and I could track you that way but fortunately, our enemies cannot track you using the diadem, at least not as far as we know. The three adornments are linked, but as we have the others and they do not have another one, you must have somehow inadvertently activated one of the consoles."

"You said 'things,'….. that's plural?" said Lilith.

"Cyrus never actually wore the diadem" said Enmerkar. "That is simply a legend."

"How can you be so sure?" she asked.

"Simple, it has been in the facility since you left it there almost thirty thousand years ago. Did it not occur to you that the Vori would have removed it from the last owner's head if they had been able to?"

"I assumed it was the poison that kept them away" she said, "at least until I saw them attack Harry."

"Initially it probably did, but the artifacts are all genetically coded to the royal bloodline of Anu. Only one of royal blood can remove it unless it is freely given, and since the owner was deceased…" he let his words fade.

"That would explain why Mr. Schmitt could not remove it" she said, "he tried first, and it would not budge, but how was I able to remove it?"

Enmerkar nodded. "Our forebears were not likely to leave such powerful technology lying around without safeguards. That makes you, all the more remarkable."

"So, what of Cyrus?" She asked. "Sometimes stories are just that, stories. It is almost certain that he was helped to create his empire by the Vori using more advanced technology. It no doubt served their purpose at the time to have him on the throne."

"Then how did he know of the diadem?"

"The Vori revered it as a symbol of their royal heritage and he no doubt adopted it. We do still owe him a debt however, his vanity in recording it at least, has led you to us.

Tell me," Enmerkar continued, "what do you know of the fifth dimension?"

"Nothing" she replied truthfully, "I am a museum Professor, remember."

He looked at Erianes, silently questioning if he should go further. She nodded in agreement.

"Then it seems we have found our third portal guardian and we need to bring you up to speed with your new partners. Come," he said, and they went to the briefing room where he once again ran through the basics of trans dimensional travel.

When he had finished, he gave the diadem back to Lilith along with a will trainer.

Lilith was stunned and un-characteristically silent, she simply stared at them in disbelief.

She soon regained her composure. "I know what this is for" she said holding out the diadem "but I have never seen anything like these before."

"Come, I will teach you how to use them" he said, "I will help you to understand the nature of the cards, how they are a key to using the portals safely and how they will help to locate and identify your targets." Now he had really struck a chord, that was music to her ears and Lilith did not need to be asked twice. She was a very quick study, and soon seemed adept at the visualization required. She even showed some conscious understanding of the shifting symbols. By the end of the day Lilith was both awed by what she had witnessed and exhausted from the mental effort required to wield her newly gifted tools.

"Enough for today" said Enmerkar.

Over the days that followed, Enmerkar and Erianes observed their three young charges closely. They noticed that having Lilith, Harry and Sofia working together, with the three adornments in close proximity also seemed to sharpen both their individual as well as their collective reflexes, making them quicker and stronger than any ordinary human being. With practice the opening and closing of the portals soon became second nature to all of them. There was something else too, Harry and Sofia had started to have visions which, to begin with, they found frightening and worrisome. Lilith had managed to calm them, reassuring them that the strangeness would pass which to their relief it soon did.

They too eventually started to remember the lives of their forebears even though there was no recognisable, genetic link between them. "How do you cope with all of these memories?" Sofia asked her, "there are so many of them and they seem so random."

"The strongest, most evocative, or most powerful ones emerge first, and they seem to flit from one lifetime to another, which makes it hard to focus. Eventually you will learn to see them in a linear timeline, much like your own life memories" she said "but even then, there are some very vivid memories that will come to stand out above all others. I always believed that these were the lessons we needed to learn most urgently in order to survive and……." she paused.

"And what?" asked Harry

"You will find that your intuition is much sharper. You will sometimes see things before they happen."

"Do you see things before they happen?" he asked.

"Sometimes I get glimpses, I cannot control it, but that

split second has saved my life on more than one occasion."

One day Lilith was studying the cards, and she took the major arcana, the twenty-two cards that Enmerkar had said would help them fix their journey on their own timeline and she thought back to her place of captivity, to the symbols of the Ouroboros that lined the corridors, the snake eating its own tail that symbolized eternity, then it struck her.

"Erianes, the facility on Mount Ararat was it originally one of yours or one of theirs?" she asked.

"It was the first genetics facility that Nin Kirshag used before they moved to the Xisudra, when the Ennead gave her permission to proceed with the genetic enhancements. Shortly afterwards Eshunna fell to the Vori."

"Tell me about it" she continued. What else was it used for? Before the war with the Vori I mean?"

"The investigations into the portals were in their infancy and we believe that this is where most of the research on them was completed, but as I said the facility was abandoned during the war when the genetics research was relocated to the Xisudra and Atlan. Why do you ask?"

Lilith continued, "The images on the cards Enmerkar gave

us. The images your forebears used and that he then used to create the cards are not random, are they?"
"No they are not, the primary symbols came down to us albeit in a somewhat different format directly from Nin Kirshag.

Enmerkar created the cards in their current form as a safety net really, in case we were unsuccessful, or we were killed before we could finish our work."

"Why did he create what are now little more than playing cards?" she scoffed. "Surely that somehow cheapens the value of the incredible information they hold?"

Erianes nodded. "Simply because he knew that if we failed to preserve the knowledge in a way that appealed to your higher instincts, using what your initiates would call 'sacred knowledge' that they would appeal to your baser instincts.

He felt that they would survive because people would use them to gamble or try to use them for deception and fortune telling. That way the core set of images would survive in the hope that one day, someone amongst you would realise what they were intended for and begin again to understand their true function. The images affect you whether you realise it or not."

A broad smile crossed Lilith's face, "You really are a sneaky lot, aren't you?"

Erianes smiled too, "Enmerkar has a deeper understanding of your nature than any of us, and perhaps deeper even than you would care to admit? No conscious understanding of the symbols is necessary in order for them to be effective because unlike words, that have specific fixed meanings, symbols work on your subconscious much more flexibly through a process of individual interpretation."

"The twenty-two major arcana don't symbolize a single life, do they? "asked Lilith. "What they really symbolize is the life of any soul being incarnated and its journey through life and back to the source."

"Yes, that is true, but what are you getting at?"

"The symbol on the floor in the laboratory, the snake swallowing its tail means death and re-birth. That is how Nin Kirshag got the adaptations to work. She couldn't make them work through linear succession; she knew it would take too long. You, said it took almost two hundred thousand years before we started to develop imaginative thinking and to begin to work with artistic or abstract concepts."

“Yes, that is correct.”

“Well at that rate you could all have been extinct long before we were developed enough to make any practical use of it and all of her work would have been for nothing.”

“Apart from her brothers Enki and Enlil she was the only one who really knew much of the way the portals worked, using a higher dimension?”

“Yes” said Erianes.

Lilith continued “So she designed the genetic traits she wanted to pass on, to be spread randomly to the entire population in dormant form, knowing that eventually nature would bring forward those who could make of use of it. Myself, Adam and Eve” she said. Thinking back to Enmerkar’s explanation of how everything is visible in each dimension below as you travel higher and higher, she added “then the most obvious conclusion is that she managed to incorporate a fifth dimensional component somehow.

Everything that happens there is recorded in that space and so any new soul that comes along can eventually access it all. That is what I have been accessing when I have recalled past lives and that is what Harry and Sofia are now seeing. The more they are inside the portals the more they are remembering too."

Erianes looked genuinely shocked. "Come we must tell the others."

Enmerkar was impressed with Lilith's powers of deduction and even Harry and Sofia now seemed to better understand what they were accessing, albeit she had to explain it to them more than once.

"So, it's like reading a book or watching a movie?" asked Sofia.

"That's right but because of the emotional feelings it is a much more intense experience but if you think about it like that, it will make some of the worst aspects a little less jarring for you both."

Harry and Sofia looked relieved, they had both been finding the experience a real strain and it had at times interrupted their work with the portals.

"Time is catching us" said Enmerkar, "soon we must finalise our plans, get some rest. Tomorrow is going to be a very long day.

"Lilith" he said, "before you go, might I speak with you please?" Lilith nodded and sat with Enmerkar as the others retired.

"It seems that we owe you an apology my dear" he said, "we have, perhaps in hindsight, been isolated here for so long and we have been so focused on our own demise that we have not fully understood either the intentions of our forebears or indeed the world outside. As a result, we have made some terrible mistakes.

We have underestimated our enemy and during the course of that we have put you in great danger. We have been blind to so many things and, as you have pointed out, we have been deceived by some of the very people we have always sought to protect."

Lilith sat quietly for a moment then she looked up at him. "Well, don't feel too badly, in my experience those Vori are really sneaky bastards too" she said smiling, "and besides mankind does seem to be quite easy to corrupt."

"They don't seem to have had any problem getting men to do their bidding, for what in the end amounts to nothing more than few trinkets. For what it's worth, I am sorry too" she said. "I guess we have all been deceived. I would gladly have killed you both too had

Harry not prevented me, and now………now that I understand you a little better, I am sorry for the burden you carry, you must both be weary."

He nodded.

"I guess I have always been so wrapped up in my own safety, hiding in the shadows for so long, frightened that one of you was waiting around every corner to kill me that perhaps all I ever saw was life after life of constant threat. I am weary too" she confessed, "weary of carrying around all this fear and hatred as I have for so long. Perhaps, one day soon, when this is all over, we can both lay our burdens down at last and know true peace."

He smiled at the thought.

"Will you do something for me please Enmerkar?" asked Lilith.

"The Covid virus you have created will kill many more innocent people as well as those who would harm us. I did not ask for the curse that was laid upon me and it has been a mark of shame that has followed me through eons of time, but my immunity and that of my sister could be the basis for a cure. No matter how these next few days play out, whether we win or whether we lose, please promise me you will make a vaccine."

He remained silent but nodded again.

She stood up to leave, lifted his hand and with genuine affection she held it gently against her cheek.

"Good night Enmerkar" she said.

24. CHILDREN NO MORE.

A week later their training was interrupted when Enmerkar called them all together. They all now had a shared sense of anticipation as they sat down to listen to the news he brought. "While you, Lilith, Harry, and Sofia have been studying and practicing over the last few days, Erianes and I have used the new knowledge of our foe that Lilith has provided us with to get to know their tactics better. I believe that we have succeeded in locating the targets that we must destroy. There are thirteen in all.

"Thirteen?" said Harry

"Yes Harry, thirteen. We must destroy each of the seven humans currently in place as well as the five apprentices who are waiting to take over from their masters. I believe we have located the rest of the Vori and fortunately they are all in one place. If we hit them too, then that is thirteen targets in all."

Lilith had been listening silently throughout the briefing "Fourteen targets" she said. Everyone looked at Lilith, as if waiting for an explanation.

"You said it yourself." She nodded in Enmerkar's direction. "During all of this time you have watched, but in spite of your best intentions you have never really been in control. You have never seen the full picture, and they have played you to the point where they have almost won this war. If not for our chance meeting with Harry and Sofia first, you would have killed me too and done their job for them. As a result, mankind is on the point of either extinction or eternal slavery if we fail. When this is over you need to leave us in peace" said Lilith, "no more interference. We have to set our own course, we have to make our own mistakes, and you have to trust us to defend ourselves. Isn't this what Nin Kirshag was trying to give us?"

Enmerkar nodded in silent agreement then he looked at Erianes. "Sister" he said softly, "Perhaps Lilith is right, it seems that we have been hiding under the ice here for so long that we have become blind to the world outside, and it is time for us to finally leave them. Erianes thought for a moment and then slowly nodded too. "Agreed."

Harry and Sofia looked at one another, then at Lilith and their Einari mentors in turn, but knowing she was right they held their thoughts, and for a while there was an uncomfortable silence in the room.

"Sounds straightforward" said Harry trying to get things back on track, "so why do I sense a huge 'but' rapidly hoving in to view?"

Erianes smiled, she had become quite fond of Harry. "There are several problems unfortunately. The Vori are located on a spacecraft in low earth orbit. As far as we can tell it is a small craft, probably originally an animation suspension module designed for deep space exploration, which may explain how some of them survived. It seems from the news reports, that a number of your governments, have been tracking it since the 1940's. They even have a name for it, they call it the Black Knight satellite."

"How appropriate," said Harry.

"Thanks to Lilith we have the advantage now" said Enmerkar. "We know how many they are and where they are and as far as we know they have no way of detecting us here beneath the ice. We don't think they can spend much time away from their ship which would explain why we thought they were long gone. We, however, cannot use the portals to attack them as they are technically not on the planet."

"Well don't you have some weaponry that can take them out from long range?" asked Harry.

"Yes" he said

"Great, let's do that then, you can shoot them down from here while we take out the others."

Enmerkar continued, "but we have got to get the Xisudra back into space in order to use them."

"Ah" said Harry.

"Can this thing still fly?" asked Sofia.

"It has been under the ice for over twelve thousand years and even prior to that, during all of its time on Atlan, it was only ever used as a laboratory. It may have been on some short reconnaissance flights, but as far as we know it has had no prolonged exposure to space in nearly five hundred thousand years."

"The ship's systems, at least some of them still work obviously, as we use them every day, but two of the four fusion fuel cells are completely spent and there is minimal charge in the other two."

"So, it's basically a death trap then!" said Sofia.

"Perhaps" said Enmerkar "but with your help we hope to avoid that outcome. We only need to achieve low earth orbit and then only for a maximum of say, thirty minutes.

We have created a substantial pocket of air around the outside of the ship to give us room to work. There is shelter from the worst of the weather outside, but it is still cold beneath the ice sheet. We need to strip off the deep space modifications including three of the external engine mountings, plasma weapon bays, communications modules, and the accommodation pods.

That will bring the ship back to its original cubic configuration of about fifty metres and we need to check the hull integrity.

For the moment, this comprises the inner hull of the ship which has been reasonably well maintained, and the outer hull provides structural integrity both in space and against the worst stresses of gravity during the take-off and landing.

We have two remaining fusion cells. One internal fusion fuel cell should suffice for a short flight. The other one we will need to use with the external weapons array to clear the ice above before take-off. We will destroy their ship and return here if we can."

"What of the other targets?" asked Lilith

"Here is the list" said Enmerkar.

"This is the second problem" said Erianes. "There are too many to be sure that we can get them all in time. As soon as we are detected they will begin to warn their followers. We do not have an answer to this yet but for now, the three of you must complete your study of the cards. By the time we are finished you must all know each one as second nature.

There will be no time to meditate on each one in turn.

Once we are above the ice in the open, even a low level Vori ship will be able to detect us. We must not give them time to evacuate or to warn their allies. You must be doing your work even as we are in flight. Come, this morning we will attend to the ship and this afternoon you will practice taking your meditations to the next level."

Later that afternoon Lilith, Sofia and Harry were sitting contemplating the four suits of cards. "Do you think they will be ok when they leave?" asked Sofia "and where will they go?" she added.

"I don't know" said Harry, "I hope so."

"I see now that they are not all evil" said Lilith, "but for the moment at least you must forget about them. Let them do their job so that we can concentrate on ours."

"We cannot open twelve portals in enough time to get through them, to kill everyone and then leave without being seen and we cannot afford for even a single one to get away," said Harry.

"So, what do we do, split up perhaps? Maybe we can each

take one at a time?" asked Sofia.

"Too risky," said Harry. "We have no idea what defenses or advanced technology they have access to. Besides we seem to be much stronger, not to mention quicker, when all three of us are together."

"I have an idea" said Lilith "come, let us take a look at the fifth dimension and see what we are able to look at of our targets."

"We have never lingered there before" said Harry, "Enmerkar and Erianes have always warned us that is dangerous and that if we get lost in there, we may never return."

"It is dangerous, for them" she said, "but we have each other, and we all know the way back to this place, as long as one of us is capable, then we should all be safe."

They held hands around the table and started to breath slowly, rhythmically. With no external destination to aim for, they did not need the cards to open the portal. As one their diadem, the golden torc and the snake ring all started to glow and there was a faint hum in the room due to the power they generated together. As one, their eyes faded, then changed colour, to a light grey. When the change was complete, it seemed as if the stars began radiating from them. The room shimmered and they stepped into the dimensional corridor in front of them without a destination.

"Stay together," said Lilith. "Now let us imagine the wave of time." Slowly the space around them changed. It began to resemble a giant sea and the three of them stood atop a giant wave moving across the surface of the water.

"Concentrate" said Lilith, "forwards not backwards. Try to visualise all of the target locations at once, like dominoes one in front of the other."

Slowly, one by one, all of their prey came into view. It was like looking into mirror that was reflecting a mirror, which itself reflected a mirror, then another and another.

"That's it," she said, "now concentrate on finding an inflection point where the lines cross over."

What seemed like just a few moments later they focused on the Xisudra. There in front of them was the room they had left, and when they simply stepped back inside, all three of them fell to the ground utterly exhausted.

"That's it" said Lilith when she had regained her composure, "that's how we do it. We need to practice it again until we get it right."

"And without it killing us" added Sofia. "I feel like every atom in my body is about to explode" and Harry nodded in agreement.

"Yes" said Lilith, "we need to rest.

"Come on, let's see how Enmerkar and Erianes are getting on with reconfiguring the ship."

Progress was clearly slow but noticeable. The weapons system was ready to melt the ice outside and they were checking the hull for any potential weak spots.

They decided to stop and get something to eat.

"What have you been doing?" asked Erianes, you all look exhausted.

"Erianes" said Lilith, I believe we have a solution to our second problem.

"Excellent news" she said. "What are you proposing". Sofia and Harry looked a little sheepish but slowly Lilith outlined their plan.

"We used the fifth dimension to look for the inflection points so that we could verify our targets in the hope that we could narrow down the number of times we needed to use the portal."

"Go on" said Erianes, curious as to where Lilith was taking this.

"It seems that their human followers meet in two places."

"When are these meetings taking place, and where?" asked Enmerkar.

"They are both scheduled for this Thursday, three days from now," said Lilith. "There is an economic forum at Davos and an interfaith meeting being held in Urumqi in Northwest China. The former is just a standard G20 economic summit attended by lots of politician and business leaders. The latter it is a cover designed by the local communist party to take away attention from their alleged ill treatment of the Uyghur population."

"Excellent news" said Erianes congratulating them on their discovery, "the Xisudra will be ready by then and that could make your task considerably easier."

"There will be a lot of collateral damage" said Lilith "but at least we are one hundred percent sure that we have the right ones. We have practiced the visualization for the portal locations, and we can open them both, but unless we are already inside the corridor, we can't see our targets are actually where they are supposed to be.

This means that if we work sequentially, we can't be sure of getting them all in time. If we lose any of them now, we will just drive them under ground and we may never find them again."

"What are you proposing?" asked Erianes.

"We will have to open both of the portals at once," said Sofia.

"That is a fair summary" said Enmerkar "but that's not how the portals work, you can only open one at a time."

"Actually" said Harry slowly "we have discovered that it isn't, and that we can open multiple portals more or less at once. That is how we discovered the convergences." Enmerkar and Erianes both looked genuinely astounded. "You have seen the great ocean?" he asked.

"I don't know about an ocean but if you mean, have we seen multiple threads of the timeline, then yes," said Harry "we have. We can't see individual events when we open multiple portals unless they are happening at the time that we open them, but when we look forward it is like watching lines of spaghetti stretching out in front of you, or maybe a tube map would be a better analogy. If we concentrate hard, we can see the locations, the places, and times where the intersections occur. In fact, this is the only thing about it that makes any real sense." He paused to let the enormity of what he was saying sink in.

Enmerkar smiled. "No one has achieved that since the time of Enki and Nin Kirshag." He looked at Erianes, "perhaps we truly have at last reached the culmination of Blessed Nin Kirshag's work." Erianes nodded, "but still we must be cautious" she said, "let us not forget that they were lost to us in the corridor, this is an incredibly dangerous thing you are attempting."

"Yes, we know it is" said Lilith, but we must learn to control the dimension when we are in it, and besides we know what is at stake here, so we are prepared for the risks."

"There is something else too," said Sofia. Then she paused for a moment not knowing how to explain what else they had discovered. "It gets weird very quickly inside the portal, it appears that we can step out of each of the portals at exactly the same time that we open them no matter how much time seems to elapse for us when we are on the inside, so to all intents and purposes as far as the outside world is concerned, we can literally be in two places at once, perhaps even more."

"If you do not focus directly on the timeline, you risk changing it, or worse, stepping into another one altogether. What happens inside the portals, can ripple through thousands of worlds. I warned you once Harry of the consequences if you make a mistake there." said Enmerkar.

"We won't" he said, "we can do this, together," and he reached out his hands to Lilith and Sofia.

"What consequences?" said Lilith, almost casually.

"Oh yes," said Harry "I may have forgotten to mention that."

"There are other inhabitants of the fifth dimension" said Enmerkar. "They are aware of everything you do there and if you transgress their rules or if they believe that you are going to disrupt their reality, they will kill you without a second thought. Do not think your new-found 'powers of three' will save you. You will have no power over them.

At the very height of our civilisation, when we

started exploring the portals, even with all of the resources we had available to us from multiple worlds, we were no more than children to them, stumbling blindly in the darkness."

For a moment they all stood in silence as they considered Enmerkar's words.

"Fair enough" said Lilith, "thanks for the warning, but it doesn't change the plan. There is no other way we can do it in time, so we are lost either way if we don't try."

"You once told us; "said Harry, looking at Enmerkar, "that for some reason they care about us and if they can see everything on our plane, in our timeline, even if they won't allow us to see it, then they must know this is the plan and everything that has led up to this point. Otherwise, why would they have allowed Nin Kirshag to incorporate a fifth dimensional element into our DNA?"

Although he was clearly troubled Enmerkar looked at Erianes and she nodded.

"Very well. Enough for today, we will resume in the morning."

The next morning after breakfast they met in the lab. “We have a problem,” said Lilith. “I was going over the timeline data last night and I noticed an anomaly. We cannot hit them when they are together and we cannot wait until Thursday, we have to go tomorrow.”

“But why? That’s a day too early” protested Sofia.

“Yes, I know” said Lilith “but we forgot to scan the timeline for the Black Knight. I have discovered that there are intersections which we had not considered.”

‘So what?” said Harry.

“It means that there will be at least one Vori at each of these events to meet with their disciples. Some, or perhaps all of them will be awoken and they will leave the satellite tomorrow night. If we wait there is a risk that we will either miss them or they may be too powerful for us if we meet them head on. Although security should not be an issue for us getting in, that adds an unstable element into the mix.”

She looked at Erianes and Enmerkar then continued, “they won’t be where you are expecting them to be, and they are significantly physically stronger than the three of us. We can either risk the uncertainty; or we are back to twelve targets plus the satellite, but I think there is a solution."

"What can we do?" asked Harry.

"We will have to open twelve portals all at once."

"But we haven't practiced with that many. Is that even possible, to open twelve?" asked Sofia who was visibly shocked by the suggestion.

"We are going to find out, but one way or another we will have to make it possible," said Lilith. "Come on, we have work to do."

"Even if we can do it" said Sofia, "we are going to need help. Even opening just two at once and trying to keep them stable was exhausting, we would be very exposed and that would make us vulnerable."

"About that" said Lilith, "I think that our Mr. Schmitt may be more useful to us than we had perhaps imagined."

"He works in a museum" said Harry, "we can't just ask him to kill random people."

"Well, he had no problem shooting you did he" she said.

“No” thought Harry to himself, “he didn’t hesitate but then he was probably quite scared,” and he rubbed his shoulder at the memory of the pain.

“Besides” continued Lilith “his background is a little more complex than you might imagine. Trust me he will be useful,” and she began to relay the story of his military service. “He won’t need much convincing, he has already seen you two” she said, pointing at Erianes and Enmerkar, “plus the Vori on Mount Ararat. While he may not know the full details, he is bright enough to understand what is at stake here.”

Enmerkar and Erianes looked worried but uncharacteristically chose to say nothing, they simply looked at one another and nodded their agreement.

“You had better go and get him then,” said Harry. “We need to plan this quite carefully and we don’t have a lot of time.”

25. THE ENEMY RETURNS.

Hans Schmitt was laying in the bath in his apartment in Yerevan. He was soaking away his aches and pains, whilst at the same time, trying to make sense of the things he had seen on Mount Ararat. His world view had been turned upside down, his life would never be the same again. He knew that he could never tell anyone of course. If he did and even if Enmerkar did not carry out his threat to kill him, his academic career would be in tatters, but then he smiled at the absurdity of his thoughts. Now he knew that a literal war had been raging across the world for thousands of years that he knew nothing about, it made everything he thought he knew irrelevant. Feeling helpless and somehow emasculated, he had been irritable and constantly on edge since Harry left him back at the camp with Mehmet and Baris.

As he was pondering on recent events, he felt a weird sensation, like static that made the hairs on his neck stand up, then a portal opened in the bathroom just behind his head and Lilith walked through. "Hello Mr. Schmitt" she said, "please forgive the intrusion."

He jumped out of the bath. "Bloody hell professor you almost gave me a heart attack," he said. Then realizing he was naked he quickly grabbed a towel.

"I am sorry" said Lilith "but we really need your help, would you mind coming with me please?"

"Not if I have a choice" he replied.

Lilith smiled at him and shook her head.

"Well at least let me put some clothes on then."

Back on the Xisudra they set about explaining their problem and secretly Schmitt was pleased that they needed him. He had sought adventure all of his life and this was beyond his wildest dreams, but over the coming hours he would indeed prove his worth.

First, they showed him their list of targets. "I don't recognise anyone on this list" he said "no heads of state, no ministers, or highly public people at all."

"That is the whole point" said Harry, "they are all meant to be invisible and to operate in the shadows."

"That's a double-edged sword" said Schmitt, "but we can use that."

"What do you mean?" asked Sofia.

"Invisible people tend to be harder to find but when they themselves finally shuffle of this mortal coil; it doesn't tend to create too much attention."

Sofia nodded. "Well, the good news is that we have found them all. We have been studying their lives in some detail but as we don't have much time; here is the skinny version of what we know about them and their habits" she said, sharing a few images and notes of their intended victims.

They gave Schmitt some time to read the notes and then they set him the task of working out the order for their targets and helping them to understand the best way to go about their work. Finally at the end of a very long day they met again for a last debrief and one final walk through, of their hastily revised schedule.

Schmitt began. "For an operation like this I would normally expect a lot more time to observe and plan, but as we don't have the luxury of time we will just have to go with the basics. Tactically, when facing a larger number of enemies, you must make use of every advantage you can. Yes, you can use the portals so you have the element of surprise, but if you want to keep this as quiet as you can for as long as you can, then there is more than one angle to surprise."

Lilith was nodding in the background, silently adding her approval to his strategic summary.

Schmitt continued, "you can't assume that your technology is better than your opponent's but," he held up a map of the earth "you are based here in the Antarctica close to the south pole, so here the time is irrelevant to you but if you look at the time zones around the world your targets are spread from Washington DC to Tokyo.

That covers how many time zones?"

"Maybe 10? What is your point?" asked Harry.

"In fact, it covers fifteen time zones. For the proposed timing of your mission, it will be anything from the early hours of the morning, say 1am in downtown Washington DC, to 3 o'clock in the afternoon in Tokyo and anytime in between."

"How does that help us?" asked Harry.

Schmitt continued, "Everything I have heard here, tells me that speed is of the essence if this plan is going to work. You said that you can't actually see the targets unless you are inside the portal, and you cannot hold them open indefinitely? Well, if you know what time of day it is where they are, the weather conditions etcetera, then you are more likely to find them quickly, but more importantly you know what kind of environment you will be stepping into. That could mean the difference between success or failure." He paused for dramatic effect. "Or even life and death."

"Although they are not high-profile individuals, they may have some security we are not aware of. I assume these people are not just going to roll over and die?

That they will be happy to kill you if they see you coming first?"

Lilith nodded in agreement, "without doubt they would Mr. Schmitt."

"So, pay attention to the details," he continued, "knowing what may seem like little things might just save your life.

The religious targets are probably the easiest to predict. They spend most of their time in the same place and by the nature of what they do, they tend to be quite secluded. Their schools will also have fixed timetables for prayers, meals, study etc. The biggest problem is that news of any incident there is likely to spread very quickly and attract attention."

Harry nodded, "that makes sense."

"Conversely," said Schmitt "the other seven are based in big cities where there will be more going on and there are more likely to be witnesses, but accidents happen every day so it will take a little while, perhaps an hour or so to hit the news feeds. Hopefully that should be enough time. My recommendation would be to hit the five religious targets first. You will need to be as clinical and stealthy as possible. I know this is a big ask at this late stage but ideally, they should look all like accidents."

"That's quite a lot to remember," said Sofia. "Is there anything else we should be taking in to account."

"Actually yes. There is one more thing that has been troubling me" he added. "Do you know why there is a female in this group, and only one?"

"No; we don't" said Sofia, "do you think that is a problem?"

"I don't know" he said, "but I don't like surprises. Nothing about any of this set up seems to be random, so you should be wary just in case. After all, you two are pretty extra ordinary women" he added looking at Sofia and Lilith.

They all nodded in agreement. "Thank you, for that summary Hans," said Lilith, before she continued with the rest of the plan.

"At 5.30am Enmerkar and Erianes will begin to melt the ice above the ship, that should take about thirty minutes to get through the two miles or so of the ice sheet?" she said looking inquisitively at Erianes who nodded in agreement.

"At 6.00am Harry, Sofia and I will begin to open the portals.

At 6.05am, you get airborne and head for the Black Knight. How long will it take to get into weapons range?"

"It should take no more than about ten minutes" said Erianes.

"As Mr. Schmitt has suggested, we target the apprentices first in order. The Vatican, The Sunni School in Saudi Arabia, the Shia school in Tehran, The Potala palace in Tibet, and the Jewish religious school in Jerusalem.

Time itself doesn't mean anything inside the portal but we have to actually step outside to execute them. I believe that it will seem to us as though we are operating sequentially, but to those outside of the portal everything will appear to be happening at once. Even if we are right and we can step out of each one at the same time it still only gives us half an hour to hit each target. Killing someone does not come easily to most rational people and you will find it a very jarring experience."

"So, we have about thirty minutes for each one?" asked Sofia not wanting to think about it too much.

"I would say twenty minutes" said Lilith "just to be on the

safe side."

Harry nodded. "That gives us ten minutes grace for each one. What about phase two? Washington, Beijing, Tokyo, New Delhi, Berlin, Paris and finally London. Erianes, you estimate that we have to hit them all by 6.30am if we are to be confident of getting them all?"

"Yes" she said. "Ideally you would look at each in the early hours of the morning but, as Mr. Schmitt has already pointed out, because they are spread globally that won't be possible so there is a real danger of being revealed not just to the enemy but to the wider world.

Killing people in prominent locations, whether they know they are really their enemies working from within or not, is bound to raise some alarm amongst their governments. It will most likely make you all targets, both in the moment, and for the rest of your lives."

"Well, we will just have to deal with that as it comes" said Harry, "now what have we forgotten? Erianes, you look worried" he said.

Erianes was indeed worried. "As soon as we emerge from the ice the Xisudra will most likely become visible to both the enemy and also to your more advanced world governments. The Black Knight will be passing over Northern Russia, then Alaska and we will almost certainly trigger regional air defence systems on our intercept course. If the ship was fully operational that would not pose even a remote threat, but in its current state, a lucky shot from either side may shorten our journey considerably."

"By considerably I assume you mean completely and permanently?" said Harry.

Erianes nodded.

"There is also a danger of a misunderstanding and starting an international incident that could trigger a war between them if they think they are shooting at one another."

"Oh great" said Sofia, "so we could stop one war but end up starting World War three in the process. You have contacts in the US and Russian governments though, can't you warn them?"

"It is a big risk to do that" said Erianes, "but you are right so we will try. Perhaps if we leave our communication until 6.05 am we may just give ourselves enough time for them to react and to contact their commanders on the ground."

"Hans" said Lilith, her voice like warm honey soothing his ears "you know what we are up against and the risks. I am sorry but I have to ask you for one more favour, but we need you to help us with one more thing."

"As I have said professor, killing a man is no small thing but I understand what you, what we….," he corrected himself, "are all up against, so yes I will help you see your task through to the end, what do you need?"

"We will talk later" she said.

"Very well" said Enmerkar "tomorrow we go hunting. Please get some rest."

As they turned to walk away, "Lilith" he added softly, holding out his hand with three vials of liquid. "Consider it a parting gift."

"Thank you" she said.

No one slept well that night. The next morning when Harry, Sofia, Lilith, and Schmitt entered the laboratory they found Erianes and Enmerkar looking resplendent in their finest robes. Both were deep in prayer kneeling at a small alter. Harry thought it seemed strange, watching what would have, to men in any other age, appeared like a god and goddess, lighting candles, and praying to their own divinity. Praying for the safe execution of their plan and for deliverance from their enemy. They all bowed their heads in respect and added their own silent prayers to the proceedings.

"Good morning" said Enmerkar momentarily, cutting through the solemnity of the occasion. "Let us take some refreshment, toast our success and prepare."

It could have been a regal cocktail party were it not for Hans Schmitt looking strangely out of place, dressed in his combat fatigues; and holding an M430A1 assault rifle.

Harry looked on in quiet admiration. "I am rather pleased that you did not shoot me with that" he said.

Schmitt smiled. "If I had known what I was walking in to on Mount Ararat I may well have."

"Mr. Schmitt has agreed to be our backstop," said Lilith. "He will come with us into the portal, but he will remain on the inside."

"Why?" asked Sofia.

"You said it yourself, last night sister. The effort required to maintain the portals is considerable and it will weaken us. If we open the portals and they are discovered, or we miscalculate, as Erianes did in the cave of the genies, we could find one of our intended targets on the wrong side of the doorway. That has the potential to unleash chaos and we have to keep the timeline as intact as possible. We have to keep our interactions to the absolute minimum to ensure that time heals quickly.

We know that the door can be held open from either side. But ideally one of the three of us should remain inside the portal most of the time to focus solely on keeping them open. If that is not possible and all three of us have to step out, then we probably cannot afford to be gone more than a few minutes."

"Can one person hold all of them open" asked Harry. "The concentration is intense, and it is exhausting."

"I have thought about that" said Lilith, we should rotate the task and as the one who stays behind will be temporarily weakened, we will need to take some additional precautions. Mr. Schmitt will ensure that no one comes through the portal unless it is one of the three of us."

Enmerkar looked concerned but decided that

voicing further concerns at this stage would serve no useful purpose; but he felt duty bound to warn their new recruit.

"Mr. Schmitt" he said, "we are grateful for your help. We have made our preparations as best we can; but you must know that there is chance that we will not succeed. Our three young friends have learned more about this dimension than we had believed possible in such a short time, but without having the opportunity to thoroughly test everything they believe they know, much of it remains highly theoretical. Should they not be able to return to the portal for any reason, there will be no help for you there and you will also be lost."

Schmitt nodded in affirmation. "I understand."

"Very well then."

"Let me have a look at that list and the photos again please." asked Harry. He scanned down the names and descriptions of their first group of targets.

"They look so normal" he said, "so ……. human."

Sofia nodded "I can't believe I am going to have to kill a priest" she said. Look at him he is just an old man."

"You are Roman Catholic?" asked Lilith.

Sofia nodded. "Of course, I am Italian."

"Do not get sentimental sister" said Lilith, "because I can assure you that they are not sentimental about you. Most importantly do not forget that these people are not their religion. They represent only their own personal interests. They are merely parasites using peaceful religions as a cover for their evil, they may look 'human' but in all the ways that matter, they have all chosen to leave their humanity behind long ago.

Your Monsignor Galaci, the Italian Jesuit priest has been responsible for perverting and distorting your religion, spreading poison, and personally overseeing the biggest child porn racket in Italy for over half a century. How many innocent lives do you think he has ruined?

Look at my own religion, Farhad Karimi and Bilal Al Said look much the same do they not? jolly, bearded old men…. but they have helped to keep the Sunnis and Shia's at war. They watched as half a million people were slaughtered in 1980 in the Iran Iraq war and today, they oversee the biggest terrorist networks in the world from Afghanistan to Europe and East Africa.

Then there is Ariel Freidman. He is a nasty piece of work who revels in violence. He has been the biggest obstacle to peace in the Middle East for over three decades. He talks peace but at the same time, he funds both sides to kill one another. He has been the instigator behind the attacks on the Palestinians in the both the West Bank and Gaza. He has also funded their fighters in turn to kill Israelis in Jerusalem and almost every other city you care to name around the world."

"Yes, I get it, but surely you don't expect us to believe that these factions will all kiss and make up when these few are gone?" said Sofia.

"Of course not, human beings are too fickle for that." she replied. "If it wasn't so sick, you would almost have to admire how they have gone about their work over the centuries. They have kept the flames fanned wherever they could, so that the fires themselves have almost become eternal. They are fed by the very souls of generation after generation, of human beings who cannot see that they are only destroying themselves. Who knows, without the constant wind blowing, perhaps anything, even peace, may be possible. Maybe we do have a better nature within us somewhere if we look deeply enough for it."

"What about Ceba Bhujel?" asked Harry. "The Buddhists are not a warlike people."

"You are still making the mistake of confusing our target with his religion. It is true" she conceded, "that the Tibetan's are a peaceful people now, but even they were warlike once in their history. They are still a proud people and individuals are just as capable as those from any other society of causing great harm. In his case, he was recruited when he failed to achieve what he felt was his right within the Yellow Hat sect. In reality he is just a hardline communist who helped chase out the Dalai Llama when the Chinese took over the country.

He poisons the well wherever he can, against the Tibetans, against the Chinese too in their ancestor worship, and against all of the other peoples that fall within their orbit from Hong Kong to Mongolia. His current focus appears to be creating tension along the Chinese- Indian border in the Himalayas. Can you imagine the devastation if 2.8 billion people suddenly find themselves in a fully-fledged war?

I cannot stress this enough Harry; you must put your" …… she paused……. "your humanity and human emotions to one side, when the time comes you must not hesitate, or all will truly be lost."

"I know Erianes and Enmerkar have trained us, but Harry and I have never killed anyone before," said Sofia.

"I know sister," she said softly, "I know."

The mood in the room had become very sombre and Enmerkar who had been listening quietly smiled and asked, "would anyone like a cup of tea before we begin?" at which point Harry burst out laughing.

"I still think it would have been easier to wait until at least some of them were in the same place, like the economic forum or inter faith conference or something" he said.

"Well, that option is not open to us, so it does not matter now," said Sofia.

Lilith nodded in agreement. "Besides crowded spaces tend to throw up too many variables. It would be difficult to control everyone one of them on such a tight schedule and I don't know about you, but I am not ready for the world to see this yet."

"On second thoughts" said Harry "you are right as usual. The general population would lose their 'shit' if they knew about this, and we would be targets all over again."

They set the Xisudra's weapons system to begin melting the ice, then half an hour later Erianes and Enmerkar said their goodbyes and made their way to the bridge.

Harry, Sofia, and Lilith activated the adaptive camouflage in their Einari robes and accompanied by Schmitt they entered the portal where they began searching for all of their targets and establishing their exit points.

A few moments later they signaled to Erianes that they were ready. At the surface in Antarctica the temperature was minus forty degrees as the ground began to shake and the steam began to rise, slowly at first and then in large swathes as a huge hole almost two hundred metres in diameter, suddenly opened in the ice.

The penguins that had at first been agitated but rather curious, now scattered hastily, frightened by the noise and shaking, caused by the pressure changes as the Xisudra slowly began its journey to the surface.

Enmerkar looked at Erianes and they smiled at one another, both pleasantly surprised that the ship was still in one piece. As the Xisudra cleared the ice and headed north they began their tracking of the new elements in their plan and Erianes contacted the Russian and US governments in an attempt to get them to stand down.

In Murmansk Admiral Poroshov, the commander of the Russian northern fleet was alerted to an unusual disturbance heading their way. Meanwhile just south of Fairbanks in Alaska, at Eielson base, his counterpart Air force Colonel Lyndon McGuire, Commander of the US Alaskan air defence was being awoken and alerted to a huge radar signature of unknown origin approaching their position rapidly.

They were both experienced commanders, well aware that each side had tested the other on many occasions. Never the less, as a matter of protocol, they ordered their respective units to a yellow alert whilst they assessed the situation. Fighters were made ready to intercept the intruder when it reached the Barents Sea and air defence systems were brought on-line.

It took them both only a matter of moments to realise that this was not a run of the mill exercise. Soon both bases had scrambled to red alert, the fighters took to the air and their missile batteries went live. Colonel McGuire barked his order to get his counterpart on the phone and then added silently, "and may God help us all."

26. THE BATTLE BEGINS.

Aboard the Black Knight too, the Vori systems came to life. The Xisudra had been detected by the automated defence systems which were coming on-line, and the ship was beginning to revive its occupants. Enmerkar knew that once they recognized an operational Einari cruiser they would have no option but to instantly attack it whilst it was still within the atmosphere. Once it achieved a high earth orbit, then from space they would be a sitting duck.

Fortunately for Enmerkar and Erianes that was not the plan, and it would take their enemies a few moments to realise it, hopefully allowing them to get close enough to be sure of their task. As the Xisudra hit low earth orbit at an altitude of just one hundred and forty miles, Erianes leveled out their trajectory and they looked down at Earth below. "This is a truly beautiful world" she said almost absent mindedly.

Enmerkar nodded as he brought the weapons online, but before he could fire them, the ship was hit with the shock waves emanating from a series of explosions from the fighters below them. Erianes looked concerned "Are they firing on us? are we hit?"

"No, the ship is fine, we have not been hit, but the fighters below have been destroyed by the Black Knight. It seems that despite its size they have significantly enhanced its defenses and they are now targeting us." Momentarily the ship shook as it was hit by an energy weapon and the systems went offline again. "They are trying to create chaos and confusion, in the hope that we will be the target of retaliation. We must hope that the governments below can stop this escalating" said Enmerkar.

"Can we get weapons back online?" asked Erianes.

"Yes, but it may not be sufficient." he replied.

"Then set a collision course" said Erianes "and divert all of the energy to the forward screens. The mass of the ship at high velocity will suffice if we can reach them before they destroy us. We must finish this now otherwise Harry, Lilith and Sofia are lost."

Enmerkar nodded, loaded the co-ordinates, then put the engines to maximum.

Meanwhile, inside the portal Schmitt took up his position behind them. He waited patiently, watching as Harry Lilith and Sofia scanned their prey. The first three they decided they could handle one on one, hoping that this would help keep any suspicion to a minimum.

Monsignor Galaci was enjoying a light breakfast in his quarters in the Vatican. The smell of warm croissants and coffee filled the room, and he was contemplating the day ahead when a portal opened behind him. Sofia stepped through put her hand over his mouth and stuck a syringe into his jugular vein before pumping in approximately 50cc's of air. Taken completely by surprise, almost immediately his body went into spasm. As it did so he turned his head, his eyes were open wide, and he looked into Sofia's own deep brown eyes, as if silently questioning why? and simultaneously pleading with her for mercy. "You deserve this you fucking pervert" she said without any tinge of remorse as if in response to his silent plea. As the air reached his heart it brought on a massive heart attack. He writhed in agony for a few more seconds as she held him tightly preventing any call for help. Once she was sure that the end was near, she let go and he was dead before his body hit the warm stone floor.

It was mid-morning in Tehran when the elderly cleric Farhad Karimi made his way to the madrasah where he would teach his final morning class before afternoon prayers. Just like his unfortunate counterpart in Rome, he too was lost in his thoughts. He glanced at the beautiful young woman walking up the stairs towards him. Lilith smiled at him and as they passed then she simply paused, turned, twisted his skull, breaking his neck before she pushed him down the stairs. She could hear people running to see what had happened to the old cleric, but she disappeared in a cloud of smoke as his body reached the bottom, so that it had the appearance of a simple accident, an old man had unfortunately stumbled on the old, worn, stone steps. Back inside the portal neither of them spoke. Lilith and Sofia simply nodded at one another to acknowledge the success of their respective missions.

In Lhasa, the Capital of Tibet, Ceba Bhujel had just finished his lunch time meal. Although he himself was responsible for it when he betrayed his country, he could not get used to eating in the middle of the afternoon, it always gave him indigestion. His body was telling him that it was lunchtime, but the Chinese communist party wanted the whole of China on one time zone, so they had moved Tibetan time forward two hours to accommodate the mandarins of Shanghai and Beijing. "Idiots" he thought to himself.

Harry was not looking forward to his task and he had been getting anxious with the waiting. "How long does this guy take over lunch?" he wondered. Ceba Bhujel eventually arose from the table and started to make his way to the temple to continue his meditation and as he walked through the shady corridors on the north side of the palace, Harry looked on at the approaching figure from inside the portal. "He's quite a portly chap" he thought to himself rather unkindly, "no wonder he takes so long over lunch," then he looked down at his own midriff and winced, he had been enjoying the food a little too much on the Xisudra. Realising that his mind was wandering, he said to himself "concentrate Harry."

Then he stepped out from the portal right behind the orange robed monk, before putting two fully charged tasers, one to each of his unfortunate victim's temples. The combined 70,000-volt shock killed him instantly. Then Harry dragged his body to the electrical junction box at the end of the corridor, opened the cover and undid two of the live cables. Anyone finding him would hopefully at first suspect he had electrocuted himself trying to rectify the power outages that were common in the temple. In time they may come to a different conclusion, but the long term did not matter, he only needed half an hour of confusion, that was all the time they had anyway.

Back inside the portal Lilith and Sofia were waiting, eyeing their next targets in Saudi Arabia, Bilal Al

Said, and Ariel Friedman in the Israeli capital.

"Harry, once we are in position, you take Friedman in Jerusalem, we will handle the cleric," said Lilith. "The portals are stable for now, better than I had expected but we need to hurry. I can already feel my strength being drained" she said, "I think we will have to risk leaving Mr. Schmitt for a few moments."

Harry felt sick to the stomach with what he had just done but the time for expressing any reservations had long since passed. He simply nodded in acknowledgement and set off into the old town of Jerusalem.

Lilith and Sofia put on black hijabs before entering the school grounds and making their way to the garden where Al Said was sitting taking his mid-morning break. He looked up, immediately alarmed, clearly enraged by their presence, and demanded to know what women were doing there. Lilith and Sofia smiled as one. "We are a gift from our masters" Lilith proffered, then as one, they moved slowly, seductively, towards the old man and began stroking his beard.

He smiled, somewhat surprised, but this was nothing that he had not received previously, although never in the Madrasah. Curiously though, this time he was feeling overwhelmed by their sheer presence, they radiated desire and sexual promise like non he had ever known. His confusion lasted just long enough for Sofia to expertly insert a delicate, but very sharp needle, coated in deadly nightshade poison, into his back just between his fourth and fifth rib, and directly into his heart.

Lilith kissed him so that he could not cry out. What seemed like a mere moment later, he slumped forward into her arms. They dragged his body out of the rose garden and sat him behind a row of pine trees where a passer-by would think he had taken shelter from the heat.

"That was a bit much," said Sofia.

"What?" asked Lilith innocently.

"The kiss" she said, "couldn't you just have put your hand over his mouth, I wanted to retch. He was disgusting."

Lilith smiled, "We all have to make sacrifices. I would also remind you sister, that you are one who happily stabbed him, beside we have a power over men, and you should learn to use it as I have. It may save your life one day too."

"I suppose so" she replied, "but there is only one man I want, and I don't need that for him," and they stepped back into the portal together.

"Schmitt was pointing his rifle directly at them and he looked very relieved to see them return."

"Where is Harry?" she asked, he should have been back by now.

In the warren of streets that is the old town of Jerusalem he had been following Ariel Friedman along the Via Dolorosa, the 'way of pain.' It was 9am. Due to the unseasonal heat and the sporadic riots, many of the shop houses had either not opened at all or had only opened briefly, but there were still too many potential witnesses. The hardier Christian pilgrims were still resolute in their desire to pay their respects on the route that Jesus had supposedly used when he carried his own cross on the way to his crucifixion at Golgotha.

Friedman looked at them scornfully. They disgusted him, so much so that his disdain would have been apparent to even the most casual of observers. Then Harry got a lucky break. The Arab uprising that Friedman had ironically fueled, had spread from the Al Aqsa Mosque complex and the Wailing Wall, forcing the police to seal off some of the streets. Friedman decided to take a short cut down a small alley and that was Harry's chance. He walked up behind him and hit over the head as hard as he could until he fell to the ground, bleeding and unconscious. He hit him twice more caving in his skull, removed his watch, took his wallet, then disappeared back into the portal.

As he did so he looked around and for the briefest instant he seemed to see a very large figure appear, then disappear. A chill ran down his spine.

"Where have you been?" asked Sofia? "And what are these?" she asked looking at the watch and wallet in his hands.

"The Via Dolorosa was busy, there were police everywhere because of the riots. It would have attracted too much attention if I had moved too soon. Besides I wanted it to look like a mugging gone wrong" he said.

"You look like you have seen a ghost Harry," said Lilith.

He thought back to the figure and then said "it's nothing. How are Enmerkar and Erianes getting on?"

"They are having some problems with the ship and the Black Knight defenses are active but that is all we know.

We cannot help them Harry, we must focus on finishing our own tasks," said Lilith. They all nodded in agreement "Who's next on the list?" asked Sofia.

It was just after 6am when Justin Boyce Stewart's train pulled into Paddington Station in London. He brushed back his long blond hair as he rose from his seat and pulled down a small suitcase from the rack above his head. He would be just in time to catch the Heathrow express and that would leave him plenty of time to relax and have some breakfast in the executive lounge before catching the mid-morning flight to Zurich.

Like his counterparts he knew that there would be repercussions, very unpleasant ones, were they to keep their masters waiting. He had seen 'discipline' being enforced before and frankly he didn't fancy being on the receiving end of the lesson so he had decided he would travel to the forum a day early.

Conferences at Davos was usually as boring as hell. He hated listening to the clueless politicians spouting endless drivel about agendas they knew nothing about when it came to the detail behind them. That did not matter to them though, as long as they could dip into other people's pockets to pay for their own vainglory, they would never care. At least it kept them busy, focusing on things that distracted them from what their masters' had spent so long planning.

The lobbying meetings were important to him though; and the private conversations were how he and his counterparts exerted their control. The vast payments that went unnoticed by watchdogs and regulators, the favors or influence they would grant, and sometimes the odd friendly warning of what may transpire if their agenda were to be derailed by the odd honest, prominent politician were the all-important tools of his trade.

He well understood that fear and greed are the quintessential twin human motivators when it comes to exerting influence, and whilst some of his counterparts relished in wielding the former tool, for him, greed had proven to be the most effective. It wasn't that he didn't like to threaten people, on the contrary it gave him a certain thrill, but the truth was he was quite lazy, and it was far easier to change a few digits on a bank transfer than to go to all of the bother, not to mention the theatrics of kidnapping someone's wife or family. Then there was the mess, he hated mess.

Despite not looking forward to his trip there were some aspects of his work that he did enjoy. He really did enjoy manipulating people, but then he was a sociopath. This was his purpose in life after all, uncovering the cracks, those little weaknesses in people's personalities and then finding the best ways of exploiting them. This is what they had all been engineered to do.

He could not help feeling that some of his colleagues lacked a certain subtlety though and, in his head at least, he relished the air of superiority that he felt this gave him. That is not to say his counterparts had not found that fear and greed were effective, but he felt that sometimes they lacked imagination. His personal favourite was flattery. Inflating the ego of his targets who, for the most part, tended to be very insecure despite them invariably being in the public eye.

He was eager for the day, hopefully not too far away now, when they could finally step out of the shadows. He could not wait to look on the faces of some of those people he had endlessly flattered but so detested. For now, they were useful fools, but in the end; to him they were just that; fools. He was also sick of travelling economy class when these idiots flew around the globe in their private jets at the slightest whim.

There was little direct contact between their group, but he was sure that he would not be alone and that at least some of the others would also take the opportunity to travel early too, so the time would not be wasted. It would be another two-hour drive from Zurich airport to Davos, so he was looking forward to having a nap in the airport lounge. Fate, it seems, has a sense of humour too and his nap turned out to be quite a long one, an eternity in fact.

As he stepped off the train and ran for his connection across the bridge to the platform where the connection awaited, a petite lady with dark hair dropped her briefcase in front of him and the contents started dispersing across his path.

Unfortunately for Justin Boyce Stewart, he had been so wrapped up in his thoughts that he had failed to notice the very still figure of Harry in his camouflaged clothing as he passed him just a few feet away on the bridge. He instinctively bent down to pick up some of the contents and suddenly felt a pair of strong hands grab him from behind and then he found himself falling onto the electrified line just as the 6.12am Great Western train was leaving for Bristol, which unfortunately decapitated him before the driver could bring it to a complete stop.

Harry and Lilith ignored the screams from the platform below them where people were gathering to view yet another railway suicide and wonder what drove this unfortunate soul to take his own life in such an awful manner. They simply walked down the steps on the other side of the bridge, turned back underneath the stairs into the portal they had exited a few moments earlier. Schmitt was pointing his rifle at them but quickly raised it away and apologised. "Welcome back" he said.

Sofia looked up and smiled. "I think we may have struck a lucky break."

"How?" asked Harry.

"I have located Kenji Akira and Gopal Singh and I think I may have found another intersection."

"Where?"

"Dubai airport," she said.

Lilith scanned the dimension and nodded. "I agree sister. It looks like they are both transiting through there. Akira's plane arrives in from Tokyo within 5 minutes of Singh's arrival. They may even be catching the same onward flight to Switzerland."

"I don't like the idea of an attack at an airport said Harry. It's very visible and the airport itself will have a high security alert."

"We have no choice," said Lilith. "Fate has chosen to help us, and we must take the opportunity. It cuts into our safety limit time wise, but we should wait until they are both together."

"One of us has to stay here from now on" said Harry, "you can see that we are already tiring, that makes it one on one and improves the odds in their favor."

"Take me with you, I can help," volunteered Schmitt.

"We can hide in plain sight with our camouflage, but if they see you in an airport with an assault rifle you would be shot on sight," said Harry. "You would be a sitting duck."

"Don't worry" said Schmitt, "we will get the job done and they won't shoot me. I am hoping that I won't be there long enough.

All you need is a diversion to get people looking the other way while you do your bit right? Look at the layout, the duty-free shop is right in the middle of the shopping mall with rows of shops on either side. There are two entrances and there are public toilets to the rear which also have an entrance on both sides."

"That might just work." said Lilith. "It should help keep any collateral damage to a minimum and we can limit any coverage later. We will be able to block the security cameras easily enough if we interrupt the supplies to the mainframe, so afterwards there would be eye-witness testimony only, but nothing electronic to back them up unless some moron happens to be taking a photograph instead of running away."

Sofia protested "there will be people in the air, won't we be risking a major accident?"

"They will have an analogue back up" said Schmitt, "but most likely the computer won't be down long. It should simply reboot, and it will take no more than a few minutes to run its internal diagnostics. They train for this sort of thing."

Harry nodded. "Ok, we are running out of options, I say it's worth a try. Give us a few moments then send the power surge to the airport mainframe and trip the computers."

In Dubai airport Musa Obaid, the tower flight controller was nearing the end of his shift. It had been another long day but nothing out of the ordinary as the massive double decker A380s came and went. These double decker planes were true behemoths, monsters almost, yet somehow, he never got tired of looking at them. To him they were strangely graceful. Taking another sip from his water bottle his mind began to wander. He was looking forward to his afternoon off and, after prayers, he was planning to visit his daughter to enjoy a leisurely lunch with her and with his grandchildren. But his plans were about to change as five minutes later all hell would break loose.

Gopal Singh was standing in the entrance to the duty-free shop staring at a large golden camel. He glanced at his phone, there was a message from Kenji Akira, his flight had just landed, and he was asking where they should meet. This seemed like as good a place as any, it was easy to find and very public, so he replied sending a picture of the camel and the duty-free sign. Kenji Akira replied with a thumbs up emoji and then made his way over from the Arrivals Hall.

Gopal Singh preferred to travel westwards, although the daylight on the outward leg seemed to be shorter, the jet lag was not so severe, and he found the return journey much more pleasant. Not that the time difference was too bad on this occasion, five hours for him and seven hours for his colleague. It was still a long trip but at least it wasn't Washington DC. He made a mental note that once they had taken control of the world he would propose a new international date line, somewhere in the eastern hemisphere where most of the world's population actually lived.

He was still wrapped up in his thoughts when, a few minutes later, his colleague arrived. They greeted one another with polite smiles and a handshake, then they started wandering around inside. Hiding in plain sight was what they did best. Although they knew that their promised destiny was to rule mankind, the mundane aspects of their work made it easy for them to blend in with the crowd and even sociopaths recognised the value of good manners.

What could be more natural to the casual observer in an airport than a couple of middle-aged men browsing the duty-free shop for some fine whisky, dates, figs, and other exotic delicacies, presumably to take home for their families to enjoy after a long and arduous business trip?

Unfortunately for them their current observers were far from casual.

"He's arrived. Go now." said Sofia "and please don't shoot anyone Mr. Schmitt."

"Don't worry Sofia, the safety is on" he said, smiling. "I will be back in a jiffy."

Inside the ladies' toilet, just behind the duty-free shop, three figures stepped out of the portal. Lilith and Harry made their way into the rear entrance of the duty-free shop and once inside they stood quite still awaiting their prey.

Schmitt meanwhile ran out of the toilet to the front entrance of the duty-free shop. He began shouting incoherent threats at the top of his voice and waving his assault rifle in the air so that it could be clearly seen. Suddenly the airport public announcement system sprang to life with a security alert, asking everyone to remain calm and to stay inside the shops and restaurants.

This was quickly followed by a commotion outside the store, security guards were frantically running through the shopping mall apparently responding to reports of gunman who had somehow managed to gain access to the security area.

They spotted Schmitt almost immediately. He had done his job, so he turned and ran around the far side of the shop as if trying to evade them, but he was slow enough to make sure that were indeed following him. The guards were screaming at him to put down his gun and as he turned the corner, he simply headed back into the Ladies toilet.

"Something's wrong" said Akira, grabbing Singh's arm as he turned frantically looking for another exit. Seeing the rear exit, they made a break for it past the displays full of cigarettes and chocolates. Unfortunately for both of them, they should have been paying attention to the large display of assorted whisky which seemed to shimmer as they passed it and two figures stepped forward and shot them three times each with their, almost silent, Einari weapons. Lilith paused for a moment, kicked both bodies then nodded to Harry.

Everyone else in the duty-free store was still looking at the commotion at the front entrance so Harry and Lilith slipped out the way they had entered.

Not wanting to be shot upon following the gunman through the door into the toilets, the security guards were exercising caution. They had stopped outside giving Harry and Lilith enough time to enter unnoticed by the other door. They stepped back through the portal where Schmitt was already waiting. "We did it." he said.

In the air traffic control tower, Musa Obaid was now ready to have a heart attack. The last five minutes had been the most stressful of his life when, for a few moments they had lost all power and they had to implement emergency procedures to stack all incoming flights. With almost eight hundred people on board many of the flights they could not afford even a minor slip up. He was staring at his screens, praying ardently for a miracle when suddenly they started to flicker back to life, as the computers began rebooting. He slumped back into his chair praising a merciful Allah for answering his prayers so swiftly.

Back inside the portal Sofia had watched events unfold and just for a moment two large Einari figures appeared on the portal horizon. She was about to sound the alarm when as suddenly as they had appeared, they simply vanished like smoke leaving her unsure if she had simply imagined it.

"How are you holding up?" Harry asked Sofia and Schmitt. "I am good," said Schmitt wiping the sweat from his brow.

"Me too" said Sofia nodding.

"I will stay inside this time" said Harry "you look drained."

"Ok" said Lilith, "Sofia you take Stefan Myer in Berlin, and I will attend to Ms. Cyrille Fournier."

"Are you sure about this?" asked Harry. Lilith nodded. "If Hans is right then she may be a handful and I am after all the most experienced at this" she said rather theatrically running her thumb across her throat.

"I will keep an eye out for you professor," said Schmitt.

"Thank you, Hans." said Lilith.

27. THE FINAL BATTLE.

One hundred and forty miles above the Earth, the Xisudra was in a death dive streaking towards the satellite. “You will not escape this time.” said Enmerkar.

He and Erianes looked at one another, he held out his hand to her. She took it and smiled. They were about to say their last goodbyes when suddenly a portal opened directly beneath them, and they fell into it. Their ship continued on its course without them and crashed into the Black Knight satellite exploding instantly. The seventy thousand metric ton craft, combined with the fusion drive implosion ensured the complete destruction of their target, killing everyone on board.

As they entered the portal, Erianes received a blow to her head and was knocked unconscious. Then a huge hand grabbed Enmerkar by the neck and began choking him. It was a Vori, but he was almost three feet taller than Enmerkar and his strength was ferocious. This is not possible he thought, even as he struggled against his assailant. As he blacked out, he heard a female voice shout, "Now brother."

As the portal closed on the Xisudra, a shock wave rippled through the open portals and Sofia screamed. "I can't hold them" she shouted, falling to her knees. The golden torc around her neck was radiating an intense light and Lilith and Harry immediately came to her aid as they too concentrated on the portals. As their eyes faded to grey, Harry's ring and Lilith's diadem began to glow too. The shock wave slowly dissipated, and they soon regained control of the portals. Unfortunately, not in time to prevent one of their quarries, Zhang Wei, from discovering the open portal and recognising that he was in imminent danger.

It had so far been a quiet afternoon in Beijing. Zhang Wei had just made himself a coffee and was sitting in the kitchen of his brand new two-bedroom condominium in the city centre when he noticed a shimmering just in front of his newly installed double oven which was his pride and joy and formed the centre piece of his new home. Suddenly he saw three figures come into view behind it and he knew this could only be the enemy of his master. He ran to the kitchen island, grabbed a carving knife in one hand and large meat cleaver in the other, then he screamed as he ran towards them hoping to catch them off guard.

Unfortunately for Wei, he had failed to notice Schmitt standing off to the left, who calmy raised his rifle and fired two shots into Wei's sternum before adding a third to his forehead. The recoil pushed most of Wei's body out of the portal. Schmitt kicked the rest out over the threshold with his foot.

"What the hell was that?" asked Harry. "What destabilized the portals?"

"I don't know" said Lilith "but something has happened, something we have failed to consider perhaps. We must conclude this quickly, the others may also know that we are coming, and they may be better prepared than him" she said, pointing at Wei's body.

When they had finished restoring stability to the portals Harry said, "Thank you Hans. We would have been in real trouble without you."

Schmitt nodded.

"Is he really dead?" asked Sofia, as Harry helped her to her feet, "we should make sure. "Oh, I am very sure" said Schmitt who had a wry smile on his face and was looking around the kitchen where Wei's brains had made a real mess of his brand-new work tops. Then he added "communism seems to pay well these days. I hope they find him last, there is no way they're going to write this one off as a suicide."

"You never know" said Lilith hopefully. "As far as we know our Chinese friend may have other enemies. But let us be cautious, I think we have to assume that the Vori know something is going on now even if they don't know the extent of it. Let's hope that Enmerkar and Erianes can keep them fully engaged. If we have another incident like that, I am not sure that even the three of us could keep the portals open and stable enough."

Lilith was correct, as Enmerkar and Erianes had just discovered, the Vori had been better prepared than they had hoped. As soon as the alarms had been activated on the Black Knight, they had immediately begun to check in on their assets.

In the ultra-modern apartment in the upmarket residential area of Bismarck, on the outskirts of Berlin, Stefan Myer was awoken by his alarm clock at 5.30am as he was every day. Surprisingly more one dimensional than his colleagues this particular sociopath was very much a creature of habit.

Although he was still tired, he did not hit the snooze button; but rose instantly from his bed. He stretched to the ceiling, took three deep breaths then dressed in his sweat pants and t shirt before making his way to the kitchen. He grabbed a small double espresso from his beloved De Longhi Pro coffee maker that was already waiting for him. He had set the timer the previous evening as usual. He sniffed it three times taking in the aroma before downing it in a single shot. Then he put on his four hundred euro trainers, and, at exactly 5.45am he headed out into the street, turned left, and admired the lightening sky as the dawn approached.

Every day he would run to the Titan gym two miles away. He would exercise for exactly one hour and thirty minutes before running back to his apartment where he would then check to see if he had broken his current record of just over fifteen minutes for the journey. For Myer, the plus side of his obsessive habitual routine was that it allowed him an unparalleled ability to focus on a single task. On any other day this may have been an advantage when carrying out his master's wishes but today was not 'any other day'.

Today Sofia was waiting for him in her camouflaged robes on the threshold of the portal she had opened, just in between two large trees that lined the corner of Scheerderstraffe and Kholstraffe. She knew Myer would pass here on his way home at 7.05 central European time and she had chosen the location for several reasons. Firstly for the cover the trees provided, but secondly because it would give her the option to choose which side of the corner that she would decide to shoot him on when the time came, depending on the location of any witnesses. That would mean either shooting him in the face as he approached or shooting him in the back after he turned the corner. At this point she was almost exhausted and despite the abhorrence of her task she no longer cared, she simply wanted to get it over with.

As it happened, fate intervened once again and she didn't have to shoot Myer at all. As he rounded the corner she stepped out of the portal. Myer had been so focused on the timing of his run that he was startled to see the movement to his left and he stumbled backwards into the road, right into the path of a large oncoming silver S Class Mercedes that was taking advantage of the green light. His body was propelled over the bonnet to the other side of the car.

The car screeched to a halt along with another that had been coming across the lights in the opposite direction. The occupants jumped out and the driver of the car that had hit him shouted for the other driver to call an ambulance. As she was waiting for the response almost absent mindedly Sofia was thinking to herself that Myer was fit and athletic. Typical Aryan blonde hair and blue eyes. It would be just as well she thought if he was dead because she didn't relish any kind of physical struggle.

A moment later the other driver shook his head, he was looking at the body and said, "Nein, er ist tot" then he made his call to the local police. With all of the drama unfolding in front of them, on the opposite side of the car no one had noticed the shimmering between the trees on the side of the road, which quickly faded and apart from the sound of distant sirens approaching, the city suburb quickly returned to normal.

If Sofia's task in Berlin had been pleasantly less burdensome than she had anticipated, the same could not be said for Lilith's target in Paris. Sofia stepped back in to the portal. Instantly she noticed Schmitt lying prostate in front of Harry inside the portal and Lilith outside with the figure of Cyrille Fournier standing over her. What could have happened she wondered? Instantly fearing the worst.

It was just after 7am in Paris and Cyrille Fournier was sitting with a coffee on a park bench in the Place de la Concorde admiring the craftsmanship of the ancient Egyptian 'Le Obelisque de Luoxor'. It was quite a cool morning, and the cold air forced her to pull her scarf a little tighter around her shoulders, but the clear blue sky above held the promise of a beautiful day ahead.

She felt at home here more than anywhere else in Paris and she had no problem reading the extensive hieroglyphics down the sides of the monument. Exaltations to their gods, stories of strange beings and spells begging for help in the hereafter, crafted by a priestly caste who knew more about the reality of the world around them five thousand years ago than almost anyone alive today.

As she mused about how pathetic mankind had become since those times, she felt the static behind her. She'd always known that one way or another they would meet. Either she would hunt them, or they would come for her. The sensation grew and the fine hairs on the back of her hands had begun to stand up as she reached inside her purse. She had instantly realised that a trans dimensional portal was opening.

Only the mighty lord Enlil amongst the Vori had ever managed to open a portal but she had studied the science and was close to understanding how they worked. That was why she had been chosen as the leader to succeed them in due course. Of all of their experiments,

Cyrille Fournier was undoubtedly the pinnacle of their success.

Lilith, they had engineered as a crude biological weapon, but Fournier was meant to be a ruler. The genetic memories of Ningal, the Ennead traitor as she had been branded, lived on in her. It was only the smallest fraction of her progenitor's knowledge they had been able to harvest without it being fatal to the host, but it was enough to make her possibly the most intelligent human being on the planet. She had been in no doubt that her manifest destiny would be to finally secure the victory over the Einari, as Ningal herself had vowed to her lover Enlil, and to rule in his place.

She turned as Lilith stepped through the portal and even with the cloaking effect of her robes, to Fournier she was now clearly visible.

"Hello sister" said Fournier instantly recognising Lilith. "So, it is true, you do still live. I am pleased, you will yet prove useful to us."

Lilith was caught on the back foot. She hesitated for a moment, it was just long enough for her foe to shoot her square in the chest and stun her. She fell to the ground on the grass behind the bench and the pigeons that had been lazily foraging for titbits immediately fled skywards.

"Shit, she's got a Vori weapon" said Harry who was watching from inside the portal. Fournier, realising where the horizon of the portal was, focused hard and seeing Harry come into focus she took aim at him and fired, but Schmitt dived in front of the entrance taking the full force of the next blast. Had she managed to hit Harry the portals would have collapsed together, and all would have been lost in an instant.

Even as Schmitt was hitting the floor, Sofia was returning back through the portal from Berlin. Seeing their peril, she grabbed her Einari weapon, fired at Fournier hitting her twice in the shoulder and arm, then she stepped out of the portal to finish her off.

She leant over Lilith who was starting to come around.

"Sister, sister, can you hear me?" said Sofia.

"Yes" said Lilith, "I am alright, help me to my feet."

Sofia supported her as she stood up shakily and they entered the portal, collapsing together once inside next to the unconscious body of Hans Schmitt.

"How did she recognise you?" asked Harry. "I

don't know" said Lilith, who was visibly shaken. "Consciously I would swear that I did not know her, but when I was standing close to her, deep inside I did feel something, a connection of sorts. I really did seem to know her too."

"Well, you recognised Sofia too," said Harry.

"That was different" said Lilith, "I knew Eve as my sister, but with Fournier, it felt like I was facing my own evil reflection."

"Perhaps she was also one of those experimented on the facility at Edin."

Lilith nodded. "Perhaps, but I thought I was the only survivor."

"Well, you are now" said Harry, "so focus, we still have work to do."

The strain of their work and taking turns at keeping the portals open was making itself felt. "How could she see into the portal?" asked Harry.

"It seems that the longer they are open and the more changes we were making to the timeline, the less fluid and malleable the portals are becoming" said Lilith, "it is getting harder to maintain them too. We have to finish this quickly, if we don't, then we risk one or more of the portals solidifying."

"What does that mean?" asked Sofia.

"From my training with Enmerkar I think it means that it would leave a permanent doorway open between the dimensions" said Lilith "and our deaths" she added almost casually.

Both Sofia and Lilith were clearly shattered, and Harry knew that both would need to stay inside the portal this time otherwise it could all come crashing down around them. He would have to take care of the final target on his own.

In Washington DC it was just after 1am and Bill McKenzie had enjoyed a very satisfying evening in Georgetown at the El Nino club, a well-known pick-up place for gay sex. He had followed this up with a brutal couple of hours with a young Puerto Rican boy in his usual hotel suite at the Flair Majeure hotel.

Now he was on his way home, walking past the Old Stone House towards the Rock Creek Bridge and

Foggy Bottom where he would catch the metro to Embassy Row on the other side of town. He liked living in the diplomatic district. There was plenty of opportunity there every day to carry out his work through the many clubs he was affiliated with, even at casual meetings in the coffee shops, hushed conversations over restaurant tables, not to mention the gay bars and sex parties that he loved to frequent. The political DC landscape was his particular playground, and he knew that although not a single voter knew his name, that he was the real king rat of this particular cesspool.

He glanced in admiration at the Old Stone House as he passed it. This famous landmark was one of the oldest surviving buildings in the capital, maybe in the whole of the USA. He liked Georgetown because it reminded him of the old colonial period in history. He didn't give a rat's arse about the founding of America; he just liked the idea that there were fewer people here then and he wondered what the excitement of the time would have been. Not to his current tastes perhaps but being a sadistic bastard he was willing to try most things at least once. Even the Marquis de Sade would have blushed at some of his antics over the years.

Fortunately for him, this was America, the mighty

US of A and he was a 'good ole boy'. If you had as many powerful friends as he had, particularly ones who owed you a lot of favours, then you could literally get away with murder and still stay well under the radar. It helped if your victims were the 'little people' because then no one cared. Despite all the fine words, the promises made in the press, the posters and the TV commercials, life was cheaper here in the heart of democracy than almost anywhere else on the planet. Thanks to his prudential choice of victims, and to what he would nominally call 'his friends', Bill McKenzie was in fact the most prolific serial killer that the capital had ever seen.

As he walked along in the darkness, Foggy Bottom was certainly living up to its name tonight. The warm night air combined with the humidity of the day, was hit by a cooler current blowing off the Potomac River. As the two air currents collided, the mist began to form before it rolled, rather theatrically, over the creek and along the road towards him like a stage magicians use of smoke. Then suddenly his thoughts were interrupted as he felt the hairs on his neck stand on end and he turned to see a burly figure approaching him and he ran.

Bill McKenzie loved torturing other people, but he was a consummate coward and self-preservation, always very high on his list of priorities, suddenly jumped to the number one spot. He didn't care where he was heading, the adrenaline kicked in and he didn't look back. He did not notice that he had sprinted the few hundred yards North along 30th Street until he came to a wall. In front of him was Oak Hill Cemetery, he climbed over the wall and continued to run over the grass amongst the headstones and trees trying to hide from his pursuer.

Harry was a seasoned rugby player and had no problem keeping pace with his quarry, who was several stone over weight and was now gasping to catch every breath. When he caught up to him, McKenzie fell to his knees in front of Harry and immediately began to beg for his life. "Please don't hurt me" he said, "I will give you anything you want, just tell me what you want, anything, I can get you anything you want, please."

"Yes, you are right you will give me what I want" said Harry taking aim.

"No, no! please don't" McKenzie shrieked, but a moment later it was all over.

For a brief instant Harry shuddered, he felt as if a thousand disincarnated souls were looking over his shoulder and they were eagerly awaiting their chance to meet the soul of their tormentor once more.

"How appropriate" thought Harry, that one who brought so much misery to others would die here on hallowed ground amongst the graves of many of his victims, on his knees and wailing for mercy. Tonight there would be no mercy his for him, not in this world or indeed the next.

"Destiny fulfilled" said Harry to himself. The rest of their work had left Harry feeling sick but this one felt different. Perhaps it was the relief of it being the last one but he felt that despite it being a baptism of blood, as if he had somehow washed the world clean. In the fifth Dimension there was a ripple and Harry knew that he was running out of time.

He had to get back to the open portal and close it if the timeline was going to heal itself. Running as fast as he could he reached the entrance as it started to shimmer. It was already becoming unstable when he jumped through it landing face down on the floor next to Sofia who was now struggling to stay conscious with the effort.

Schmitt who had recovered from his ordeal was standing over him with his rifle.

"Oh thank goodness it is you. I almost shot you again." he

said smiling.

Harry was panting heavily with the exertion of the run. “Close them all now” he said and together the three of them concentrated as hard as they could. Their eyes began to fade as all three adornments began to glow, the ring, the torc and the diadem shone brightly and suddenly they seemed full of stars.

“It’s not working.” said Sofia. The ripples their actions had created in the fifth dimension were now reverberating like a wave and seemed to be fighting against them. With one final herculean effort the open portals began to close one by one, then suddenly all of the remaining ones closed together.

Harry, Sofia, and Lilith collapsed together and Schmitt sank down to his knees too.

“Have we really done it?” he asked.

Harry nodded, “yes.” he said, “we have done it.”

We need to check over the timeline” said Lilith, “but I think it is finally over.”

EPILOGUE

When their task was eventually complete and they could be sure that the timeline was resetting itself, Harry, Sofia, Lilith, finally opened a new portal. Then together with Schmitt they stepped over the threshold as one, to emerge at the rear of the security hut, just outside the entrance to the British Museum in London and they closed it behind them.

When the fresh air hit him, Harry fell to the floor, he was still exhausted but delighted to feel the cool stones on his back and a slight breeze on his face. Schmitt was holding up Lilith and Sofia who were also both visibly drained now by their exertions. They looked up and saw an orange glow in the heavens above them. At first it almost looked like the setting of the sun, but it was still early morning and as they watched it seemed to be moving, like a liquid fire rolling across the sky from North to South.

Harry sat up abruptly and reached for the communicator "Erianes" he shouted.

"Erianes, can you hear me?

Enmerkar, please answer me."

His only reply was static, and he slumped back to the floor to catch his breath for a moment. "There must be another way?" he thought. Then he stood up, "the sensors" he said. "Lilith do you still have the portable sensor that Enmerkar gave you?"

"There is no sign of the ship on the sensor," said Lilith. "They have gone, they must have crashed into the satellite or been shot down."

Harry crumpled. Sofia put her arm around him, "I saw them Harry I am sure I did?" said Sofia.

"Who did you see, Enmerkar and Erianes?" asked Lilith.

Sofia hesitated. "I don't know" she said truthfully, "but someone helped us, who else could it have been?"

"I saw something too," said Harry. "When I was leaving Jerusalem, but it didn't feel like them, it felt……. 'wrong'…." he said.

"What do you mean, wrong?" asked Schmitt.

"I can't explain it" he said, but he felt that same chill run down his spine as he had, just after he had killed Friedman.

Harry tried the communicator once more, but all that remained was static background noise. "Come on" Sofia said, "there is nothing more we can do now, let's go home."

All of them were utterly exhausted.

"I have to see my father first" said Harry, "and Uncle Geoffrey, I just want to make sure they are OK."

Lilith turned to Schmitt, and she kissed him gently

on the cheek. "Thank you, Hans," she said. We owe you a great debt, how shall we repay you?" Schmitt smiled, "I will think of something Professor, but right now I could sleep for a week, those weapons may just stun you at first, but they really do hurt."

Lilith nodded. "Yes" she said, feeling her own body aching, "I think they were made to subdue much bigger prey than us."

"I would not have missed this for anything" said Schmitt "but I am truly sorry that Enmerkar and Erianes did not make it. Might I trouble you for one last trip home professor?" He pointed to his assault rifle. "I will find it a little difficult to take this as hand luggage on an international flight" he said, and they all laughed.

Two days later, back in Harry's childhood home in Great Ayton the three of them were drinking his favourite tea in front of a roaring fire as they sat looking at one another. "Let's toast our lost friends Enmerkar and Erianes" he said. "I will miss them." Sofia nodded in agreement, and even Lilith had a tear in her eye.

"Yes" said Lilith, "in the end they were true friends and

brave to the very end. I wanted them to leave us alone, …. to go… somewhere …., anywhere… but I too wish we could have saved them. They gave their lives for our safety. We shall not forget them."

"No, we won't" said Sofia, "but the rest of the world will never know them or what they did for us."

"How do you feel now Sofia?" asked Harry "I mean…" he paused struggling to find the right words. "….. about the things that we have done."

"Honestly, I have tried to rationalise it to myself a hundred different ways but in the end, I still feel dirty and ashamed" she replied.

"You had no choice sister, none of us did" said Lilith, "but we won."

"I know" she said, "but that does not make me feel any better."

Harry nodded in agreement, "Hans did warn us that killing a man was not an easy thing, but I guess I didn't really understand what he meant until now.

What shall we do with these?" said Harry, holding up the three vials containing the vaccine that Enmerkar had prepared.

"I will take one back to Italy" said Sofia "and the hospital can replicate it in quantity, we have some links with the Swiss pharmaceutical companies just over the border, but even so it will still be a few years before it will be rolled out across the general population."

"We need to get one to the British government Harry, and perhaps Yasmina should visit her parents in Tehran?" she said looking at Lilith.

"Yes" she said "I will, but I think I am going to keep my original name. I like Lilith."

"It suits you" said Sofia, "no offence but you don't look like a Yasmina and, well, you are rather deadly, aren't you?"

Lilith laughed, "yes" she said, "I suppose I am. What about you Eve, what will you do…will you return to Edin with me?" she left it hanging.

"Maybe one day" said Sofia laughing, "maybe one day."

"Is it really over?" asked Harry. "Half a million years of history and conflict all resolved in just a few short hours?"

They had saved the world. There had been a dozen unexplained human deaths and a new story in the fringe press about a UFO being detected by NORAD over Alaska, but apart from that almost no one had even noticed, nor would they ever know.

"Yes, we beat them this time," said Lilith "but I can't help wondering how deep their influence went and how many men are still waiting out there ready to take their place."

Sofia nodded, "and if the memories we seem to be having are the genetic memories encoded in the Einari gene sequence, then why can we not remember back past the first Lilith? Nin Kirshag made these modification hundreds of thousands of years before the original Lilith was even born."

"I wonder what my dad will make of all this," said Harry.

"Forget it Harry, and you can't tell the British Museum either," said Sofia.

"No, I suppose not" he said, "they wouldn't thank me, they would probably have me committed."

"Come on," said Lilith. "It would seem that there is still a lot more for us to learn about these cards, about the fifth dimension and perhaps about ourselves."

"We have one loose end to tie up first," said Sofia.

Harry looked puzzled. "What loose end?"

"Have you forgotten about Abbas, Harry? He thinks we disappeared in the Majis Al Djinn. After he lowered us down in to the cave, we never contacted him again."

"Yes, actually I had forgotten, but in our defence were quite busy, weren't we?" he said. Then his lips curled up in to a wry smile, "you are right, but can we wait just a little longer?" he asked. "I quite like being part of a legend."

Inside the portal Enmerkar awoke to see Erianes leaning over him. "Enmerkar, wake up brother."

Slowly she helped him to his feet. "What happened?" he asked. When he saw his assailant stretched out on the floor in front of him, instinctively he pushed Erianes behind him.

Then he heard a female voice behind him "It is alright Enmerkar, you are safe now" it said. "He can do you no more harm."

Enmerkar turned and looked startled, he was staring at a beautiful Einari woman about twelve feet tall, dressed in robes of the Einari royal house.

"It cannot be," he gasped.

The giantess smiled down at them. "Greetings Enmerkar. I am your eternal mother, I am Nin Kirshag, and this is my brother Lord Enki" she said as another giant stepped forward from behind her.

"Enmerkar and Erianes were both stunned but they bowed their heads almost instinctively. "My lord, my lady" they said as one.

"My sister and I would like to thank you for your help and for all of the sacrifices you have made," said Enki. "We have watched your struggle. I am sorry that we could not have helped you more, but we have at last prevailed. This is our brother Enlil" he said pointing at the figure on the ground. "Our war is finally over."

"If I may my Lord. This is a truly wonderous day; but how can it be that you are both still here?" asked Enmerkar.

"In the final days of our civilisation, we were trapped inside the trans dimensional portal."

"Trapped? How is this possible?"

"When Enlil finally realised that he had lost, he fled into the portal and I followed him but when I caught him, the madness was so strong in him that I was not powerful enough alone to subdue him."

Enmerkar involuntarily felt his own bruised throat, he could certainly testify to that.

"Nin Kirshag came to my aid otherwise he would probably have killed me, but in the struggle, we lost him, he managed to evade us in this place. It is much stranger than you would imagine here in this dimension."

"We knew of the legends that the dwellers of this realm had restricted the access, but we never dreamt they could have trapped you here" said Erianes.

"At first we were trapped against our will" conceded Enki "but we came to realise that it was necessary. We have allies here, there are those who care for this world regardless of what species, or what civilizations rise or fall. Although we have been able to leave this dimension for some time, even when we knew that this was possible, we have chosen to remain.

Our brother Enlil, however, could not leave, but

he could hide. We had to find a way to draw him out and the final battle for us, had to be here, in this place safely away from the humans. The guardians here, realised that with us gone, Enlil would be far too powerful if he were ever to find his way back into your world.

We did manage to get the artifacts outside of the portal, we sent two of them back to Nin Kirshag's laboratory on the Xisudra and the other, …" he paused, "somehow Enlil diverted the corridor as we threw it out and it was lost to you. Although he could no longer make use of it, as long as it remained outside of the possession of the Einari, we could not be sure that you would be safe, so we have continued to pursue him in this dimension. Had one of the Vori learned its true secrets, discovered how to make use of it, they would perhaps have freed Enlil from this prison and your destruction would have been assured. This we could not allow."

"Is that what they were doing experimenting on Lilith at Mount Ararat?" asked Enmerkar.

"Yes," said Enki, "and she was not the only one. Your protégés have remarkable potential but your idea to make the will trainers, and to use the symbols that we passed down to you in this way, was what gave them their true advantage. It reduces their dependence on the artifacts, they will realise soon enough that they no longer need them.

For you, outside of this dimension this war has raged for half a million years, for us it is has been as the blinking of an eye. Our race owes you a great debt. Without you we would not have survived."

"I don't understand said Enmerkar, have we survived?" Erianes and I are the last of our kind."

"No," said Nin Kirshag, "you are not," and she waved her hands. For an instant they could see Harry, Sofia and Lilith drinking tea and toasting their friends.

"Rest now" she said "gather your strength, in time I will explain everything, but you need not fear for your young friends.

You will see them again."

THE END.

OTHER BOOKS BY THIS AUTHOR

FROM THE BORO TO BILBAO

In From Boro to Bilbao, Craig tells the story of finding his feet in a new country against the backdrop of the great financial crisis. Striving to cope with different work and social cultures, and of how he threw himself into the joys of his new country. He came to love the richness of Spanish life; from simple tapas to the rich glories of the country's history, architecture, and landscape.

Sometimes funny, sometimes moving, Craig describes with affection and in detail the people he met along the way; the experiences shared, misunderstandings overcome, and friendships forged for life.

Without Banks the world we know today would not exist but… Have you ever thought the odds were stacked against you and never really understood how?

It has never been more important for us all to understand what banks are, how they work and why our banking system is not fit for purpose. Craig Iley has been involved in the development of two new challenger banks and 'SHAKING THE MONEY TREE' explains how we can develop a new financial covenant, to regain control of our economic destiny.

ENGLISH ONLY ENGLISH

There is an old expression, that says "when life gives you lemons, make lemonade". Well, life has just turned up with a very large bag of lemons. A big enough bag in fact, to make sufficient lemonade to give me diabetes. Well bugger that! I have no desire to dive into a sugar induced death spiral, so I decided to re write it. "When life gives you lemons, go on a road trip. Ask the universe what the hell is going on and see if you get any answers." Amazingly it worked!

Printed in Great Britain
by Amazon

45849957R00225